Constance
Beresford-
Howe THE
MARRIAGE
BED

Constance Beresford-Howe

THE MARRIAGE BED

A Totem Book
Toronto

First published 1981
by Macmillan of Canada
a division of Gage Publishing Limited
Toronto, Canada

This edition published 1982
by TOTEM BOOKS
a division of Collins Publishers
100 Lesmill Road,
Don Mills, Ontario

Canadian Cataloguing in Publication Data

Beresford-Howe, Constance, 1922-
    The marriage bed

ISBN 0-00-222198-5

I. Title.

PS8503.E72M37   1982   C813'.54   C82-094962-0
PR9199.3.B47M37   1982

Printed in Canada

To
my son Jeremy
with love

Monday

SOMEWHERE ON THE FRONTIER between darkness and light, I was detained by a dream. Like my daytime existence, it was obscure and cluttered with detail of bewildering insignificance; but as dreams so often do, this one seemed to have a meaning beyond the sum of its parts.

I was visiting a prison — or was I the jailer? — in any case, the cell was a mediaeval affair, stony, dark, and cold, where a prisoner sat fettered with heavy chains. It was my husband Ross, but his seat was the low rocking-chair where I nursed our children, and I felt the weight of those chains as if they bit into my own flesh. Somewhere in the background (which suddenly became an airport Departures lounge) my stepfather Max and my mother were dancing, and I could hear seagulls. I was weeping, because we all knew that Ross, who had left me five months ago, was as free as a feather in the air. I was the prisoner loaded with chains, namely my two children, my current pregnancy, and my own temperament.

Snowlight at the window pulled me into the day. The dream faded and vanished. Awareness came first: the sleepy, fragmented chat of Martha and Hugh from their cots in the

1

next room, like the conversation of birds; the kick of the fetus in my imprisoning belly. Next my identity came back — the who if not the why of Anne Graham, with her honours degree, her double heartbeat, and her dishevelled life. The dream, of course, was nonsense. Besides, it was plagiarized. It came from one of those metaphysical Body-and-Soul debates, a poem I'd read the night before. Just the same, there had to be meaning, if not answers, in things like dreams and books. I fumbled for the anthology on the bedside table among a clutter of socks, letters, and kids' toys. Yes, here it was — a poem by Marvell.

> Oh, who shall from this dungeoun raise
> A soul enslaved so many ways?
> With bolts of bones; that fettered stands
> In feet, and manacled in hands;
>
> . . .
>
> A soul hung up, as 't were, in chains
> Of nerves and arteries and veins;
> Tortured, besides each other part,
> In a vain head and double heart.

A nice bit of imagery, that, even if my pregnancy gave it a new dimension Marvell never intended. But answers? — No. The arts, like the sciences, could provide no more reliable clues to my future than the entrails of a bird.

With a great sigh I wallowed up out of my blankets and sat on the edge of the empty bed to brush and braid my hair into its thick rope. Sad that my library card, in so many ways a passport out of chaos, took me nowhere in particular. How could it, when I read more for escape than enlightenment? Just the same, I devoured piles of books weekly, searching for some kind of reconciliation with this narrow house, or my failed marriage, or my stalled academic career. Now I reached again for the Marvell poem and read the next verse with my unfinished plait in one hand like a loose tether.

> Oh, who shall me deliver whole
> From bonds of this tyrannic soul?
> Which stretched upright, impales me so
> That mine own precipice I go . . .

A crash from the next room, and Hugh's wail. Downstairs the dog began to bark hysterically as the postman pushed a handful of bills through the slot. The day had begun. I tossed back the braid and slung on my tentlike dressing-gown, thrusting my feet into slippers.

But when I opened the kids' door, the sight of them gave me a crazy lift of joy, as it did first thing every morning. Hugh was on the floor howling, having tipped over on his head as he tried to climb out of his crib. Martha, her stout, naked form precariously balanced on a chair, was trying to drag her best smocked dress down off its hanger. She eyed me with truculence, as if I were the one caught red-handed.

"Put on the blue overalls, Mar. Then you can run down and get the mail for me."

"No."

Ignoring this, I peeled Hugh out of his sodden pyjamas and began to dress him for the day. From below, our Siamese cat Chairman Mao yowled imperiously for his breakfast. Scuffling on her out-turned feet, the basset nosed open the door, then histrionically flopped down and began to scratch herself. On one flank I spotted a new red patch of eczema. And that meant, oh God, a trip to the vet — our supply of ointment was all gone.

At this point the phone rang in the hall. "Go and answer it, Martha," I said cunningly. At once she dropped the dress and ran. She loved dealing with the phone; it fed her self-importance and love of management, and made her forget the major frustration of her life, the fact that she wasn't yet three. I hung up the small frock, closed the cupboard door, and followed her with the blue overalls. Hugh staggered after me.

"Hullo, Granny," Martha was saying into the receiver. "I have no clothes on." Craftily I began to ease her into pants and T-shirt, a manoeuvre she pretended not to notice. Hugh squatted down near us to chew a small toy dog.

While my mother-in-law's slow voice quacked out of the mouthpiece, it suddenly occurred to me that this was not the day for her regular weekly call. What the hell could it mean, then? — had Ross at last told her about us? In an effort to instil calm, I laid a hand over the unborn one as it kicked into a somersault.

"Let me speak to your mother now," the voice said.

"No. *I* want to talk."

"Thank you, love," I said, and ruthlessly twisted the receiver out of her fat grasp. She promptly tripped over Hugh, who broke into a shrill wail and kicked at her. With a groan I hauled him up and slung him over one hip, rocking him to and fro soothingly. Martha stumped off downstairs singing "Stayin' Alive" in a loud and tuneless voice.

"Good morning, Mother."

"Is that you . . . Anne?"

"Yes, it's me." Edwina Graham never believes anything, however self-evident, until she's heard it at least twice; but this was only one of the reasons why talking to her made me wonder over and over again whether it's possible actually to die of boredom.

"Um — is everything all right, Mother?"

"Everything is fine." (He hadn't told her, then.) "And how are you . . . *feeling*, Anne?"

"Oh, great. Just great." My distended belly began to itch fiercely, perhaps with relief. While not as total a coward as Ross, I wasn't looking forward either to the day when she had to know he was living with his secretary Larine.

On my hip, Hugh grizzled away drearily, his nose running. Teeth or another cold? All this time, Mother's calm, oblivious voice went chuntering on:

"Not due for my checkup till April, but this weekend at Lucy's bridge party . . . never could resist peanut brittle . . . so my — there's a small Adjustment the dentist will have to make to my . . . so I'm coming in to the city this afternoon."

"Your plate has cracked again," I thought. "Why the Christ can't you be a woman and say so?" But Edwina was haunted by a suspicion that most plain English nouns and *all* verbs of action were potentially dirty words. This, of course, made her conversation quite indecent with all its meaningful pauses and strange, embarrassed italics. Hard to believe a mind like this could exist in the year 1977; but there we were.

"And so if you're not . . . *doing* anything special around tea-time, Anne, perhaps I could just . . . *drop* by and say hello to you and the Little Ones." There was a brief pause while in a lull of Hugh's squalling I nearly fell asleep. "Maybe I'll be lucky," she went on, "and Ross will come home early for once. It's months since I saw the boy. . . ."

In another, longer pause, I scratched my belly and tried

5

to think of something reassuring to say.

"Sure, come whenever you like; Mother. I'm not doing a thing. See you, then."

But I might have known better than to hope for a quick escape. She now launched into one of those timetable chats so dear to the hearts of all true bores, in which her most trivial move for the next eight hours would be described and revised like the strategy for some obscure battle.

". . . so Dr. Payne has very kindly offered to . . . *squeeze* me in around two-thirty, which I can just manage if I catch the one-forty-two. I'm not sure, of course, just exactly how . . . *long* he'll be, but I suppose he'll be finished by four. If it's later, I'll take a taxi so as to be with you at four-thirty, or at the very latest a quarter to five. . . ."

My own watch was seldom wound or accurate, and I rarely knew or cared what day it was; but dear old Mother made me feel that these were virtues, not faults.

"Just a cup of tea now, Anne; you're not to dream of going to any trouble." (This meant the tea party had better be perfectly organized and presented or she would be horribly understanding about it, and mention me to all her friends as Poor Anne.) But my attention was briefly distracted by an ominous silence from downstairs. Sometimes, to mark her disapproval of long phone calls, Martha would retire to make a puddle (or worse) in a corner of the sitting-room.

"Look forward to seeing you," I said hopefully. But with Mother, phone conversations were never for anything so crass as communication; they simply existed as models of good form.

"And how is Ross these days, my dear?"

Once more the fetus, curling, dived and kicked me

under the ribs with acrobatic accuracy.

"Oh, Ross is fine, thanks."

"Still working much too hard, I suppose. I just hope setting up his own place wasn't rather . . . *premature*. He's a really bad worrier, that boy; and as for overwork, I well remember that in his second year at Osgoode I simply had to — "

"Look, Mother, there's somebody at the door — I'll have to go. See you this afternoon; we'll talk then."

And I hung up smartly, ignoring with dignity Martha's loud shout: "Nobody's at the door!" As I made my ponderous way downstairs, lugging Hugh, I thought defensively that it was not a question of dislike. From the wedding-day onward, Edwina had been flawlessly kind and generous to me. To all of us. It was not her fault, maybe, that this calm, superb kindness was such a devasting commentary on her only son's marriage — that rash, over-fertile, and wholly deplorable union.

In any case, she would arrive this afternoon like sweet Vengeance itself, with a bag bulging with homemade marmalade, something useful hand-knitted for the unborn, educational toys for the children, and in a tactfully small envelope something she would slip under a pot-plant, murmuring, "I'm sure you and Ross could use a little . . . *something*, my dear." No, it wasn't dislike, really. More a sort of fascinated loathing.

Well, Camus said somewhere that it's cowardly to despair over the human condition, but Mother's upcoming visit would sure as hell put that theory to the test. For one thing, it meant hearing Ross (who is twenty-seven) referred to as "My Boy". It also involved polishing up every sodding piece of the silver tea-set, unused for months. No choice there: she gave it to us after her own mother — as she puts it — "Went". In order to present the image of the perfect homemaker, the gracious chatelaine (which of course was vital, because of the way I felt about Mother), I would also have to make a cake. And that, in turn, meant going out to buy lemons and walnuts, though I'd planned to skip the walk today. A grey rigour of cold air was pressed over the whole city of Toronto like a steel helmet. From time to time the windows trembled in a sharp little wind that would soon crystallize in icy particles whipping horizontally through the streets. Ah, well. War is hell. On with it.

But before getting on the treadmill that would convey me to the kitchen sink for a confrontation with neglected stacks of dirty dishes, I picked up the mail from the hall floor, where Martha had left it. As predicted, it was mostly bills. The one item of any interest was a postcard from my neighbour Margaret. In her neat hand she neatly discussed the weather in Boston. It was evidently as nasty as the weather here. There was no letter from my stepfather. This depressed me considerably. Max used the phone only for business, and he was too busy for much visiting. But he sometimes found time to scribble me silly, wise, funny, loving notes; and since Ross's departure, these had become more and more important to me. The medium more than the message was the point; but both seemed to be addressed to the true and innermost me, seen by no one else now that Ross was gone.

"This afternoon," Max might scrawl, "I spent three hours organizing the arrival from Taiwan of five thousand dozen pairs of men's Y-front underpants. What a way to spend your life. Send me a bagel by special messenger." Or a wire might arrive: "Thinking of joining the Flat Earth Society. Members so crazy they could just be right. Love, Max." I kept all these bulletins, however ridiculous, partly because I had a superstitious fear that one day — perhaps soon — they might stop.

With some force I tore up a circular from a newly open pizza parlour, and a folder advertising smoke detectors. Ah, friend, if I installed one of those things here, it would ring so often I might never forget where hell is.

After feeding the kids their cereal, I drifted reluctantly to the sink to tackle the dishes. Once actually eye to eye with the buggers, though, I lost momentum abruptly. There was a brief lull in the city's grinding, daytime tumult. I gazed out blankly at the grey sky. A little galaxy of dust held in suspension by a weak glint of sunlight floated in my line of vision. Outside, an oil truck groaned as it filled our tank, and a dog barked importantly at nothing. A pigeon flapped across the cloudscape and made me for some reason think of seagulls. Kent. Max. Who was that plethoric old man with the red, bald head? Of course, the Captain. And the two pelican maiden ladies in cardigans, his daughters. Coffee after dinner eight years ago in the lounge of the Sea View Hotel, Broadstairs.

A depressed little family of Swiss holiday-makers looked out at the pearly rain-clouds. Alone in a corner sat Max, the newest guest, reading *The Daily Telegraph* with the help of a balloon glass of brandy. A gust of laughter came from the bar across the hall, where my mother Billie was making life amusing for a group of American tourists.

"Care for a game of chess, young Anne?" inquired the Captain in his cement-mixer voice.

9

"No, not tonight, thanks. I've got to study. O-levels begin next week."

He gave his sharp bark of a cough and one of the thin daughters jumped as if pinched. "Game of cribbage then, Father?"

"Oh, all right, if you like." And out came the cribbage board and the dog-eared pack with Tower Bridge on it. Max took off his thick gold watch and laid it absently on the table. Why, I wondered, just as I wondered why such a man should ever have come to our hotel. Dressed in the most beautifully tailored lightweight suit I had ever seen, he looked like some exiled duke or inexplicably displaced millionaire. Or perhaps he was some special kind of diplomat or spy, I thought, mooning and doodling over my Latin textbook. Nobody remotely like him had ever in my time walked into the dining-room of the Sea View Hotel with its smell of brown soup, proprietor's Peke, and damp table-linen.

And I had a special reason for observing him so intently. For some time now it had been clear to me that the only way to get the kind of life I wanted was to marry a rich Older Man with the least possible delay. I wanted a first-rate university education. Here was the old millionaire. Now all I had to do was get one to provide the other. After all, a degree wouldn't cost him more than a mink coat, the sort of thing doting elderly husbands often provided for young wives. I'd given it a great deal of thought; there was no other way. My assets were only two: my brains, which I knew without vanity to be first-class, and my looks, which since puberty had attracted a wide variety of unwelcome attentions, specially from Older Men. For some reason, boys of my own age appeared totally uninterested in me, which was on all counts just as well for my plans.

Public libraries, where I spent most of my leisure time, had provided me with detailed technical information about the sex act, without revealing to me why on earth any woman would permit such a silly thing to be done to her. Men, however, seemed very keen on it for some reason. And Max was a handsome man with his thick, nearly white hair and magnificent dark eyes. One could imagine he was the sort of person who would at least be polite about it. The whole nasty business might be endurable with someone like that, as long as it didn't last too long. To be sure, a chambermaid's overheard complaint about her husband ("'E's never *orff* of me") was not encouraging. Better not to think about the bed part of it.

The young waitress Vera (as distinct from the old one with the varicose veins) came in to clear away the cups. Her hair was newly back-combed up into a great beehive that made her profile look vaguely African. Max reached over his cup to save her trouble, but she neither smiled nor thanked him, only flounced out with the tray as if offended. I knew, as only one teenager can know another, that she was annoyed because it was clear the beehive amused him.

After a few minutes, Max dropped his folded newspaper on the table and stood up. The Captain's daughters eyed him furtively. He looked irresolutely across at the bar, then strolled out to the entrance hall, where glass doors framed a moody view of grey water tumbling under a grey sky. He opened the door and stepped out into the soft English air.

"Oh, please, sir, you forgot your watch," I said, bursting out abruptly after him. It was not, perhaps, a very subtle approach, but the best I could think of at the time.

"Ah. So I did. Thank you very much."

I handed over the watch, hoping it was not embarrassingly hot from my moist hand.

"You're from America, aren't you?" I asked breathlessly.

"No, Canada."

"Really? Are you on holiday? I'm afraid the weather hasn't been very nice here this summer."

His dark eyes looked at me quizzically. "Think it's going to rain again? Can I risk a walk?"

"Oh, I'm sure you could. There's a nice sea-front promenade just along here. I don't suppose — I mean, would you like me to come along to — to point things out? It's quite an interesting town, actually. Charles Dickens lived here off and on."

Once again he looked at me and the faint smile spread from his eyes to his lips. "I'd be delighted," he said. "But you'll have to get permission first from your parents. That was your mother with you at dinner, wasn't it?"

"Back in two seconds," I promised, and shot upstairs. With frantic speed I tore off my ugly school shirt and tie and put on a too-small blue satin blouse I'd recently bought at a sale. I flung on my mac but left it unbuttoned, and hurried past the bar without troubling Billie with news of my immediate plans. Billie never worried anyhow where I went, or with whom, as long as I got home before dark. She was touchingly sure that nothing illegal or immoral could happen to a girl until after the pubs closed.

He was lighting a cigar when I hurried out, the open coat flying around the blue blouse at which he glanced with those casual dark eyes that looked so sleepy, yet seemed to miss nothing.

"Still at school, are you?" he asked.

"Yes. I'm in the Fifth at Broadstairs Grammar."

"That's about like our last year of high school, right? What are you going to do when you graduate?"

This was marvellous, I thought. He was interested. It could turn into one of those whirlwind courtships. So I let it all come tumbling out, too fast, repetitive, confused, as we walked along the sea-smelling promenade.

"I want to go to university, but unless there's some kind of miracle I won't be able to, because I'll never get a scholarship. You don't know what the competition's like, and we've moved about so much, my mother and I . . . she gets restless. This is the first decent school I've ever been to, where they really make you work. Only Billie — that's my mother — is getting bored with Broadstairs; we've been here nearly two years. She just doesn't understand about good schools. Of course, to be fair, neither did I, until it was really too late."

"I see. How old are you, then?" Max asked, though he hardly needed to.

"I'm nearly sixteen." Like everything I'd told him so far, this was close to the truth.

"You seem older than that," he remarked. "More mature." Then he added, with more truth than tact, "In some ways."

I kicked a small pebble several forceful yards ahead of us. After a brief pause he went on in his rather thick, slow voice, "Your name's Anne, isn't it? Well, if you did get a scholarship, Anne — I mean by some miracle — and go to university, where would it be, and what do you want to study?"

"Oxford, and it's botany I'm keen on. Billie just

thinks it's silly, fiddling about with mounting specimens and all that. So even if we had the money, which we don't ... Anyhow, she used to like it because it kept me busy; but reading botany as a subject is something else; all those Latin names annoy her. She's a bit against education anyway. Puts ideas into girls' heads and makes it hard for them to marry people. For instance, I wanted to go to boarding-school in the worst way when I was young; but Billie said I must be mad to think of playing hockey and getting thick legs. She's an awfully *opinionated* woman.''

He gave an abrupt snort of laughter and I paused, too, for a brief giggle. "Just the same, ever since I was twelve or so, I've been going up to London every Saturday from wherever we happen to be, on a day return, to make drawings of things at the Natural History Museum at Kensington. It's a marvellous place, they have all sorts of lovely things. I'll show you some of my work if you like.''

"I'd like that very much. But where's your father, and what does he think about botany for girls?''

"Oh, he died when I was getting on for six. He was a classics don at Exeter. I don't remember him, except sort of dimly when I see my two old aunts. They're poor and have rheumatism and dote on the Vicar ... you know. They'd help me if they could, but ... Anyhow, there it is. The minute the funeral was over, Billie and I got on the train, and we've been moving from one seaside place to the other ever since. I don't know why she's so restless.''

"So your mother never remarried?''

"Oh no. I think she's afraid of being bored.'' A belated loyalty kept me silent about the two or three surrogate husbands Billie had over the years lightly and briefly held. Though one was deplorable — a seedy ex-R.A.F. officer called Fred, who had disappeared with some of her money — none of the others, at least as far as I could tell at the time, had ever done her or me any harm. She had never neglected me any more or less for any of them; they had too little importance for that. It was only, she explained to me once, that she had to have a man to laugh with once in a while.

"She doesn't like being cooped up," I said, in an effort to summarize the situation. "When we first unpacked our things in Brighton, she said to me, 'We're not a family any more, you see. Just a couple of people travelling together. Trying to be considerate to each other, and amusing company. That's all.' "

Max gave me a quick glance. Then he took a last draw on his cigar before tossing the butt into a tidal pool. "I think we'd better turn back now," he said quietly. "It's getting late."

There was no sting in the words. I knew I hadn't bored him, even though the blue satin blouse had not had anything like the impact I'd hoped for. In fact, it was high time, I thought, for the whole conversation to get off its present level. Then, perhaps, he would begin to look at me the way so many Older Men did, that rather absent yet purposeful look that meant their penis was thinking.

Somewhat desperately, because the flat, white face of the Sea View Hotel would soon come into view, I began, "Do you believe in affinities at all? Because I felt very . . . attracted to you, the minute I saw you at dinner-time."

"Thank you. That's very complimentary."

There was a silence. Then I blurted out, "Are you married?" Too late I regretted the blunt directness of this question, even though the answer was vital to my plans.

"I was married."

"Oh, you're divorced, then."

"No. My wife died of cancer eight months ago."

"Oh, I'm so sorry," I said, trying not to sound cheerful. "Is that why you're here, then? To recover from your grief?"

The twilight almost hid his grave smile. "No. I'm here on business — a conference. But there was some mix-up about reservations at the Grand; instead of a single room they booked me in with a guy from Hamilton, and I could tell with one look he was a snorer. So I came along to your hotel."

"Rotten luck," I grinned, diverted. "And I should know. We live there."

"Jesus," he said, " — if you'll pardon the expression. Are all the meals as bad as tonight's?"

"They used to be much better. But there's a new cook from Athens, and he isn't concentrating."

Suddenly Max laughed out loud. "Anne, you make me wish I wasn't flying back tomorrow."

"Oh, so do I!" There was so much fervour in my voice it embarrassed both of us, and I ground my nails into my palms in an agony of self-punishment.

"Never mind," he said cheerfully. "Maybe you'll visit Canada some day, and when you do, be sure to look me up. Here's my card."

It read "Maxwell Ehrlich, Import-Export Consultant, Toronto, Canada". I put it into an inside pocket with care.

"And now it's time for me to return you to your mother and say goodnight. Thanks for a very enjoyable walk, Anne."

I offered my hand and his big, warm one swallowed

it. There was nobody in the lounge. I moved a little closer to him, face lifted as if by accident to a convenient angle. He could kiss me if he liked. It might not be too awful, actually. But just then the bar door opened and out straggled the last customers, Billie among them. She had evidently been saying something absurd to one of the Americans, who was guffawing. In a shy mumble I introduced her to Max, and over their handshake she gave him her enchanting, crooked little smile. I saw his face change at once. A kind of delighted surprise lit up the experienced dark eyes as he looked at her. And there went, I realized with a pang of real regret as well as chagrin, all my hopes of a May-December marriage. For a few minutes I actively disliked my mother.

"It's a pleasure to meet you," he said. "Your daughter has shown me a bit of the town and made me forget I was lonely."

Billie gave me a somewhat sharp parental glance, under which I blushed angrily. As soon as possible I muttered goodnight and marched upstairs with such rigid dignity my knees would hardly bend enough to climb the steps.

A few minutes later in our room Billie said lightly, "That was rather a smashing man you picked up, sweetie."

"I did not pick him up," I said, indignant at her accuracy.

"He told me after you went up that he thought you were a very valuable person."

"Did he." I flounced sulkily over to my own side of the bed. Well, that was that. Valuable, indeed. And nobody else in sight remotely available to marry except ghastly Captain Blackburn.

"Pity he's off tomorrow," yawned Billie.

And Canada being, to my mind, a place as inaccessible

as Mars, I thought that would be the end of it. A pity in
more ways than one, too. There had been something power-
fully appealing about Max. And for some reason the name
Canada had a vague but stirring association for me: it
meant discovery, a land of wonders; it formed a fleeting
image of wild birds. But it was not a place I ever seriously
expected to see. I was both too old and too young to have
any real confidence in miracles.

Abruptly the sun went in. I blinked, disoriented, at the
piles of our dirty dishes. But in the cluttered kitchen, one of
those rare domestic lulls lingered like a gift. Martha murmured, "Bugger you, Cindy," to her doll, and Hugh,
plumped down over the short V of his own legs, silently
inspected a broken toy car. He turned it over delicately in
his small hands, frowning with concentration and pushing
out his lips. As usual when happy, he looked worried.
Under the table the dog scratched herself voluptuously.

"All right, you guys, we'll do the dishes later, and take
old Violet to the vet. Bring me the snowsuits, will you,
Martha? Get up, Hugh; we're going out. Where the hell are
all the boots? And Violet's leash?"

And with a loud groan I began the long, heavy-
breathing business of stuffing the kids into their winter
armour, forcing their passive feet into boots, dragging on
mittens, winding scarves. As I squatted there yanking at the
stuck zipper on Hugh's jacket, it suddenly occurred to me
to wonder what the hell I could or would say to Mother
Graham if by any chance she did know about Ross, and was
only waiting to confront me in person this afternoon with all
kinds of terrible questions like Why, and How Could, and
What Now. The thought of it brought a sour return of

breakfast coffee into my throat; because there were no answers to such questions, except grossly indecent ones. At this point I began to cry, as from time to unpredictable time I so often did now. Tears dripped down in a loose rain on my hands and Hugh's fine, floppy hair.

Once years ago in a museum I saw a painting of Saint Lawrence being grilled like a cheese sandwich. It was refreshing to think of it now and wonder what would be the appropriate treatment for My Boy, after leaving me the job of telling Edwina the tale of our failure. No, I thought grimly; come what may, I will tell her not one single word about it. Some of the things I could say to the lady would provide a positively criminal pleasure, and I didn't deserve it. He, on the other hand, did.

Though now fully dressed, Martha was pulling off her woollen hat. "Crybaby," she said to me with scorn. Then added, "I need to go peepee."

In the vet's waiting-room, Violet shivered and whined non-stop, her voice rising to an occasional yelp, presumably whenever she remembered her hysterectomy. Quite a crowd of dogs, cats, and hamsters waited for attention, all of them reacting to the reek of creosote and drugs with a variety of snarls, whimpers, barks, and caterwaulings. It was easier for me to empathize with these lower animals than with most of their owners, notably a fearfully dirty old man with a loose cough, two chattering girls with gum, a fat lady leashed to an equally fat cat, and a horsy, weatherbeaten woman with two huge borzois. My children sat quietly, watching the scene with simple spectator pleasure, though Hugh had the dubious look of one not absolutely sure of getting out of there without an injection.

". . . so I went Yeah, and she went That's right, you don't believe it? and I just freaked my *mind*, because there was this neat guy just in the next seat — man, was it ever funny. . . ."

These girls seemed to have no pet with them. Perhaps they'd just dropped in for a place to sit and chat. Still, they did appear to be in charge of one of those folding canvas push-chairs that hump babies' backs. They might have brought the fat baby in it here to have his nails cut. He had been so casually stuffed into his stroller that his hooded blue coat was shoved up around his ears; but he was sucking one of the buttons on it philosophically, with a vacant look of satisfaction.

The old man shuffled his feet. His clothes released an eye-watering smell of tobacco and onions. To evade it, I got up to choose a magazine from the rack. The talking girl paused to eye my huge form in a long, incredulous stare. Obviously she saw not the faintest connection between her conversation and my condition, of both body and soul. She couldn't have been more than three years my junior, but because I knew the connection and she didn't, a whole generation yawned between us. This was not a thought that cheered me up at all. Soon she was plunging on again, faster than ever to make up for lost time — "like I mean *funky*, and then Arlene went — "

Just then I suddenly noticed that the fat baby had turned a darkish shade of purple. Loose threads on his coat marked where the button had been before he began to choke on it. The girl was now leaning on her friend's shoulder, eyes squeezed shut in an ecstasy of giggles. Reaching over, I plucked the child fast out of his canvas sling and up-ended him. A smack on the back failed to dislodge the button, so I reached a finger down his throat and hooked it out of his airway. Instantly he sucked in a deep breath and began to roar.

"Well done," said the horsy woman briskly.

The girl, her eyes still swimming, looked at me with a dignified air of offence. She took the baby from me and doubled him up, still yelling, into his chair. I felt too intimidated to offer her the wet button, so I dropped it into an ashtray.

"Now then, Mrs. Graham next," said the vet, poking his grey head out of the examining-room. I dragged the unwilling Violet after me, all her claws scrabbling on the polished floor.

"Here, I'll lift her up," he said cheerfully. "Don't want you delivering those twins in here, ha ha ha."

I forced a wan smile. Dr. Cook might not be much of a humourist, but he was a good vet. Without him we would have lost our cat to pneumonia the year before. It was a pity he'd never bothered to replace four missing top front teeth, because the gap provided a whole orchestra of piping, fluting noises whenever he spoke.

"H'm. There's a nice new outbreak, eh?" he whistled, knitting shaggy grey eyebrows over Violet.

"It's nothing in her diet, is it? She's just a complete neurotic."

"Right. Keep her spread out like this and I'll rub in some ointment. That's it." Violet rolled up her eyes and groaned with pleasure as the tarry stuff eased her itch. "Do this a couple of times a day, rub it in well, and she'll settle down. I'll give you a mild tranquillizer, too, for the nights. . . ."

One of his vein-roped, freckled hands accidentally

brushed against mine. And this produced in Mrs. Graham a sexual urge of exquisite, ludicrous urgency. In my present state of unwelcome celibacy, I sometimes had these spells, brief and irrelevant, but severe, and always at times and in places where no relief was remotely possible. There was no dignity in a fate like mine, I thought angrily. Could there be anything more ridiculous than feeling horny about a toothless old vet? It was either tragic or wildly funny. I had to bite the insides of my cheeks hard to hold in a lunatic grin.

"Now stop that, you silly bitch," he said to Violet, who was trying to lick off the ointment.

"Yes; cut it out," I added severely. But I was talking to a different bitch.

We paused to peer wistfully through the frost on Jennifer's Craft Shop window with its bright patchwork quilt and spinning-wheel, trying to find an excuse to go inside. None came to mind, but I steered the kids in anyway. Jennifer, otherwise known to us as the Loom Lady, had opened for business about a year before. She stocked wool, thread, buttons, and so on, but chiefly sold wall-hangings, cushions, and fabrics woven by herself on a loom in the back room. She appeared now in the doorway, a tall figure in a caftan, and at once ducked back inside.

"Oh, it's you, Anne. Come on through."

She knew I loved to watch her weaving. Her brown, pink-lined hands moved the shuttle and lowered the bar in a kind of slow, dancelike rhythm that fascinated me. And there was something important about that simple web of material, its pattern emerging in a sequence as simple as cause and effect, each related to the other in the most satisfactory possible way. She was creating something both useful and beautiful with a sort of meaning one hopes without much confidence that life itself may have. These feelings had some months ago made me very much want a loom of my own; but when I proposed it to Ross, he instantly said, "No."

"But why not, love? Think of all the lovely curtains and bedspreads I could make, and tweeds for coats and suits — "

"*No*, Anne."

"Well, I know the initial outlay's pretty big, but in the long run it would be really econ —"

"No. No. And *no*! Is that clear?"

"Not so loud, you'll wake the kids. But for pity's sake, what's wrong with wanting a loom? It's not all that hard to operate, once you get the hang of it. Jenny's been teaching me how."

"Anne, I said no and I mean it. For Christ's sake, what next? There isn't room now to move around the dining-room table since the sewing-machine moved in there. That's all we need, for God's sake, a goddam six-foot *loom* cluttering up the place."

"Well, of course, if that's how you feel about it." I disentangled my legs from his with dignity, shifted to my own side of the bed, and subsided into a huffy silence.

"Yes, that's how I feel about it."

"Fine. Forget it, then."

"I already have."

But ever since then I'd seized every opportunity to drop in and watch Jenny working, her long back straight as she sat on the bench. Though her ancestors had come generations ago from Ethiopia, she herself had been born on Queen Street, and somewhere along the way a little white or mixed blood had lightened her colour to milk-chocolate and given her nose a bridge. I thought the total effect very handsome, with just the right touch of the exotic; but Jenny once told me dryly that her own people considered her a sad comedown from the ideal, while of course people of my race had the same opinion, for different reasons.

"Made something new since I saw you last," she said now, gesturing at something on the floor beside her. With considerable astonishment I saw a carry-cot down there among the cartons of wool, with a sleeping infant in it. He looked prematurely resigned and old and his small hands were clenched defensively.

"Why, Jen, you sly fox. I had no idea you were—"

"Well, I'm large. Always been large. Always will be. It has its advantages."

I longed to ask her a dozen questions, but couldn't. There were some people, like Max, you could ask almost anything; there were a few like my dim-witted neighbour June you could ask absolutely anything; and there were private people like Jennifer Mugabwe whom you could ask nothing at all. Occasionally I'd seen men of various colours fleetingly come and go about the shop, but she never referred to them, verbally or any other way. I vaguely assumed she was or had been married, because she wore rings on all her fingers; but I never asked. Quite possibly the rings were just a send-up of the whole matrimonial scene.

The kids stood by the carry-cot looking down critically at the newcomer. "He'll look better, maybe, next week," said Martha.

Jennifer laughed. "Don't take any bets," she said. But she touched the carrier lightly, just once, with her long hand.

"You must find he complicates things for you here, don't you, Jen?"

"Sure he does. But what the hell. I got lonesome."

And indeed a profound and permanent loneliness enfolded Jenny as palpably as her long, rich-coloured gowns, and gave her a dignity never seen in simply happy people. Yet you could not possibly feel sorry for her. She seemed to have no particular attachment to anyone, despite the existence of a large, gregarious family. In fact, she ran her life, like her business, with a cool detachment I admired and envied. And the boy in the cot would not alter her basic quality; you could see that by the way she looked at him. Her kind of motherhood would be aloof without being cold, proprietary without being possessive. When I thought of future likely developments in my own she-wolf relationship with my kids, I wondered whether I couldn't use lessons from Jen in more than weaving. For a minute I stood there watching her thread the shuttle back and forth, back and forth, and her silence rested me. Then the shrill bleat of a noontime factory whistle recalled me to the business of life.

"Oh God, is that noon? Come on, kids. Health Shop next."

"It's Monday," Jen said. "They're closed today."

"They would be. It's shaping into that kind of day. Come on, then, Hugh. Hup-hup, Mar. See you, Jen."

Doggedly we set out once more. The little Greek everything shop that was the nearest thing to a supermarket our district had to offer lay two blocks south along the groove of a sawtooth wind off the lake. Violet shuffled along cheerfully enough, the vet now being safely downwind, but Martha paused to slap every bare and creaking tree we passed, and Hugh began to grizzle again, his nose cherry-red in the cold, as the stroller jolted him over ice shards on the pavement.

We were all glad to dive into the shop's cosy fug smelling of coffee and vegetables and sugary packaged biscuits. The aisles were crammed with every conceivable kind of tinned, packaged, dehydrated, and frozen food. Senior citizens inched up and down the gangways as if mesmerized by such a choice of evils, and over our heads Muzak speakers oozed the kind of vapid tunes some baleful expert had found stimulated consumers to consume more.

I hovered a long time at the bakery shelf, trying without success to find brown bread that wasn't full of sinister chemicals. One of the many things motherhood had done to me was produce a deep suspicion of all preservatives and artificial flavours added to food. I'd even gone so far as to shape a theory that these additives fostered not only allergies but drug dependence, personality disorders, depression, violence, and racial tension. As theories go, mine seemed to explain the seventies as well as anything else; not that there was much satisfaction in that. Gloomily I chose a small ready-sliced brown loaf loaded with preservatives, as Martha duck-footed toward me lugging a huge box of sugared cereal.

"No, love, we don't want that kind." Too late, I remembered that the word "No" invariably triggered a head-on collision with Martha's will-power, a force Ivan the Terrible himself might have respected. She clamped herself now so tightly to the box that when I tried to get it out of her arms by pulling up, her feet dangled six inches above the ground. With a final jerk I separated her from the carton and set it out of reach on a shelf. Shrieking with rage, she aimed a kick (which luckily missed) at a display of pet food and rolled herself like a dervish down the narrow aisle. Various elderly shoppers nervously stepped aside to avoid her flailing arms and legs. It was hard to believe, I thought, going in pursuit, that here was a child whose diet was almost entirely free of preservatives.

By the time I reached her, Martha had already attracted a small group of spectators watching the performance with pleasurable horror.

"Well, that one's got the devil's own temper, for sure," said one old man with munching relish.

"Honestly, I don't know what's the matter with kids today," a middle-aged woman with a tic murmured.

"I'd give her a good slap if she were mine," contributed a grim old person of unidentifiable sex.

"You better be careful, young lady, or a policeman will come and take you off to jail," a fat woman said, bending menacingly over Martha with her bifocals flashing.

In other circumstances, I would have hauled young Martha to her feet, adding a brisk smack if necessary, and that would have been that. As it was, I gathered her up tenderly and gave her a number of kisses, at the same time spraying the audience with a dismissive glare. The woman in bifocals had a cruel, beak-nosed profile that reminded me of Pamela, a waitress from my childhood, who had the same kind of furrowed face, like some barbarian chieftain slow in the head but nifty with the battle-axe. Just to think of Pamela brought me a retrospective qualm of fear. I must have been about seven when Billie hired her to look after me the three or four evenings a week when she liked to go to the pub.

"Of course, you could easily put yourself to bed," she

27

said, "and if the hotel bursts into flamés, you've got two
perfectly good legs, which is more than can be said for most
of the poor old bods here. But Pamela will keep you company, and help with your bath, and that will be nicer for
you." What she meant was that this way she could both
have her evening out and feel like a wise and generous
mother. I grudged her neither of these pleasures, but I did
protest.

"Bill, I don't like Pamela."

"Why on earth not? She can't help being fat, you know."

I thought she could, since I'd seen the number of Mars
bars she could put away at a sitting; but this wasn't the
point. Pamela had heavy eyebrows that met and mingled on
the bridge of her large, hooked nose. A peculiar metallic
smell hung about her, and on one of her broad hands she had
a rudimentary sixth finger, a little stump that made me
flinch every time it caught my eye. One of her pastimes was
to tickle me with fingers that grew increasingly hard and
probing, adding sharp little jabs with this deformed stump
until my laughter turned to sobbing under the red mask
grinning down at me.

"I don't like it when she tickles me," I said helplessly.

"Oh, don't be such a stick-in-the-mud, Anne. Can't
you enjoy a game like anyone else?"

All children learn in ways like this that they can expect
no justice in this world. I was no exception; but to this day, I
think having Pamela as a babysitter was unusually bad luck
in every way. Not only were her looks — and her smell —
repulsive, they were deeply disturbing, because I knew
these things were the outward signs of her true inner self.

On some evenings she brought along reading matter
like *Woman's Own* and the time went by more or less

peacefully; but more often she preferred to talk, thus preventing me from diving into a book of my own, where I was already finding refuge from the world and some of the people in it.

"What's this, then?" she would say, riffling the pages of *The Magician's Nephew* or *The Phoenix and the Carpet*. "Rubbish, I call it. Un'ealthy stuff for a kid. Give you nightmares, that will. Now you take my cousin Ede's boy, 'e's just about your age, and that kid 'asn't never 'ad 'is nerves right since the teacher read 'is class some rubbish about a dragon. Walks in 'is sleep, 'e does, like some kind of a zombie, arms 'eld out and 'is eyes wide open, while Ede and 'er friends are trying to get on with a card game or that. It's 'orrible to see 'im. You want to give 'im a clip round the ear'ole to wake 'im up, I tell 'er, but Ede won't do it. I shouldn't wonder it'll end in 'im going mental. But there, Ede's got one boy already stealing knicks off of clotheslines, so maybe it's in the blood."

The thought of this corrupted blood creeping along with stolen underwear on its sinister tide was disquieting enough, but as the evening wore on, Pamela often had worse revelations to make.

"No, I wouldn't want no kids; none of that for me, thank you," she would go on. "Too much can go wrong, and that's a fact. There's my sister, waited ten years and then 'ad 'er first, all them fancy vi'amins and a great big modern 'ospital — and then what 'appened? I'll tell you what. That baby when it was born 'adn't got but the one eye, right bang in the middle of its fore'ead. Know what they done? They drowned it, that's what, right there in the delivery room, in a pail of water."

Nothing about this narrative struck me as even remotely funny at the time. She would watch me closely all through these accounts, and when I began to swallow and hide my cold and sweating hands, her face would darken with a heavy flush. She saved up for bedtime tales of the psychic experiences of her niece Doreen, who once heard a voice in the wind on Margate sands calling "Beware", and on another occasion, just before getting into bed, felt a skinny hand grasp her by the ankle and hold her fast.

Unfortunately, as far as I could tell, the things Pamela liked to talk about were just as inescapably true and real as she was herself, and there seemed no way I could discuss either of them with Billie. So I simply accepted fear of the dark, fear of blood, fear of the wind, and fear of Pamela as part of living. When Billie suddenly announced one spring that she thought a few months in Boulogne might be amusing, for once I had no tears to shed at the thought of lost friends and a school actually conducted in French. It wasn't till years later I realized that I would never be free of her; never. Which may explain a good deal, if not everything, about the way I am now.

I bent over Martha tenderly.

"Now come on, lovey, and we'll all have a nice ice-cream, how's that?"

A smile of blissful triumph spread over her fat face. The audience scattered, amid disapproving murmurs. As we all emerged once more into the wind, licking our cones, I muttered "Beware", and the memory of Pamela shrank just a little.

Halfway down the block we met my neighbour Junie and her two kids, Darryl dragging dough-faced Charleen along on a toboggan in a series of malicious jerks to make her cry. Snow was now driving in stinging gusts through the grey and bitter air, forming as it fell a layer of hard little pellets underfoot as dry as salt.

"Hi, June. Ugh, isn't this awful?"

"Mo-om-my. Make Darryl stop that."

"I need a drink badly," said Martha.

"Don't we all. Stop that, Violet."

"Want to come over for coffee, Anne? Bring the gang, then."

"Mo-om-my . . ."

"Shut up, Charleen."

On we went to this reiterated theme through the blast, pushing or pulling kids and parcels and dogs and ourselves. Under our plodding feet the snow crunched like the salt of Siberian mines. Our street soon mercifully appeared, with its terraced rows of ex-slummy houses, their doors and woodwork painted bold fuchsia, lime green, or yellow by their trendy occupants. I admired these Depression-built houses for remaining, in spite of everything, stubbornly dated, incorrigibly lower class, with their mean little bay windows and prissy gingerbread trim. What's more, though they were cheek to cheek, as it were, and blandly similar, each one had none the less an air of separateness that seemed to me very Canadian and satisfactory.

"You sit down, Anne. I'll get the baby's stuff off. Darryl, you help Martha with her boots. Coffee or a beer, Anne? No kidding, you look awful. God, when are you due? You must be five feet round, I never saw anything like it." And she actually pushed a hassock under my feet.

This solicitude was vaguely alarming, because Junie so rarely expressed concern about or even interest in anyone but herself, with the possible exception of the shadow-people in afternoon soaps like *As the World Turns*. In fact, the flickering action on the small screen seemed to her the one reality: life itself from day to day was an illusion she moved through like a somnambulist. Now, though it was only midday, she automatically turned on the set like someone plugging into a vital source; but to my relief she forgot to turn the sound up. The kids immediately squatted around the TV, Charleen sucking her thumb, to watch the host of a talk show bare all his glittering teeth at his guest, a frightened middle-aged lady novelist.

"I saw Ross when he called in last week," June called from the kitchen, where I could see her stirring tap water into the powdered instant.

I'll bet you did, I thought unkindly. When I say June Williamson isn't interested in real people, I mean with the exception of one and all circulating in and out of our house next door.

"Well, anything new with him?"

"Nothing much. He did the ironing. As usual. Fixed the bathroom tap. Read a story to the kids. And then took off."

"That was Tuesday. Haven't heard from him since? Sheesh. Aren't men the pits." Junie's idiom was terrifically with it and up to date; but I sometimes wondered whether it meant she was advanced or retarded for her age, which was thirty-four.

Now should I tell her Mother is coming for tea, or let her have the thrill of catching it without preparation? Decisions, decisions. Christ, it was delicious to be sitting down. While June rummaged biscuits out of a packet, I sighed and closed my eyes to the rhythmic scratching of Violet;

opened them a minute or two later to find the talk-show man now looking rather nervously at the novelist, who was laughing.

"Not asleep, are you?" demanded June's thin voice. My eyes blinked to focus her long, narrow face, green eyeshadow over close-set eyes, the whole in a lavish Botticelli frame of dry, frizzy hair.

No such luck, I thought ungratefully, and sipped my lukewarm drink.

"I mean like what are you going to *do* about that guy, Anne? Call him up and tell him to get lost permanently, I would."

"I can't call him up."

"Good grief, why not?"

"Too proud or something. Or just bloody-minded. I don't know. It's being in the wrong, it makes me stubborn as hell."

"In the wrong! What next. He's the one shacked up with someone else. I mean this is why divorce was *invented*, right?"

"I know."

"So you might as well face it, the marriage is over."

"No, it isn't, really."

"Come on, what's this really —"

"Can't explain. Just it isn't over."

There was no way to explain to Junie or even to myself why and how this was true. But Ross and I both knew that in spite of everything, some kind of tough, durable bond still linked us — something that had nothing at all to do with love and less with sex. Whatever it was, it made Larine with her long, lank hair and waif's eyes almost irrelevant. But it was not a situation anybody else could be expected to understand, no matter how often they watched *Family Court*.

"Ask me, I'd lock the bastard out next time he comes by," said Junie.

"You wouldn't. He washes the floors."

She shrugged eloquently. And because we were friends of a sort, I tried to think of a change of subject. Among the many things she didn't believe in was housework in any of its many forms (slavery); so they lived in a morass of discarded copies of *The Sun*, choked ashtrays, more or less empty tin cans, and a series of hamsters that kept disappearing into the walls. Whenever Ross grumbled about my casual housekeeping, I used to point out to him that at least our sink wasn't full of silverfish, nor did our sofa smell shrilly of pee like June's.

"Grand or petty larceny," he sighed, rolling his blue eyes upward. "First- or second-degree murder. You're the family lawyer, all right."

"Oh, do stop nagging."

"Listen, in this kitchen you could do worse than latch onto the old line about 'cleanliness is next to godliness'."

"Cleanliness is next to goddam self-righteousness, if you ask me."

"I didn't ask you. I know better than that."

I shook my head to scatter this line of thought. "Want some lunch?" asked Junie, and I said "Yes", though I knew that she didn't believe in cooking either (waste of time). Lunch would therefore mean a tin of something, and for the kids mugs of coloured water made from crystals called Yum, easier to carry home than a jug of milk. Just the same, it was so beautiful to keep sitting down that none of this seemed to matter very much.

The kids were now fighting over possession of a box of

popcorn. Darryl, aged seven, was an easy winner. Clad in a torn, oversized T-shirt that read "Great in Bed", he had his father's basketball-shaped head and small, nailhead eyes. Charleen, with a loud, nasal whine, grabbed away Martha's share, and Martha promptly hit her across the arm with a toy truck. Hugh began to wail because in watching the fray he'd relaxed his clutch on his own popcorn and Violet swiftly gulped it down. The whole scenario was so familiar and so bloody awful it was like an old friend.

I thought of struggling up to interfere, but the effort was too much. I closed my eyes again. Junie, returning with a pot out of which she ladelled a mass of gluey pasta into bowls, did not appear to notice the fracas at all. How superb, I thought enviously. How great it must be to rise with such sincere indifference above nearly everything, including your own kids. Once she'd chosen their names, they no longer appeared to involve her at all. And this was probably no more ridiculous than going to the opposite extreme, like me. I was already worried that Martha's nose might be a shade too long, and that Hugh's wife wouldn't understand him.

"What's your feeling about my hair. Be honest," Junie asked as I poked at my spaghetti.

"Your hair? Why, it's great stuff."

"No, I mean the style. I'm thinking about going short. Eh? What do you think?"

"Sure. Why not."

"Why don't you too? That huge braid down your back, Anne, is it ever weird. I mean nobody else . . . and it's a gorgeous colour, you know. You could have a perm and —"

Fighting off sleep, I said, "Oh, too much bother. I'm used to it this way."

"But that's just it, man. What I mean, maybe we're both ready for a new self-image. Now this radical Afro's been out, actually, for ages, right? A real short job you can blow-dry. Like Liza Minnelli? How about it, you and me both."

"Mm. Might look great."

"Plus I'm thinking of getting into acupuncture. My back gives me hell these days. This winter's been such a drag. What do you think?"

"Dunno. Might help."

"Cagy you. Never say. When were you born? I bet you're Scorpio."

I was born when my daughter was. But there was no real point in saying this to June, so I said nothing.

"I'm Pisces, but Clive's Leo, that's probably why we're so maladjusted sexually. I'd like for us to get into bondage, something kinky, you know, just for a change? But he just grunts and says a screw's a screw, the quicker the better as far as he's concerned. . . ."

I shifted my weight to ease a cramp. Once June got started on her sex life, the monologue could run a long course. By rights I should have found the topic quite riveting, now it was a purely theoretical or philosophical one, removed from the arena of the marriage bed for me, perhaps for keeps. Instead, I stifled a great yawn as June droned on about uterine orgasm. Darryl, on the other hand, was listening greedily. Still, it might have been only coincidence that his hand was on his genitals. It was there most of the time anyway.

Idly my mind drifted to Clive, with that chest hair of his, thick as a hearthrug, and his habit of scratching himself through it with an absent smile. At least *he* wasn't coming home to me every evening. Yes, it was quite good therapy to think about Clive.

Snow was still hissing against the windows. June was silent now, sitting hunched over, pushing back the cuticle from her bitten nails. Without wanting to, I said, "You ever sorry you quit at the bank, June? Ever wish you'd never started all this . . ." and I lifted my chin at the room, the kids. "I mean, for you it was all chosen . . . not like me, where the whole damn thing just sort of happened."

"Are you kidding?" The cigarette bobbed between her lips as she lit a match for it. "Smartest thing I ever did was get out of that lousy job. When I think of that bitch of a supervisor pussyfooting around, and all that nitpicking every day about a few lousy cents . . . oh God, no. What's a man for if he doesn't get you out of all that."

"Well, he gets you into a lot of other stuff, though."

June shrugged. "What stuff? Couple of kids — six-room house — nothing to it, if you know how to operate. You're your own boss, that's the point. Time's your own. You can, like, get yourself together. . . ." But her voice petered out, unconvinced. Then she began again, perhaps remembering which of us was the real failure. "Of course, it's different for you, with your college degree and that. No way, you were out of your mind to bog down with all these kids. And now with Ross . . . well, I don't know, but in your shoes I'd dump the whole gang of them on his doorstep, or on your family or somebody, and just take off. Get some really great job. . . . And get rid of that braid."

A fleeting memory of chains made me twitch aside the heavy rope of my hair. "Every single, solitary person I know agrees with you, June." And I began to cry again, the tears running down warm and comforting into my neck.

June pushed a Kleenex into my hand, muttering, "You poor kid." I blew my nose. Hugh headed over to me with his drunken stagger and tried to climb the mound of my belly. He was considerably wetter than I was.

"Right, Junie, we have to go. Ta for the lunch, and the cry. And I honestly think you'd look great in a short hair-style — shaped into a side flip, you know?"

June's narrrow face at once turned to the hall mirror. She stared at it intently, trying for the how-manyeth time to get her own identity into some kind of permanent focus. I stuffed the kids into their clothes without help; in fact, she was so absorbed she hardly seemed to notice our departure. And as I herded the kids and Violet out of her house and into ours, I felt the usual guilty relief at having escaped from her. Guilty because often, comparing our failures and frustrations, I knew she was my sister, my double.

Home again inside my own walls, I felt a little lighter and brighter, for no good reason at all. After changing Hugh, I plopped him into his crib; then, using rather more muscle, I put Martha down for a nap. There was no point even in thinking about one for myself, much as I craved sleep. At night I could only doze in snatches, what with heartburn, fetal acrobatics, and backache; but all these things had been going on for so long I hardly noticed them now, any more than I missed being able to see my own feet.

Anyhow, at this point even sitting down was out of the question. It was half past one, and there was all the silver yet to clean, the Coalport cups to get down, a cake to make, and the sitting-room to dust before Mother (promptly on the tick of four-thirty) arrived with the goddam marmalade. Having all this to do was useful, though, if only because it annoyed me and pepped up my circulation. Quite possibly Edwina was mustering a little adrenalin of her own for this encounter. Because by this time she almost certainly realized that calling on me amounted to an invasion of alien territory.

As I beat eggs fiercely into the cake batter, I thought about my own first discovery of how militant a house visit can be. It was the night when I first called at that house on Prince John Street where Ross lived with Larine. They shared the place with four or five other people, including a student librarian and a man who made trusses in the basement apartment. I knew all their histories; Ross often discussed their problems at length with me. It was one way of avoiding confrontation with our own. The result was that I knew the Chinese girl's grades, the truss-maker's gambling debts, and why the math teacher's dropout son Jamie was cheerfully earning a living playing the guitar in subway stations. But I'd never met any of them, apart from Larine. For a long time some ridiculous kind of delicacy — or maybe it was simple cowardice — kept me from going there, even when warmly invited. Disturbingly enough, Larine had from the start been as friendly to me as her unfocussed nature would permit; and as for Ross, as soon as he had moved out of our house, he became more affectionate to me than he'd been for a long time. Still, he'd been gone for over a month before I could bring myself to go where the two of them lived.

Presumably by accident, Ross had left behind some legal papers I knew he would need next day in court. And so, carefully allowing myself no time to get agitated about it, I put on my new eyelet cotton and my best white sandals, and installed a sitter for the kids. My current pregnancy didn't show yet, which helped give me confidence.

"Come in, come in," said a pretty little Chinese girl in jeans. "I think Ross is in the kitchen."

From the hallway I glanced into the sitting-room, where Pink Floyd was bursting out of several speakers and a couple danced at opposite ends of the room. A huge dog of no identifiable breed was asleep or dead in the hall, where a long macramé ornament hung. I stepped over the brute with some difficulty and trepidation.

"It's okay," said a voice from the stairs. "He only bites people he knows." Glancing up, I saw a boy on the landing fingering a guitar — Jamie. Long, curling Jesus hair fanned out on either side of his freckled face, which was dramatized by a strip of beaded leather tied across the forehead. He smiled at me happily.

In the kitchen I found Ross perched on the counter eating a bacon-and-tomato sandwich. He hopped down at once and came over to give me a friendly kiss on the cheek. "Nice of you to drop by," he said. He'd been urging me to do so for weeks, because that would force me to recognize his new identity. So I smiled at him without warmth and said, "It isn't a social call. But I knew you'd need this stuff for tomorrow." And I handed over the papers. The idea had been simply to deliver them and go, after giving an impression of supreme unconcern. But of course with little or no persuasion I accepted a cup of coffee and sat down at the kitchen table to drink it. There, with as much strategic coolness as possible, I assessed enemy movements.

Larine was stirring something highly unsavoury in a pot. She wore no shoes, and a length of frayed clothesline belted her tattered jeans. Through the thin cotton of a very tight T-shirt, the nipples of her tiny breasts stuck out like two mosquito bites. Except for these, she looked like a deprived nine-year-old, which in many respects she was.

"You eaten yet?" Ross asked her.

"No. Later, maybe." This I found understandable. The kitchen smelled of stale oil and chemicals. Aside from tins of dogfood, there didn't seem to be anything to eat around anyway.

"Larine's on a macrobiotic diet," he told me, "so I eat alone not to gross her out."

"Do you?" I said unpleasantly. "Should have thought it might work the other way."

But this only made Larine smile kindly and Ross give me an indulgent pat. To be showered with so much serene goodwill of course infuriated me, and I stood up to go. But just then Larine forked up the contents of her pot, and I saw it was a blouse she was tie-dyeing, which helped to explain if not excuse the smell. "I'll hang this out and then split," she said to us. "You guys maybe want to rap."

I muttered something and she disappeared.

"She's a good kid," Ross said fondly.

I looked at him. "Well, the kid part is right on. Most of your chums here come on like maybe eight years old. And I happen to know Larine is twenty-five. I mean, doesn't it embarrass you to be with them, for God's sake?"

"No," he said coldly. The eyelids dropped sulkily over those very blue eyes of his. I had never attacked so directly before. "Sure, it's easy to be stuffy about people living like this. But get this straight — they're people with guts. They're finding their own way. Even the kids. They aren't afraid to be themselves, not their parents' puppets. Anyhow, for the first time in my life, just about, I'm easy. They give me space."

My mouth trembled. I pushed away my cup. The enemy had been located and identified: me. It was time to go, and I went. But on the way out, I noticed a splintered hole in the lower panel of the vestibule door. In spite of all that courage and space, somebody had raised a foot and kicked that hole in who knows what rage of frustration or disillusion. I wondered which one of them it was, and by the time I got home, I felt almost cheerful.

Once the cake was in the oven, I dragged up a kitchen stool to prop under my broad bottom, and with a sigh uncapped the silver polish, trying not to let the smell of it get to me. Luckily, despite my feelings about Edwina and her marmalade, I really liked the silver tea-set. Each piece was designed with classic simplicity, without any silly bulges or ornamental fuss, and it was actually a pleasure to turn the bronze tarnish into a bright, silky shine.

Perhaps it took someone with a rootless past like mine really to value everything this silver stood for, namely continuity in an incoherent world. A long, tranquil sequence of time produced both Ross and the tea-set that was a natural part of his heritage. It was carried in every afternoon at four by his grandmother's lame old maid Gwen, who had been with the family for forty years. On the tray was always the same array of things: a faded Crown Derby bowl for slops, a delicate little sterling strainer, and a set of embroidered cambric napkins. The food was always paper-thin bread and butter, a plate of oatmeal cookies, and a fruit cake. The thin little George III spoons were brought over to Canada by Ross's great-grandfather. Also part of his luggage was a velvet-lined leather case for his top hat. It was a world where young Malcolm Graham was expected to become a Supreme Court judge, and did, just as Ross Malcolm Graham followed him to Ridley and Osgoode Hall as naturally as he breathed.

All this made me think with some bitterness of the five suitcases Billie and I used to tote from seaside hotel to seaside hotel, like a pair of travelling actors. I see now that Billie probably felt the need to play over and over again the role of pretty young widow with child; but in those days I never really knew my part. Children get their sense of security from their background, and I had none that lasted; it kept folding and dropping away like stage sets. Bournemouth, Brighton, Felixstowe, Broadstairs . . . it was there at the Sea View Hotel where I first felt that almost desperate need to find some kind of stability. Perhaps that's what first attracted me to science, a branch of study where change was not a threat to be struggled with in confusion and dismay, but a natural process to be observed, codified, and documented. A career in some lab or lecture theatre would give me a persona, a settled place to be in. . . . That was what I craved, and why I made that childish grab at Max.

It wasn't until much later that I realized how much of this Max perceived. I was completely astonished when, a few months after that night on the Promenade, he wrote to Billie.

"There's been a kind of miracle," said the thin blue air-letter, and the slow smile in his dark eyes came right up through the flimsy paper like something palpable. Business would bring him back to London in December, and he went on to suggest that we join him there and do some theatres over Christmas weekend. So for several days Billie and I ate with him in grand restaurants, and looked at crown jewels and zoo tigers and the pantomime, just like a family.

I hardly dared to breathe for happiness and hope. He was clearly attracted to her. Unfortunately, he was not at all the kind of man Billie generally fancied: she preferred them to have mustaches and fast cars. It seemed so unfair that I had the agility and common sense to want him now for Billie rather than for myself, and yet had such poor chances of success because his sideburns were short. The day he was scheduled to fly back to Toronto, fog delayed him a whole extra day with us and I rejoiced; but Billie had caught a heavy cold. Instead of being sparkling and silly she looked small and miserable, the end of her nose bright pink and her eyes puffy. I was sure then there was no more point whatever in thinking about a future with Max in it.

But on our first morning back at the Sea View, an overseas call came for her while we moped over a sausage-and-egg breakfast. She came back to the table looking flushed and astonished.

"I may just die of complete surprise," she said.

"Why, what's the matter?"

"That was Max Ehrlich. It's three in the morning in Canada. And what an awful connection; it was like trying to talk at a dogfight."

"But what did he want?"

"Well, he said, 'Billie dear, why don't you and Anne come over to Canada this spring and look the place over.' His exact words. I think."

"Oh, Bill. That means he wants to marry you."

"He's much too clever a man to say that yet, sweetie. But, yes, that's exactly what he means."

"You don't think it was just crossed wires or wishful thinking, do you? It would be awful to go all the way over there and then find out he only wanted to show us Niagara Falls."

Billie gave a snuffling little laugh. "What a funny, middle-aged sort of kid you are, ducky. But what do you think of the idea? You like him, don't you?"

"Would you marry him, then?" I asked, hardly daring to believe it. "I mean, if he asks, would you accept?"

"Of course I would. That is a very special man, and I know it. He's about a hundred times brainier and nicer than I am, but if he doesn't mind that, why should I? No, I think it would work out very well, mostly because of the way Max is. Good without being dull. So rare, that, when you think about it. As for his being Jewish, I like that too. It's part of him, maybe the nicest part. He knows how to laugh, anyhow, better than any Christian I know."

I listened in some surprise to these tributes. Billie stopped talking for a minute as if she were a little surprised herself. Then she added briskly, "So you approve, then? I thought you would. And of course it's lovely for both of us that he's quite rich into the bargain."

"Yes."

"Then there's Toronto. I like the sound of it. Right on that huge lake, and everything so new and busy."

"Yes. And if I get my A levels, I could go to the university there, couldn't I?"

"Of course, if you're really bent on it."

Billie poured us more tea. There was a sudden rather awkward little silence between us. I glanced at her to find that all the gaiety had faded abruptly out of her face, leaving it with a rather pinched look that had nothing to do with her cold.

"What's the matter, Bill?"

"Oh, nothing really. Only I'm forty, you know, sweetie, and he's over fifty. We're both pretty wise birds, in our different ways . . . you get to a point in life when you know more than you want to know ... I mean when there are absolutely no starry-eyed delusions about anything. Marriages, for instance. They are *deals*. Max and I both know that. A sort of trade-off on both sides. Nothing soppy and romantic about it at all. I get security and companionship. He gets ... well." She pushed away her tea without finishing it.

"Of course, you realize he's marrying both of us," she went on. "He thinks the world of you — admiration, respect — the lot. Me he will keep as a pet."

"Billie!" I said, shocked by what I recognized as the naked truth. It alarmed me considerably, because I thought no one having such thoughts could possibly marry in spite of them. In this, as in so many other things, I was, of course, wrong.

The timer buzzed, jerking me back to the present, where my own bed was made — i.e., my cake baked, my silver polished, and my bloody mother-in-law due for tea. How queer that Ross's stable past and my rootless one had twisted together like this to produce today, with all its possessions, its ironies, its insoluble problems. With a great sigh I stooped and lifted the cake from the oven as Martha called to me from upstairs. Christ, it was nearly four o'clock and I still had the kids to dress and the house to tidy. ...

Promptly on schedule, Mother emerged from her taxi and minced daintily up the path, crocodile handbag in one hand, bulging plastic carrier in the other. A face flashed at Junie's bay window. Intermittent gusts of dry snow spat at Mother's mink. "Why does she walk as if her sodding *legs* were nailed together?" I wondered as I went to the door.

We exchanged the light ritual kiss she had taught me to receive and give. The kids watched with large, surprised eyes while the fur coat was taken off and hung up. Most of our callers wore duffle coats, so I think as she first approached they'd seen Mother as some kind of fur-bearing animal, a bison for instance, which God knows wasn't far from the truth. For various reasons (flu, Florida), she hadn't paid us her usual monthly visit since Ross left, and they had forgotten her.

"Well, and here are the dear little . . . *children*!" she said, exposing for their benefit the full expanse of her newly mended bridge. They both backed off, looking hunted.

"Haven't you got a kiss for your old Granny, then?" she asked.

"No," returned Martha bleakly.

"At least say hello, can't you?" I urged, mortified.

Just the same, as they stood shoulder to shoulder looking up at us, I was proud of them. Hugh was balanced firmly on widespread legs. His Ogilvy tartan shorts and white shirt hadn't been on long enough to be more than slightly crumpled. And although his nose was running, he took his favourite three fingers out of his mouth long enough to give Edwina a wide, wet smile.

Martha's black hair was brushed smooth and pinned back with a silver clasp, and she was smugly conscious of her pink smocked dress (kindly ironed the week before by Ross). She had actually stood still willingly while I forced little silk loops over twelve small buttons down her back. I just hoped she wouldn't repeat to Mother any of the words I'd mentioned at the time.

"Do come in and sit down, Mother, and I'll get us some tea."

47

"Is there presents in that bag?" demanded Martha.

"There might be, for a good girl," declared Mother coyly. "Come and let's see. My, how they've grown, Anne. Hugh has changed so I'd hardly know him. He's the perfect image of my father. How has he ... *been* lately?" she added rather less cordially when he toddled over to lay a wet hand on her knee.

"Well, this winter he's had one long cold, or about sixteen short ones. Still, that bad go of croup he had in December was the last — he hasn't been to hospital since, thank God."

"What does Dr. Marshall say about all these colds?"

"Mother, we left Dr. Marshall years ago. The kids' doctor now is Jeff Reilly, an old pal of Ross's. He's young but awfully good."

"And why do I say 'but'," I thought crossly. Why did I ever endure the austere régime of her old buddy, Dr. Marshall, who had no lips and no compassion — likewise no interest in Martha's five-month colic.

"Hm," said Edwina, exercising restraint.

Hugh listened to this exchange pensively. In his sixteen months of life, he'd learned more than some people ever know about the frailties of the flesh. In that short span, recurrent ear infections and bouts of croup had fetched us running into Sick Kids' Emergency several times, and he'd been in for six days in the fall, having a hernia repaired. Neither he nor I would ever forget the suffering of that separation, the twice-daily agony of the visits when we met and parted and tried to control our tears. Poor old Hugh had a naturally cautious and pessimistic nature, and his experience of life so far tended to confirm his worst misgivings. That was why I so loved his patience and gentleness. Now he looked with speculation at the carrier bag; but he would never, as Martha did, lay bold hands on it and shout, "Open up!"

"Now just a minute, dear," murmured Edwina, meaning "What foul manners your child has." I escaped to the kitchen to boil water and cut lemons, but out there I could hear amicable sounds of mutual approval as she doled out the gifts. Martha actually said a gruff "Thank you!" and ran out to show me a Lego set. On Mother's large, bland face when I returned was a faint, gratified smile, although she said, "I really meant it for Hugh; but the tea-set seems to be what he likes."

"Yes, I think Martha's going to be an engineer, she's such a Lego nut. As for Hugh, he may well wind up as a nurse."

Mother chose to regard these remarks as jokes, and attempted to smile. A balloon over her head said in large letters, "They're queer youngsters. But what can you expect?"

"Let me see," she said. "Martha will be three next month, won't she? I must say she has a very large . . . *vocabulary*, for such a little girl."

"Well, it's my guess that she's got a higher IQ than either Ross or me. They say you should never do this, it makes problems later on at school — but she is *forcing* me to teach her to read. Already she does quite well with things like Dr. Seuss."

"Go, dog, go," said Martha complacently.

"Now, Mother, come and sit at the table, there's less chance of spills that way with the kids. Come on, you two."

The table with its bright silver and best china looked orderly and gracious. The children's faces shone over their clean white bibs. Gently I removed Martha's hand from the cake knife and gave her a marmite sandwich. The tea ritual unfolded with propriety to the tinkle of spoons and inane remarks about distant relatives and the weather. By Mother's standards, it was all going extremely well. But just as I thought this, the napkin slid off my lap and as I bent to retrieve it, I spotted on the carpet, close to Mother's foot, a large human turd. Martha, of course. It even had a cheeky little curl on the top of it.

Swiftly I dropped a Kleenex and with a scoop and a twist recovered this deposit before beating a swift retreat to the kitchen to dispose of it. Once safely out there, I leaned against the counter to let a wild, silent fit of giggles come and go.

"And now do tell me all about Ross. How is my boy these days? It seems so long since I saw him last. He's still working up to all hours, I suppose."

"Well, we knew setting up his own practice would mean a rough year or two, even with partners as good as Tim and Randy. Luckily, though, the business is rolling in. No trouble about that side of it." (And just how lucky, Mother dear, I hope you never know.)

"So he's still getting home late every night, I suppose, and working every weekend? Well, it's a mercy you live downtown — at least he's not commuting at all hours. But when does he ever see the children? I must say, it's rather ∴ . . *hard* on you, specially with this new one coming. Well, he'll simply have to take a little time off then. Pity there's no such thing as *paternity* leave." And she gave her little tittering laugh.

I stared into my half-empty cup. Then I wiped Hugh's nose. "Do have some more cake, Mother."

"No, thank you, dear. I'm glad to hear the practice is thriving. But what about that girl Larine?"

By a superhuman effort I kept astonishment off my face, and resentment. It's cheating when predictable people say something totally unpredictable.

"Why, she's all right, I guess." But my voice was high with surprise. Was it possible that good old Mother had resources of insight, or sheer, blind guts, that in these four years I hadn't yet recognized?

"I did so feel," she went on, smoothing a hand over her large bosom in the complacent, preening way she had, "and I still do, that Ross was taking a quite unnecessary risk, hiring a girl with that kind of . . . *background*. I mean drugs — a police record — in a law office? With all the . . . *decent* girls looking for work, I really can't understand it."

"Yes. Well," I mumbled.

"After all, Ross is just at the beginning of his career. It's not as if he could afford to take risks at this point, do you think?"

"Maybe not."

"But perhaps he hasn't asked what you think."

My heart was pushing up into my throat. Did the bloody old trout know about the whole thing after all? If so, why was she sidling around the point like this? And if she didn't know, what hell-sent hunch had made her start discussing Larine? My palms were damp with sweat and the table seemed to swing loosely under my elbow. But I kept my voice calm and level. Nothing like rage, terror, and hate, aimed like ray-guns in several different directions at once, to produce the old fighting spirit.

"Well, I think Ross felt a bit protective after he got her off that pushing charge. The drug laws are pretty silly, as you know. And the poor kid has a lurid history . . . did Ross ever tell you the story? Her mum was a lush and her dad a religious nut. Or was it the other way round? Anyhow, one of her uncles when she was twelve — um, I guess you get the picture. So Ross thought it was time somebody gave her a break. And so far she's done the routine typing and filing at the office quite well, so he's probably right.''

There was a brief silence. Then she said, ''Ross's father was a *very* difficult man, you know.''

I looked at her. ''Was he?''

''Yes. He'd make a decision like that, on impulse, and then, right or wrong, he'd stick to it, stubborn as —'' She shook her blue-rinsed head. ''He insisted my mother must come and live with us, when my father . . . Passed On. Before six months were over, he knew as well as I did that it was a *mistake*. She didn't mean to interfere, but — well, he died at sixty-one, while she lived to be ninety. You see, he never would admit . . . never. Yes. A really . . . *difficult* man.''

I waited, hoping for more, but she only smoothed her bosom again as if to placate it. Then, after a long pause, she muttered, ''Better say no more. I tend to say . . . *the wrong thing* so often.''

For the first time in our acquaintance, I caught sight of a life's disappointment, frustration, bewilderment, in the pale blue of her foolish eyes. It amazed me to find she knew herself so well. Poor woman. What a fate, to be trapped like that for all those years, between two egos. It was a surprise — almost a shock — to find myself feeling real pity for her; even a flicker of genuine loving-kindness. But what a rat-hole life is, I thought angrily, if it can actually make you love an ass like Edwina Graham.

But like most moments of its kind, in our house at

least, this one was promptly attacked by the forces of chaos. Our Siamese cat, who loved Ross, liked me, and tolerated the kids, had little or no use for the rest of the human race. He now decided that Mother had stayed quite long enough. With a lightning dart, he pounced out of ambush and bit her in the calf. She gave a thin little shriek. The children, who had been quietly stuffing down cake, shrieked too, wildly excited. I got up and flapped a napkin at Chairman Mao, who fled, pretending to be terrified. Then I inspected the wound. Only one small, restrained drop of blood, like her confession.

"I'm so sorry, Mother. He's terrible, that cat. It's a warped sense of humour or something. Let me get you a Band-Aid."

With my head bowed over her stout leg, I fiercely ordered myself not to cry. Or laugh. But Edwina victimized was once more comfortably armoured in her invincible rightness — the perfect guest, grandmother, mother-in-law; the Christian soldier marching as to war. She said, "It's nothing, Anne; nothing at all — it barely ... *penetrated*. Now I really must be going or I'll miss the ten after six. Just let me call a taxi. You sit down, my dear, you look a little tired. Thank you so much for the ... *tea*. I do hope Hugh's cold improves. You'll be sure to give Ross my love, won't you. Ask him to ring me up some time, if he ever has a minute to spare. And by the way, I have a little something here for you both ... I'm sure you could use it."

"Thanks, Mother," I said meekly. And I thought almost with relief how much more comfortable it would be if we could just keep on wearing our old attitudes.

Energetically I cleared up the tea débris and settled the kids with paper and crayons before going upstairs for a peaceful bowel movement, an event harder to fit in than people without small children would ever believe. Behind the blessed privacy of the bathroom door I managed to read several pages of Oscar Browning's *Life of George Eliot*, savouring particularly the words, "She talked to me solemnly about the duties of life, about the shallow immorality of believing that all things would turn out for the best. . . ." Ah, the wonderful toughness of women. What a comfortable inheritance. Nothing else could possibly have kept me in one piece (more or less) in the disaster area of today. The girl I was when Ross and I first met was a stranger I could view from this distance with compassion and forgiveness. She was somebody not yet initiated. Somebody who hoped for the best, and believed in happiness as a real commodity.

He was asleep on my bed when I first saw him — flaked totally out. Lying on his back, arms tossed out recklessly, but legs pressed almost primly together. He was snoring softly. Down the hall in the sitting-room, my roommates Karen and Bonnie with various boys were sort of listening to Janis Joplin while they laughed and popped open beer cans and argued about their karmas. Ross must have adjourned to my room to get away from all that; but I needed my bed. I'd just come home from a long session at the library, because I had a final exam coming up in zoology, and I intended to get the provincial gold medal.

I leaned over him, my mouth opened to say "Hey", and then it happened. In books I'd often read about this emotion without ever feeling it myself, or even believing it really existed. Now here it was, like a punch under the heart. I mean, I'd seen Ross before, plenty of times. For some time now he'd been Karen's steady. She was even beginning to talk about getting engaged after he graduated.

Now I looked at him while a westerly wind blew the light rain of a March thaw against the window. His black eyelashes made stiff crescents on his thin cheeks. The inside of his lower lip was a bright coral colour. His head was big, but the neck looked childishly frail. Something made his hands twitch as I watched him, and maybe the same something made me sit down on the edge of the bed, pushing him over slightly to make room.

"Wake up," I said.

He did, instantly. His blue eyes snapped open; he drew in his long arms and folded them defensively across his chest.

"You've been sleeping in my bed."

"Sorry. Just goofed completely off."

"It's this thaw. And exams looming up." A breeze smelling of wet earth and lake water stirred the curtains. After the winter's long austerity, there was something disturbing and delicious about this mild, moist air. It made the blood slow and the sex organs heavy. Doubtless that was one reason why I couldn't take my eyes off his bearded face, and also why he didn't move away from contact with my hip.

We said nothing for a minute. Beyond the door, Joplin's meandering, sorrowful, self-pitying ballad went on, and we listened, loving it. Then I leaned down and kissed him on the mouth. He co-operated with a warm, trusting friendliness that made my whole body ache with tenderness. I leaned on him and traced the line of his bearded jaw with my fingertips.

"What the hell's your other name, Anne?"

"Forrest."

"Honours Botany. The literary mag and all that."

"Right."

"How come you hardly ever hang around with Karen and Bonnie? Where's your guy?"

"Oh, I mostly mooch around on my own. Got nobody special. If it interests you, I'm known around as 'The Ice Cube'."

"No kidding," he said with interest. We looked at each other thoughtfully. Then he said, "Care to try that again?" and we did that. Several times. Nobody out there seemed to miss him. I forgot all about the gold medal. Sleep no longer seemed in the least important. Eventually we took our shoes off and lay back together on the pillows.

"This is nice," he remarked. "You are nice."

"You are Karen's. That we'd better remember."

But my hand, which had no ethics, was smoothing the shirt over his warm chest.

"I'm nobody's. Don't you believe rumours."

"What's this ring you're wearing, then?"

"It's a seal ring — used to be my grandfather's."

"No kidding. What's that on it, an eagle or something?"

"To be exact, it's an eagle displayed, in his dexter talon a sword erect, proper."

"How bloodthirsty."

"My clan ancestors were a pretty fierce bunch. But the blood's got very thin by now. They'd be ashamed of me. I came in here, actually, because we were trying some Mexican pot earlier on, and it made me feel sick. See what I mean? And you're pretty straight too, right? I like your Rapunzel hair, it feels like a big silk rope."

At this point, Karen opened the door. What happened then — what we all did and said — is blank now. All I can remember is laughing. And then came those spring weeks of new green in parks under the cool, cloudy sky, and in his narrow student bed. ... One brilliant afternoon in particular, I remember, we lay on the young vegetable grass and watched a child in a red dress play in the sunlight with a white cat, and joy distilled itself in those shapes and colours like a real and lasting thing. ...

Sitting on my ignoble throne, I stared down at the chipped tiles of the bathroom floor. We never had got round to remodelling this room, which still had a chain-pull toilet. Without warning my head dropped forward in a short doze, even while one ear kept awake for the kids. Very shortly Hugh's cough jerked me upright, and I rose heavily, flushed the apparatus, and washed my hands, gripping the basin midway to ride out a cramp. While it lasted, I studied the blistered green paint of the cracked wall as an alternative to any encounter in the mirror with my own blotched and pallid face. What a vision, the eyes sunk in dark pits, the big lips cracked, a pregnancy mask over the cheekbones giving the whole thing a crude, animal solidity. Incredible to recall that people once used to call it beautiful. That was indeed in another country, in the cool, sterile latitudes of virginity.

Martha's feet stumped up the stairs and she pushed open the door with a peremptory "Hey!"

"We knock, please. But come in here if you need to, for God's sake. Don't let me find any more poop in the dining-room, *ever again*."

She stared at me, all injured dignity. "That was not me," she said severely. "Granny did it."

A great grin split my mouth. "Nonsense. Do you want to go now?"

"What?"

"I said do you need to go now?"

"Go where?"

"Oh Christ, Martha."

"I'm hungry. I want some strangled eggs."

"All right. Come on, then. You can stir them up."

One of her rare smiles spread across Martha's fat face. She cast short arms around my thighs and pushed her head hard against the low-slung drum of my abdomen, creating a warm patch there with her flesh. I smoothed the thick silk of her hair. Here at last was something of value salvaged from the trivial chaos of the day — something beautiful, perfect, and undeserved. I was humbly grateful for it.

Because it was not moral purity or any lofty sense of values that made me stubbornly adhere to my children once they were so fecklessly conceived. It was just some kind of blind, irrational instinct that appalled me as much as anybody else.

"But Anne," Ross said in a voice slow with shock, "that's impossible. You're on the *pill*, for God's sake. You've got to be wrong."

"No, I'm not. The test was positive. The doctor says I haven't been on the pill long enough. Before you, I wasn't — you know that. So there hasn't been enough time."

"Jesus, Anne. Jesus."

"I'm horribly sorry. Not that it helps much."

"Well, but look. Hospitals look after this kind of accident all the time. I mean, it's perfectly legal. And done by experts and all that. So —"

"No, Ross."

"But —"

"No."

He looked at me in blank dismay. "You don't mean you're actually going to go through with it? But that's *crazy*."

"I know it is. I *know* that. I can't help it. For one thing, I know something about genetics and embryology, so the thought — but it's not just that . . . I don't know what it is."

"But where does that leave me? Tell me that."

"Look, it leaves you just wherever you want to be. This isn't a trap. You're free to do whatever the hell you want. And so am I."

He put his head in his hands. "For God's sake, Anne, how can I get married and start a family right now? You know damn well I've got years to put in before I can earn enough to — "

"I know that. Try to get it through your head, I'm not asking you for anything. I've done a stupid thing; it's my fault entirely. It's also my responsibility. That's all there is to it."

"Oh, don't be such a fool. You know it's mine too, even though — oh Christ. Look, you've got to be reasonable. You're not *thinking*. What about your demonstrator's job? — you said yourself it could be a toehold in the department — for three years you've worked your brains out for the chance. Now for God's sake, go to the doctor and get yourself fixed up. It's the only sane thing to do."

"I can't do that, Ross."

"But why *not*?"

"I've told you why. I just can't do it."

He looked at me desperately. "You scare me, Anne. You scare the hell out of me. Please, change your mind. Please."

"I can't. Everything you say is true. But I can't."

"Then I can't help you. Sorry, but that's it. It's my whole future on the line here too, you know."

"I know that. So we just come apart, that's all. No hard feelings. I'll manage somehow. There are clinics, day-care places. Other people get along, why shouldn't I? You're free; I have no claim on you."

"It's not as if I knew — I mean, I thought you were protected — "

"Of course you did. Stop tearing yourself to pieces. It's all right, I tell you. I'll get along fine."

"Anne, it would be so simple if you'd only — "

"Don't say it again. I can't."

There was a truly terrible silence. Then suddenly, without taking his eyes off mine, Ross broke into clumsy sobbing. The tears tumbled out of his eyes in great round globes and poured down his cheeks, and I put my arms around him protectively.

"Now Ross, will you listen to me, love. Get this straight, once and for all. There's no need to go on about marriage and all that. If you want to — and you may not — if so, okay — we can just go on living together. In any case, I can work at the lab right up to the time and again after. You can be involved as much or as little as you like; but understand me, you are *not* trapped."

"Of course I bloody am," he sobbed indignantly.

"Not by any ring or licence you're not."

I felt his muscles relax a little. He turned away to blow his nose.

"Of course I want us to keep living together," he said. "First thing to do, I guess, is to tell your parents and, oh Christ, my mother, and in general share round the misery, see what they have to say. Better get it over with as soon as we can."

"All right. Only let the poor things see us graduate first. It's only a week to convocation."

"Yes, yes," he broke in. I knew he was grateful for any excuse to put off these encounters, as who wouldn't be. I also knew he still hoped I would change my mind and extricate us both from the whole situation. Perhaps I myself hoped somehow I could, but with no real confidence.

The kids and I ate scrambled eggs out of a communal bowl. I spooned bites into their mouths in a game called Not For You that Hugh enjoyed so much he forgot his dislike of eggs. By the time I got them into their warm, footed sleepers, it was getting late, but instead of putting them to bed, I let them play with their stuffed animals by the sitting-room fire. This indulgence was more for me than for them. While I washed up, I needed to hear their voices, because after dark was the worst part of the day for me. The house developed oppressive creaks and sighs. The empty bed upstairs yawned. Loneliness sneaked up to me, as dangerous as a tangible intruder.

It was hard to believe now how often gregarious flocks of people used to swoop into and out of this deserted house. Natural for them to stay away now, of course. People feel uneasy in disaster areas. Even Bonnie, my best friend since college days, seldom came here now. As I dried Martha's bitten, battered silver mug, I thought yearningly of Bonnie, my onetime roommate. She had come to her god-daughter's christening in a tight skirt slit so high that the entire length of her gorgeous legs could be enjoyed or deplored by the other guests, depending on age or gender. Edwina's face was a study in repressed offence. Billie looked openly and keenly annoyed. Her skirt was slit too, but not that high.

Who else was there that day? Bonnie's current man, a quiet little Chinese dentist who, she once told me, specialized in delicate oriental love-pinches of quite amazing potency. Tim and Randy, soon to be Ross's partners, and their wives, one glacially blonde, one shy, pale, and pregnant. Max was in Japan at the time, but a cousin looking like a poor Xerox copy stood deputy godfather for him.

The christening service itself, with its strange, heathen elements of exorcism, was something I was surprised and pleased to find intact in a modern Toronto church presided over by a breezy young curate who smoked cigars. Billie, of course, had no religion at all, but it had suited her to send me to church and Sunday school all through my childhood, with the result that I was an unbeliever with a sound Christian education. This, oddly enough, was from time to time a sort of comfort to me. The teachings of Christ, while they had no noticeable influence on my behaviour, were at least a point of departure. And churches were friendly, familiar places, their austerities always comfortably similar.

Bonnie, on the other hand, had belonged in her small-town youth to a fundamentalist sect of some kind that worshipped by shouting ''Yeah Lord'', and drinking grape juice out of tiny paper cups. I don't think she'd ever actually been in a church with candles on the altar and a red sanctuary lamp, and the whites of her eyes showed as she took her place at the font. She had Martha tucked in her arm like an awkwardly shaped parcel, and kept looking down, fascinated, at the small, wincing red face. It was only a few months since Bonnie had been promoted to a corner desk in the big black-glass tower on King Street, and there were moments when the kid from Red Neck, Ont., could be seen like the fading ghost of this chic person in the slit skirt, owner of the yellow Mustang at the church door. She'd been thrilled to be a godparent, and spent half her month's salary on a cascade of toys, baby clothes, and silver engraved with Mar's initials in the curliest possible script.

Martha herself was decked out for the occasion in a flowing, hand-embroidered gown three generations old. When Edwina produced it, creased and yellow, from its blue tissue wrappings, I gazed appalled at all those rows of fine tucks and delicate frills, and took it straight to a Chinese laundry. They did a lovely job of bleaching and starching it, but as the priest traced his blessing on her forehead, Martha's face turned plum-red, straining in a way Ross and I understood only too well but Bonnie mercifully didn't know how to interpret. Before the ceremony was over, Martha had begun to scream in piercing, rhythmic squalls. On the way home in the car, she spat up over her pin-tucked bodice and the lacy shawl Edwina had knitted. The world, the flesh, and the devil were clearly far from licked on this occasion.

Everyone, of course, came back to the house for champagne. After I'd hastily cleaned her up at both ends, Martha was photographed yelling in various poses. She screamed on energetically in one pair of arms after another while the flashbulbs popped and our ill-assorted guests tried to make conversation with each other. Ross, looking harassed, wrestled out corks and poured foam into glasses. I tried to soothe the baby, who responded by arching her back and shrieking even louder. Randy's wife put down her glass and retired to the bathroom to be sick. Max's cousin made a polite little speech and escaped the party with a look of profound relief. Billie said, ''Sweetie, too sad, I'm booked for a deadly dull cocktail party," and twinkled off swiftly on her little high heels.

"This must be why they used to give them opium," Bonnie said, raising her voice over Martha's. "Kids, I mean."

"It's colic," I said, not without a gloomy sort of pride. "The pediatrician says it may go on till she's five months."

"Jesus. Want to let me hold the little fiend? I think she likes me."

"No, Bon, I think I'd better try feeding her. It's nearly time." Shifting Martha to the other arm, I unbuttoned the front of my dress and fumbled with the ample cup of my nursing bra. Edwina's pale eyes froze in unbelieving shock.

"My dear," she whispered, leaning forward with a warning creak of corset, "whatever are you thinking of? Leave your guests to Ross and me, and take the baby upstairs." Tactfully she tried to interpose herself between the company and the indecency of my exposed breast.

"Not to worry," I said, trying to keep my voice polite as Martha latched rather noisily onto the nipple.

Mother rose sharply to her feet. Her pale lips moved in inarticulate protest. Eyes averted, she muttered something about the GO Train, and went. Ross followed her out. After a considerable interval he came back looking tired.

A welcome lull had by that time descended, during which Martha suckled and the rest of the gathering relaxed. Freed from the presence of the older generation, we abandoned champagne in favour of beer, slipped off our shoes or lit up a joint as the spirit prompted. Ross stretched out full length on the sofa and closed his eyes. After watching Martha feed for a while, with a curious look on her face of mingled fascination and revulsion, Bonnie sat down beside her dentist and lit a cigarette.

"You're still up all night with Baby?" Randy asked. He glanced with some apprehension at Martha as she vigorously rooted and sucked.

"One of us has to rock or walk her half the night. Anne does the feed and walks the floor awhile, then I take over, rock and walk. If that doesn't work, I put her in the pram and we go out. Motion therapy. Last night I shoved her all the way to Ontario Place, nearly, at ten miles an hour. Anyhow, that's how it felt."

"What an awful warning," murmured Bonnie.

"Neither of mine ever had colic," remarked Tim's wife, touching her blonde chignon complacently. "In fact, I don't believe there is such a thing. You shouldn't give in to her when she cries. You're making yourselves into slaves."

Ross and I both eyed her without friendliness.

"Maybe those kibbutzes are the best places for little kids," somebody said vaguely.

"No, there's no good, cheap substitute for marriage," said Randy's pale wife wistfully, her hand creeping into his.

"Man, haven't you heard? It's been *found*," said Bonnie. She shot one smoke ring neatly through the other. The dentist looked at her with his shallow black eyes that could not be seen to express anything.

"Nobody — but nobody — " she went on, "needs to hold out their wrists for the old cuffs. Holy matrimony my ass. It's the biggest con game ever sold to generations of suckers."

Somebody loyal among the married raised a mild demur, but Bonnie only crossed her magnificent legs and focussed on him the full beam of her bright, intelligent blue eyes.

"Listen, friend. I've got a sister now thirty-one. She

got married at nineteen. Two instant kids. Hubby still in college, so they're poor as lice for years. Finally he gets qualified, but they're still all screwed up with a mortgage and kids' teeth to get straight. Year after year, no holidays, no decent clothes, just running between supermarkets to pick up specials. Freezing the old home-grown vegetables, you know? Scraping wax off the goddam kitchen floor. Like that. And for what? Because last month hubby dear told her he'd like a divorce, please, so he can marry a drive-in waitress. That's the reward she got for following all the rules."

"Oh, come on. Marriage doesn't work by rules," I protested.

"No, it works because a lot of crazy women are still willing to give up their own lives and live in chains. They still believe all that jazz about Adam's rib, I guess."

One or two of the wives began to speak at once, but Bonnie's voice, with a considerable edge to it, overrode theirs. "Balls," she said. (How I wished Edwina were still with us.) "Finks like you only show how brainwashed you are. It's all those centuries of it — lying on your backs in the victim position. Some of you actually *like* it there. But that's no excuse."

"Bonnie, you're too naive," said Ross. "You actually believe there's such a thing as freedom? For male *or* female? You know damn well nobody's free. Nobody human, that is."

"I am, chum."

"Come on, be honest. When a woman blames male-dominated society and all that crap for her personal unhapiness, she is just a whining cop-out."

"I am not personally unhappy," said Bonnie with cold distinctness.

"Wait, I never said that."

"Just the same, personal failure is personal failure," I put in, attempting to soothe what was evidently keen irritation on both sides. "It isn't marriage that's wrong, it's your sister's priorities. Scraping wax — Christ, no wonder he took off."

At once Bonnie turned a flick-knife glance on me.

"You know damn well — or you ought to — for a bright woman, marriage is one those torture beds, too long or too short, she can never really fit, even if she kills herself trying. You'd admit it, Anne, if you had the guts."

"Now just you hold on," said Ross sharply. It was rare for him then, though not later, to lose his temper. "What makes you think you can speak for Anne?"

"Good grief, there's no need to get personal," said Randy's wife, her cheeks now a hot pink. "There's not one martyred wife in this room, if it comes to that. Marriage is sharing. Look at how Ross shares the housework and the baby. It's like that with all of us."

"Only sometimes it's hard to tell in a marriage which one is the wife," Bonnie said unpleasantly, looking at Ross.

"On the other hand, some females never make it into women."

There was a tight little silence. Then a babble of talk welled up, with a general shift to refill glasses or drift homeward. I was surprised at Bonnie for being so neurotically dogmatic, specially on an occasion like this. It wasn't till a couple of years later that I guessed why and forgave her.

Anyway, it all passed over smoothly enough at the time. Tim, who had been conspicuously silent, avoiding his wife's gimlet eye while he quietly topped up his Scotch, now began a discussion of the Leafs' Stanley Cup prospects. For the rest of the evening, Ross was not very cordial to Bonnie, though she made a point of being charming to him, as if that proved she had won the argument.

When they'd all gone home and I'd finally managed to get Martha off to sleep, I went downstairs to find Ross. I wanted to do or say something reassuring to him, almost as if we'd quarrelled. Of course, I knew Bonnie couldn't threaten or damage our relationship, only — well, words are dangerous things, and she'd sprayed around quite a lot of live ammunition. Perhaps, to be honest after the event, I wanted to protect him from knowing how right she was. But when I found him in the sitting-room, stretched out again on the sofa, he was fast asleep with his glasses crooked and a book slumped on his chest. I put a blanket over him carefully and switched off the light. I was bone-weary myself, but it was a long time before I could relax in our wide bed. I promised myself to give Bonnie a large piece of my mind the next time I saw her.

Now it seemed like ages since night-time meant Ross and sleep. These days the dark brought round only an empty bed and dreams about chains and cells. And waking up meant only fatigue, a dogged resumption of the daily round. For the last half-hour, for instance, I'd been moving as heavily as someone in leg-irons. It would soon be time to tuck the kids in and lie down myself; but I felt a restless urge to talk to someone — almost anyone — as if just an exchange of words might by accident or design magically release me from all my dilemmas.

I dialled Billie's number, but their phone repeatedly buzzed a busy signal. Oh well, I thought, putting down the receiver, Billie's always shied away from talking about anything serious. For one thing, she didn't really think there *was* anything serious, as far as I could tell. And she hated being depressed by other people's troubles. Or even her own. One of the first really adult conversations I'd ever had with her — I was about thirteen — only made me feel more totally alone; and things between us hadn't changed much since then.

We were in our room at Margate or Folkestone, getting ready for dinner — or rather, I was fidgeting while Billie sat at the dressing-table doing her face. It was a still autumn evening with a low mist that induced melancholy. Distantly the high tide could be heard thumping on the shingle with a muffled, grinding pulse. Billie leaned forward to her mirrored image and delicately, holding her eyes wide open as if in amazement, darkened her eyelashes with a little brush.

"Why ever do you bother?" I asked fretfully.

"Because white eyelashes make one look like a frightened rabbit." She paused to take a gulp of the drink she'd had sent up from the bar. In those days it was most unusual for her to do this — normally she drank only as a social gesture, in a crowd of other people. I disapproved, in my priggish way, of her drinking anywhere, and I looked at that large gin-and-tonic beside her with keen disfavour, even suspicion.

"Can't you hurry up? I'm starving."

For something to do, I opened the little cedar box where we kept our small collection of jewellery: Billie's rings, my birthday lockets and bracelets from aunts, and three or four heavy, handsome brooches that had belonged to one of my grandmothers. It was a queer and disturbing little shock to discover nothing in the box but a few gimcrack necklaces.

"Bill — where's my gold locket — all your pins! They're gone!"

I held out the box to her. She gave it one quick glance and then looked away. There was no surprise in her face, only a tight bitterness that for a second made her look like a stranger.

"They've been stolen!" I said dramatically. "We'll have to tell the manager right away. And report it to the police. Those rings were *valuable*! Who on earth could have done it? They must have been taken while I was at Cheltenham with the aunts, because I took my silver cross and left everything else. It's awful! Somebody must have broken into our room!"

"Nobody broke in," said Billie.

"What do you mean?"

"I know who took them."

I stared at her. She was now concentrating intently on shaping her eyebrows with a tiny pair of tweezers.

"But who, then?"

"Fred, of course." She paused to toss off the last of her drink before adding in her shallow, indifferent little voice, "He's gone, you know. For good."

"Gone!" I said stupidly. Not that I regarded this as bad news. Fred's watery eyes and weak mouth under his would-be jaunty mustache had never endeared him to me, nor had his recent habit of placing a flabby hand on my knee. But Billie had for some months past regarded him with favour as "amusing" — her highest tribute. One way and another, he'd spent a lot of time with us lately, his wife having some time ago (as he often mentioned) left him. Like us, he seemed to have no home apart from the hotel, and no ties other than those formed in the bar or the lounge.

But he'd grown more and more attached to Billie; so much so that just before going off to my aunts for the half-term holidays, I'd asked her, "You aren't going to marry Fred, are you?" To which her airy reply was, "Of course not, ducky. He *is* married. This is just a fun thing." I didn't ask what she meant by "this", because I much preferred not to know.

"Yes, he's gone off. Just last night, apparently. Everybody down there is buzzing with it, but nobody knows where he went. Or why."

"But you mean he's actually taken our —"

"What's even more annoying, he's taken the fifty pounds I lent him last week. Serves me right, of course. I *knew* he was — oh well. Not to brood. But all those old biddies downstairs are watching me and whispering away behind their knitting, damn them. That's why I can't have pale eyelashes tonight, sweetie."

"But the jewellery — how did — you mean he's been up here in our room while I was away?"

"Of course," she said impatiently.

I gave her a look of contemptuous disgust which she didn't appear to notice. A rush of anger made my cheeks burn.

"It's so *humiliating*," I said. "I don't know how on earth you could do it."

"No, you don't," she said lightly. "And I hope you never do."

The sea ground and thumped on the beach below. "Why do we live like this?" I burst out. "Why do we stay in these places and have such awful people for friends?"

"Come down and eat," she said, and got up gracefully, giving a last touch to her newly set hair. Sullenly I clapped shut the lid of the cedar box and followed her out of the room. And I never saw Billie more animated, charming, sparkling, and attractive than she was for the rest of that evening. She never mentioned Fred again.

"Mum," said Martha, pulling at my trouser leg. "Let's play Cave Bears."

"Sure, love. Let's go."

This was a game we'd evolved through all these lonely months: we nestled together at bedtime in front of the fire in a warm muddle of blankets and pillows while I told them a rambling story about bears. Like my own disjointed history, it had no beginning or end, no meaning or moral. It was just there, something for my voice to say, and it seemed to satisfy them completely.

Listening in silence, they curled their small, hard bodies close to mine. The wood fire fluttered and hissed, and its light comforted us. In the bay window, my orange tree, pots of split-leaf philodendron, ivy, aspidistra — a mini-jungle — dozed too in the warm twilight. Violet lay down near us, head on paws, with a contented sigh. Mao crouched as close as possible to the fire-guard, contemplating the heat with approving blue slits of eyes. It was a lull in the good old mortal storm; an illusion that the wild world was tamed.

After the kids had dropped into their dense sleep, I dozed around the unborn one's gymnastics. My hand rested sometimes on Hugh's little arm, sometimes on the small chain of bones seaming Martha's back. Soon I would carry them up to their beds, and it would be another day survived.

The night wind blew against the window. Winter pressured the roof, the walls. Ross would not come home. At night I knew this. Nor was it safe even to think about Ross after dark, because that made my double heart jump and twist with rage and grief, those two cripplers. He had wakened long ago from that long-ago sleep. He agreed with Bonnie now about that Proscrustean marriage bed.

Outside, the snow lay like a deposit of anger and sorrow, a bitter crust under the feet of strangers passing by. It was cold everywhere but in our cave. Tomorrow was waiting, with God knew what contests and ordeals up its sleeve. But inside the cave, all my young were warm, breathing, safe. It was enough. It bloody well had to be.

Tuesday

*I*N THE BASEMENT, where a weak early sun streaked the dirty windows, I threw wet wash rhythmically into the maw of the drier. With one still in diapers all day, and two at night, laundry devoured a large share of my daily time and energy. Sometimes I thought acceptance of this mechanical routine was the most significant and awful thing about my present life.

June hated the whole business so much that she sometimes waited weeks before taking a huge load to the laundromat. There she would cast it all recklessly into the largest machine, and to avoid further effort dump in such lavish quantities of bleach and detergent that her laundry always came out queerly mottled and demoralized. But I didn't mind washing, really. I quite liked the primitive noise of the water, and the feel and smell of it. And then the piles of soft, fresh clothes that emerged at the end of the whole process were a modest accomplishment of sorts — clean deeds in a naughty world.

This underground room had the further advantage of being some distance away from the kids and from life in general, but in touch with both. A locked gate at the top of the stairs kept Hugh and Martha from falling down and killing themselves, but I could hear them playing up there, just as I could hear the morning rush of traffic grinding past, and the scutter of people hurrying to the subway. It was a kind of isolation cell that encouraged retrospection, even resignation of a sort — for instance, it was some kind of austere comfort to reflect that nothing happening to me at the moment was anywhere near as awful as some of the things that had happened in the past. It was almost satisfying to think, for example, about that night when Ross and I told my parents I was pregnant — the great thing about the experience being that it could never possibly happen again.

For some reason we felt it would be easier to confront the two sets of parents separately. We agreed, also, that it would be better to face mine first. On both counts we were dead wrong. All it resulted in was two horrible scenes instead of one. It also created a sort of competition to see which of our parents could behave worst. In fact, much the best judgement of anyone concerned was shown by Ross's father, who had died a few years earlier, thus cleverly avoiding involvement of any kind.

We thought the truth might not come as a total surprise to Billie and Max; but if this was true, it certainly turned out to be no help.

"As you know," Ross began, clearing his throat, "Anne and I have been . . . seeing a lot of each other lately."

"Which has been a bit of a surprise to me," put in Max, "seeing that Anne has so much ambition for a career of her own." His dark eyes regarded Ross with a tough look in which there was no discernible friendliness, though on various earlier meetings they had hit it off very well.

"Yes, well . . . yes. Only now . . ." His voice trailed away miserably. Max waited, his face grim. Two initiation ceremonies in one week, I thought. But getting our diplomas under the elms was sheer irrelevance compared to this.

With a sort of desperation, Ross jerked up his chin and said, "What we've got to tell you is that Anne's pregnant by me."

The silence that followed frightened me physically. I was afraid even to look at Max. I saw Billie's little high-bridged nose start out tightly from her face like a bird's sharp beak, as if she were frightened, too.

"So," Max finally said, in a thick, brutal voice. "You college guys aren't even smart enough to use a —"

"Max," Billie said quietly.

"It was my stupidity, not his," I put in. At this, Max jumped out of his chair as if something had bitten him. His face looked dark with rage, but he said nothing more, only went to the window and, after jerking the curtain back violently, stood looking out at the night.

There seemed to be no small talk possible in the circumstances, so we *all* sat there locked into the grimmest of all possible silences.

"Well," Billie finally remarked in a small voice, "I must say you've been madly silly and careless, the pair of you. We'd all better have a drink at once. I'll be right back."

She disappeared. After what felt like a couple of years, she came back with a drinks tray. Max still stood at the window with his back to us. "Now, duck, come and sit down," she said to him firmly, and touched his wooden shoulder. I marvelled at her bravery. He jerked around savagely, but then went back to his chair and sat down. She unfolded his clenched hand and put a very dark Scotch into it. I took a beer for something to hold. Ross shook his head mutely at the bottles. When I· dared to steal a glance at Max's face, I saw that he was still deeply, even· dangerously, angry.

"So somebody's got to get you out of this mess, is that it?" he asked Ross, still in his thick, insulting voice. "I understand you just got your law degree. That means for the next couple of years you file paper clips for the Q.C.s, right? Not exactly good timing for fatherhood. And Anne just beginning her university job. Ask me, this kind of irresponsibility is just plain goddam immoral." He stared straight ahead of him, breathing heavily. His broad hand clenched his drink like the throat of an enemy.

"Look, I know you're upset." Ross took off his glasses and rubbed his eyes. "In fact, you couldn't feel worse about it than we do. Only please get this straight — we're not asking for help, or trying to get out of anything. We only thought you had some right to know how things are."

By this time Billie had sunk her first drink and poured herself a second. She now said crisply, "All right, then; it's time to be practical, all of us. There's no need to have a whole lot of hard feelings or arguments, or anything dire at all. We're civilized people. There's no need to come all over portentous about this little blunder. In this day and age, thank heaven, nobody's life needs to get messed up by this kind of mistake. That's all it is — a mistake. The obvious thing to do is get the abortion over with as soon as possible, sweetie, and carry on from there."

"No, that I can't do," I said.

"What on earth do you mean, can't?" Billie's voice

had a sharp edge of exasperation. By her lights she was being admirably rational, even morally right, and she looked at me for the first time that evening with real indignation.

"I mean that's the one thing I know I'm not going to do. It's the one thing I'm absolutely sure of."

"Well, I think you must be completely out of your mind, then."

"Please, nobody pressure her," Ross put in. "She has a right to go through with this if she feels that way about it. And I'm going to do whatever I can to help her, even if that isn't a hell of a lot."

"I will always love this man," I thought. "Always. Whatever happens."

"But Anne, you can't mean you'd actually saddle yourself for the next twenty years with a — "

"Billie," Max said gently. "Shut up, sweetie."

"Look, women have been known to survive these problems," I said, trying to sound sure of it. "I can work, at least until — and get most of my master's credits as well. But the thing that matters to me right now is not to back Ross into any corner whatsoever. There's going to be no garbage about getting married. I've made that perfectly clear to him."

"Well, at least you got *some* sense," remarked Max grudgingly. He looked at the drink in his hand as if wondering how it got there, and then took a gulp of it.

"Of course it's the only way. This is the worst possible reason to rush out and get married; we know that. Completely unfair on all three of us. So we've decided to keep on just as we are, hold on to Ross's apartment till next winter. . . . Of course afterwards it'll be too small, but — anyhow, we're going to save all we can until — and after that, we'll just see how things work out.''

While I made these not very coherent remarks, Ross stared intently at the carpet. He looked profoundly depressed. But Max threw one leg over the other and set down his glass with an almost cheerful air.

"So. Well, I'm glad you got enough sense not to go making it legal, setting up a divorce for later and all that mess.''

"That's what we think. It wouldn't make sense." Ross's head hung low and his voice was almost inaudible.

"That's right. Well, the two of you have your heads on straight about that much, at least. Now you'd better have a drink, Ross. Give the kid a Scotch, Billie, he looks like he could use it.''

He was almost friendly to Ross from then on, but it was months before Billie and I were able to get back on our old comradely footing. Both these reactions surprised me at the time, and in a way they still do.

Upstairs the phone trilled, recalling me sharply to the here and now. "Answer it, Martha!" I called up the stairs, and waited till I heard her scampering feet.

"Anne Graham here," said her gruff voice, and with a basket of diapers cumbersomely in hand, I toiled up the stairs as quickly as I could. Last week, before I could intervene, she had said, "No, I'm too sodding busy now," and hung up on some unknown caller. I took the receiver from her, proffering a cheese cracker in trade.

"Sweetie? Are you there, Anne?" It was Billie's lilting, little-girl voice. Before sinking into a chair to ease my back, I glanced around swiftly to make sure the box Hugh was playing with no longer contained steel wool. Martha climbed into the diaper basket to set up housekeeping with her cracker and a bunch of keys filched from my purse.

"Hi, Billie," I said loudly. She was getting just a little deaf, though she would never admit it.

"Only me, sweetie," she trilled. "How goes the battle?"

"Oh, everything's okay. I mean, there's nothing new." Of course, Billie had known from the start all about my separation from Ross. Such things never seemed to her to call for negative moral or ethical judgement of anyone concerned. So many lapses were far more damning in her eyes — wearing crimplene dresses, for instance, or saying "anyways". Yes, she was a supremely silly woman, my mother, and I loved her a lot.

"Look, ducky, I want to see you. Got some rather nice news. Grab a sitter and meet me downtown somewhere nice for lunch."

"Oh, Bill, I'm afraid it can't be done. Margaret's in Boston with her girls, and there's nobody else I really trust."

"But surely that other neighbour of yours — Joanie, or whatever her name is — "

"Billie, they could *die* and she wouldn't even notice it if *The Edge of Night* happened to be on."

"Oh, ducky, don't be such a drag."

"I could bring them with me, but you wouldn't like that, I'm sure."

"Out of the question, sweetie. Martha got mashed potato in my diamond *earring* last time."

"Yes, I remember. Well, then, if you want to see us, you'll just have to come here. Why not do that?"

She sighed. "It's just that I frankly find little kids so

horrible, even when they're yours. That funny smell they have, you know, like damp biscuits, all of them. And their voices go right straight through your head like a drill.''

I sighed, too; and with an effort made no comment. Billie had never allowed me to call her Mummy or even Mother — not so much because it dated her as because the relationship seemed to her irrelevant. As for being a grandmother, the very thought of it was in her view a feeble joke. She regarded Hugh and Martha (when she couldn't avoid directly confronting them) with amusement, even a sort of remote affection; but their company bored her to desperation. Oddly enough, I resented this far less than Edwina's dutiful parade of concern and attention. Which just shows how unjust one's deepest feelings can be.

''Max sent me a note this morning,'' I said, in an effort to smooth her feathers. ''Want to hear? He says, 'Annie dear, I sat up late last night going through a poetry book you left behind. A little culture and I haven't enjoyed my cigar since. How come these poets are so depressed all the time, even about sex? Here's this guy Auden and all he can say is

> Plunge your hands in the basin,
> Plunge them in up to the wrist.
> Stare, stare in the mirror,
> And wonder what you've missed.

I understand the guy was a fag, but that's no excuse.' How is my dear Max?''

''Oh, he's fine,'' she said carelessly.

''Look, Billie, I'd really love to see you — '' and as I said this, the need to see her came over me with the physical urgency of a stitch in the side. It wasn't enough to hear her tinkling voice — I wanted to see that little beaky nose with its twitch of amusement, that expensively tinted and coiffed hair, the pink small hands all atwinkle with Max's diamonds.

"Do come here," I begged. "It's your birthday tomorrow, isn't it? I've bought you something pretty at the Craft Shop. I really want to see you."

"No more official birthdays. Too sordid, sweetie," the little voice squeaked. "Change the subject."

"No, drop in just for an hour or so this afternoon. Ross often comes by around five to take the kids for a walk." (Well, he used to. But there are times when a lie is justifiable. Even essential.)

"Oh well, all right then. If he doesn't come, you can just tie them to their beds or something. About the Happy Hour, then, doll. See you then." And she rang off before I could get out of her what her good news was.

Idly, as I folded laundry, I speculated what it might be. Probably only that Max was going to Korea or somewhere on one of his business trips. She loved it when he was away. Then she needn't plan and eat sensibly balanced meals but could nibble bits and pieces at all hours as she chose. Instead of doing her exercises, she could spend all morning in bed with a thriller if she liked, or sit in front of TV all evening sipping stingers from the pitcher she kept on call in the freezer and visited only discreetly when he was home. Not that Max ever said a word about her large daily intake of alcohol, either because she never showed the slightest effect from it, or because he was much too wise. All the same, she drank considerably less when he was around. I sometimes suspected also (though this was pure speculation) that Billie, fond as she was of Max, preferred sleeping in their king-size bed alone. Of course, she adored all the stages of courtship — she had always been a superb flirt in the teasing manner of the forties. She even used to try a bit of the old fluttering allure from time to time on Ross, just to keep in practice. But basically I thought she could never much have liked the final act itself. She had too keen a sense of the ridiculous, and too little love of sports.

As I lumbered upstairs with clean linen for the beds, the kids scrambled up after me, followed by Violet and the cat, in a ragged little procession. None of them liked being left alone downstairs.

It was a pity, in a way, I thought, stepping over the dog to strip Hugh's cot, that I'd never been able to model myself on Billie as some girls do on their mothers. Because in her feather-weight way she probably had some of her values a lot straighter than I did. In my place, for instance, she would have regarded going to bed with Ross for the first time as simply a lark, a fun thing, not for a moment to be taken seriously. Whereas I for days and days hesitated, agonized over the decision, and postponed it, until both of us were in the last stages of emotional hypertension. I'd begun to take the pill, but for some inexplicable reason couldn't bring myself to take the plunge.

Finally I said in desperation, "Look, this is crazy. Let me get up. I've got to get out of here. I'll fail my exams. We'll just have to keep away from each other, at least till they're over."

"It would be perfectly simple if we just went properly to bed," said Ross. "It's all this messing around that's bad for your nerves. Not to mention mine."

"No, no, I haven't got time. I've got to get that medal."

He rolled away from me abruptly and sat up. "Right. You're perfectly right. This is crazy. You go off and hit the books."

While he fished under the bed for his shoes, I buttoned my blouse, shivering though his tiny bedroom was at least eighty degrees in an unseasonable heat wave. At the spotty mirror over his chest of drawers, I rebraided my tangled hair. Whistling under his breath, he pulled a clean T-shirt over his head.

"Guess I'll go over to the club and see if I can pick up a game of squash."

"Right."

"See you, maybe, after the exams."

"Sure."

"Take care."

"Right."

"Good luck."

"Thanks. So long."

With extreme dignity I preceded him downstairs and out into the blaze of sunlight. At the corner we parted silently. Halfway between the student ghetto and the library I met Karen, who had not spoken to me for several weeks. I smiled. She ignored me. "Silly bitch," I thought, "you're way behind the times."

I crossed the road, entered the chill stuffiness of the library, sat down in my carrel, took out my books, and began to cry. Fifteen minutes later I was climbing the long walk-up to his apartment, only to find him just steps behind me.

"Thought you might be here," I said, as he pulled me in and locked the door.

"I thought you might be, too."

"It's too hot for studying anyway."

"Or for squash."

"Oh. Oh. Do that again."

We sank onto the bed and all clocks stopped. It became evident after a time that, for all his apparent sophistication, Ross had little more expertise than I. This in no way impeded our mutual pleasure, only prolonged it deliciously. But was it ignorance, or simply innocence, that made us unable to separate emotion from those acute bodily pleasures? Most of my friends and his had no trouble keeping the two apart — Billie had always been able to — but we didn't know how. Freaks that we were, we lay in each other's arms afterwards and mingled tears. For us it really had been nothing less than an act of love; a final and permanent commitment.

Or so it seemed at the time. In retrospect, though, I had to admit it was inexcusable to be less with it than my own mother. Because what could be more ridiculous, after all that, than to find yourself three years later all alone, perpetually doing laundry, shedding tears into children's socks, and making up this rotten, vacated double bed? Irritably I plucked Mao out from under the sheet, where he was catching an imaginary rat. And while we were asking silly questions, why did I need to see my mother so badly now, all of a sudden, when all our lives till recently I'd considered Billie the child and myself the adult? Oh well, what was the point of brooding over such things now. In a few hours she would be here, and that gave me something to look forward to.

"Come on, you lot," I said to the assembled kids and animals. "Let's start getting ready for the Happy Hour." Putting it this way made the snowsuit routine easier to face,

likewise its grim sequel — shopping for gin at the Liquor
Board outlet half a mile away. This meant wrestling the
pram out of the front porch, always a test of muscle and
character. However, the thought of a ride in their beloved
pram spurred the kids into active co-operation, and, getting
into the spirit of the thing, Mao shot up the curtains like a
flying cat and made us all laugh.

A few torn scraps of bright blue sky fluttered like flags
overhead. The high-sprung pram lurched over the icy pavement in a slow progress that had a sedative effect on me as
well as on the children. As we bumbled along I planned the
day with some kind of confidence that I could control at
least minor events. A macaroni-cheese casserole could be
prepared in advance for supper, so I needn't be in and out of
the kitchen while Billie's visit lasted. The TV could be
pushed into the dining-room to occupy the kids there. Violet
would have to be shut into a bedroom — Billie was afraid of
dogs, even craven, dim-witted dogs like ours. And I'd buy
mushrooms and make some of those nice little hot canapés
she liked to nibble with her drinks. And somehow or other,
at some point, I would have to scrounge time to brush my
hair and change out of this grotty old smock, or she would
say in her tinkly voice, "Sweetie, you mustn't get *drab*."
Yes, this visit, like yesterday's with Edwina, would have its
strains; but at least I wouldn't be bored. Billie might be
trivial, but, after all, so is most good entertainment.

The children lolled happily one at each end of the
pram, gazing out with a sort of vacant approval at the
skeleton trees, the shop fronts, the passing cars hissing over
salted roads. They even sat contentedly outside while I
rushed into the library to change my pile of books. One

of my happiest recent discoveries was that Trollope wrote forty-seven novels, most of them good. In minutes I emerged with about five pounds of fiction, enough to see me through quite a few white nights to come. Hugh and Martha were still in a benign mood. Instead of being bored, which I well remembered as the chronic childhood disease, they seemed to be diverted by everything. Martha beamed broadly and called "Hi!" to a passing postman with bow legs, and Hugh raised a wondering face to the remote silver toy of a transatlantic plane and murmured "Bird".

"Plane," I corrected him. One of the sharpest disillusions of my young life was discovering how unlike a bird a jumbo jet is. I thought before I tried it that air travel would truly be like flying, and when Billie and I boarded the plane for our first trip to Canada, I was all aflutter with anticipation and a little tremor of fear. For her part, Billie was so sharp and cross I knew she was simply frightened.

"You sit by the window," she said. "I have no intention of looking out at any time."

Throughout the take-off procedures she kept her eyes firmly on a copy of *Vogue* and didn't look up till a stewardess pushing a drinks trolley bent over to ask what she'd like.

"Oh but Bill," I said, peering down as the horizon tilted under us and we began to climb. "Look at the little fields down there and the river — look, there's the Thames, that sort of snake." But she refused even a glance through the little porthole across which drops of moisture climbed upside-down but never fell. "A vodka martini," she said to the stewardess. "A large one."

Seconds later we were enveloped in billows of cloud; then we emerged into a bright blue, limitless sky in which from then on we seemed to hang perfectly motionless. The

Constance Beresford-Howe

only movement to be felt was a slight vibration. Billie's drink on its little tray stood without a tremor. Occasionally there was a slight bump, but the muffled thunder of the engines never changed volume or pitch. Before we'd been airborne an hour, my legs felt restless and the seat too small. "What a swiz flying is, after all," I thought, deflated. "It's not half as exciting as riding a bike downhill."

"Great, isn't it," remarked the bald man in the aisle seat beside Billie. "Cruising at 32,000 feet. Gives me a thrill every time. This your first flight, young lady?"

"Yes," I said, politely concealing my boredom.

"First trip to Canada too, maybe?"

"Yes, it is."

"Got relatives there, I suppose. Everybody has."

"No, we're — just visiting." Remembering that Max would meet us at the airport, I tried to cheer up; but it was hard to imagine this ponderous robot was actually taking us anywhere. I pushed my lunch about fretfully in its divided plastic container and suppressed a sigh.

"Well, you're in for a great experience, then, I can tell you that, even if it does sound like bragging. Canada's just plain the best damn place on earth anybody can be in A.D. '70, and I'm not afraid to stand up and say it."

He didn't look as if he knew how to be afraid of anything, this big man with his broad, fresh-coloured face and the easy, confident smile all North Americans seemed to have, as if they trusted everybody and liked everything. Billie was pretending to doze in order to avoid being drawn into the conversation, but I said. "Do you live in Toronto, sir? What's it like?"

"Well, I'll tell you something, young lady. It's a place we bought off the Indians in Mississauga a couple of hundred years ago. The price included a bunch of brass kettles and a few carrots. Now there's upwards of three million people living there in one of the handsomest cities going. I mean it. The place is huge, booming, runs like some big, clean machine — but somehow it's a town that's managed to stay human. You get trees growing downtown. Right in the middle of the city you can go fishing in High Park. You can take the subway even late at night without any real serious risk of getting mugged. In other words, Toronto's still a neighbourhood. Sure, people out west and in Quebec like to make fun of good old TO, but I figure they're just jealous. Or they haven't looked lately. You just wait till you see it.''

"It sounds marvellous," I said, trying to sound convinced. Surely no city could be that impressive, or need that much salesmanship. Besides, it didn't exist. Nothing did. We weren't going to Toronto, or any other destination. The plane droned on like a mechanical bird caught forever in the monotony of space, while people tried to doze in their cramped chairs or pacify whining children.

After a vacuum of time, some quite dreadful tea was served. I clambered over Billie's magazine and the bald man's knees to visit the tiny loo, all its conveniences trembling slightly as we hung there in limbo. But when I flopped back into my seat, the bald man leaned over to the window with a smile and said, "Look."

I looked down and at an acutely tilted angle saw, scattered in casual gaiety over the bright blue expanse of Lake Ontario, a sprinkle of tiny red and yellow sailboats, and several green islands. Then the horizon tipped and our porthole framed a vast sweep of level land bound by multiple threads of roads on which coloured beads of traffic hung. Under a blazing sun the flat factory roofs, the needle spires and silver pencils of skyscrapers, winked like mint coins. Excitement buzzed through me like an electric charge. Out of nowhere the phrase New World jumped into my head, as if I'd invented it. "You've *got* to look, Bill," I said.

Cautiously she leaned forward and took a quick glance. Then she said, "Oh. Good heavens."

A little later, after a bunch of pink roses flourished at the Customs window revealed Max, wearing a new suit and a nervous smile, Billie took his arm and chattered away about how marvellous flying was, and how gorgeous Toronto looked from the air. I said nothing, because no words seemed really adequate. I looked around for the bald man, to wave a special goodbye to him, but he had disappeared.

When I parked the pram outside the Liquor Board store, the children were so fascinated by a micturating dog at a nearby lamppost that they hardly noticed me go. As the dog moved round, repeatedly lifting its leg, Martha gazed at the spectacle, enraptured as the witness to a miracle, while Hugh strained so far out for a better view that only the harness kept him from falling out on his head. This reminded me of Billie's favourite story about how, trundling me along one day in my push-chair, she'd absent-mindedly not only tipped me out, but run over me. This was so typical of both of us that I had to smile, forgetting for a moment that stepping into the Liquor Control Board of Ontario premises was no laughing matter.

There was no Muzak here. Indeed, the general aim seemed to be to discourage buying, as far as possible. If you insisted on spending your money on alcohol, of course the provincial government would let you do it; but they made sure that pleasure played no part in the transaction. No shelves of glowing wines or bottles of spirits colourfully labelled were on display to encourage impulse buying; all the merchandise was hidden away at the back. You had to write down your choice by coded number on a grim little form to which a pencil was tethered, and present this to a civil servant behind the counter, who consequently never had to speak to you. This functionary, buttoned into a grey dust-jacket, was only a shade less dour than his colleague in a glass cage across the room, who took your money through a grill and returned change down a small metal chute, as if customers were carriers of some dread disease. It always surprised me how forbidding the atmosphere was in these places, in view of the indecently huge profits made annually by the province in its monopoly of liquor sales. Perhaps they wanted to spread the guilt around, and if this was the aim, they were highly successful. No matter how cheerful you might feel on going in, you were sure to emerge rather depressed.

There was a long queue at the counter which I meekly joined, clutching my little order form. An electric clock on the wall jerked off the minutes like a *memento mori*. Notices here and there informed us that smoking was forbidden, persons under eighteen would not be served, dogs were banned, and cheques were not accepted. The only advertisements were posters promoting Canadian wines, and these were so small as to be almost furtive.

At the head of the line was a man engaged in buying the booze for some unimaginably huge party. Our queue shifted patiently from foot to foot while two grey clerks paced to and from the nether regions carrying bottles, and packed cartons with his purchases, while a third glumly ticked off the items. The customer kept glancing around at us as if embarrassed. From time to time he coughed behind his hand, and the cough spread down the line.

It was not consoling to look along that queue and find that everyone in it was, as it were, single — a sort of discard. The fat woman, the little man in the baseball cap, the thin lady in fuchsia trousers — old and young, they all had the stamp of the loner. Even the austere tall man with the fur coat, and the dyed woman with the sapphire ring, were somehow recognizable as exiles from the cosy, nuclear family. And there I was with all the rest of the sad, defeated ones — widowers, divorcées, bachelors, survivors. When they coughed, I coughed too.

At last the big buyer seized his purchases and scuttled off with them in instalments. From his pessimistic look, one could tell the party was going to be a failure. His place was taken by a diminutive old lady in a black hat with ear-flaps. She had no order form, and the clerk frowned at her.

"I wonder if you'd be good enough to tell me the name of a really nice wine," she asked in a clear little thready voice.

The clerk looked at her briefly. "List over there, lady," he said. "Hundreds of 'em. Take your choice."

"But that's just it, there are so many. You see, I don't know which one to ... it's for my son's birthday," she added helpfully.

The clerk sighed.

"My husband's dead now, and even when he was alive we never — but Bob went to France last summer, and he — since then — well, of course I never have anything in the house now except maybe a bottle of sherry at Christmastime, so I really don't know what kind of wine would be nice for him, you see."

The clerk shrugged. A little stir went down the line. "He's coming for dinner," she went on. "I don't see very much of him — he's a busy man — but I'd like him to have a nice wine. I'm making his favourite — "

"List is over there, lady," repeated the clerk. His dead eyes were already looking over her shoulder, but nobody stepped forward to take her place.

"You want red or white, dear?" spoke up the fat lady two places ahead of me. Her coat was held together in front by an inadequate safety-pin, and her vast legs overflowed a pair of unzipped, flopping men's boots. She was probably spending her welfare cheque on liquor, and I warmly approved of her. She had a hoarse, fruity voice, and eyes of a jovial blue shone in the fat red expanse of her face.

"It rather depends on how much you want to spend," remarked the tall man, looking down at the little lady through the bottoms of his bifocals.

"Yes, but don't you muck around with any of that Hungarian or Chilean stuff; go for a nice clean claret, or maybe a good Liebfraumilch." This was contributed by the sapphire woman behind me with the frizzed, purple hair. She looked like a semi-retired call-girl.

"Look, there's a South American burgundy I picked up here on sale last week — ask Laughing Boy there if he's got any of it left." The little chap in the baseball cap fixed us with the cheeky, cheerful eye of a town sparrow and added, winking, "It went a treat with my baked beans."

"Why don't you try some Australian —" contributed someone else.

"No, no," protested the fur man. "That stuff takes the enamel right off your teeth."

The little lady in the ear-flaps looked hopefully from one face to another, and we all felt protective of her. Thinking of my mother coming for the Happy Hour, and my children parked out there in their pram, I suddenly felt rich, powerful, and generous.

"Look, if you'd like to come over here with me," I said to her, "we could look at the list. I'll show you some of the good ones that don't cost too much. There's quite a good range of —"

"The price doesn't matter," she said rather stiffly. "I don't mind paying as much as three-fifty or even four dollars. After all, it's his birthday, isn't it?" She looked at me severely, and I hastily said, "Of course. Right. Now let's see what they've got here. . . ."

The tall man and the fat lady both tagged along as advisers. After a lively discussion that soon got nowhere, it was clear that the old dear was going to be dead long before she found the ability to choose between red and white. Finally, after some argument, the committee chose a Portuguese rosé, and I filled out the form for her.

"That won't be too strong, now, will it?" she asked, frowning doubtfully. "The Portuguese, after all, they're like the Spanish aren't they, such violent people?"

"No, no; it will be mild as milk," we assured her, and sent her off to the counter with smiles and encouraging pats. We fell into line again behind her with an obscure sense of accomplishment. We had defeated, for the moment anyway, the forces of indifference, so much more deadly than the forces of evil. I hoped the old lady's busy son would appreciate his wine.

Whistling, I packed my bottles in among the kids' legs and pushed them off at a brisk pace to the greengrocer's. There the pyramids of bright fruit and scrubbed vegetables, and the fresh, green smell, were so alluring that I bought a number of things we didn't really need. As I manoeuvred myself and my purchases out of the doorway, I all but collided with Margaret Neilson coming in with her two big girls.

"Why Margaret — hi, kids — I thought you were still in Boston."

"No, we got back last night. How are you doing?"

"Well, as you see —"

"Nine more days, isn't it?" It was typical of Margaret to know my delivery date as well as or better than I knew it myself.

"That's right. You still willing to take over my menagerie daytimes while I'm in hospital?"

"Of course. It's all organized."

I knew with humility that it was. Margaret was the kind of woman who sewed on buttons before they fell off, and baked and froze Christmas cakes in July. As for perfect motherhood, she might have invented it. Her children were planned, and arrived accurately three years apart. She had even organized their begetting to the day and the hour, in order to ensure females. This impressed me enormously when I first heard her account of it, even though it was hard after that to look her husband in the eye. As they grew into their teens, she kept the girls so fully occupied with swimming, music, karate. and yoga lessons that they had no spare time whatever left over for sex or drugs. This, at any rate, was the idea; but those kids had a demure look that sometimes made me wonder. It was impossible genuinely to like Margaret, of course; but you had to admire her.

Unlike me with my haphazard, small-hours reading, Margaret belonged to a Canadian-book-review group and a left-wing book club. She had season tickets for an experimental theatre. One night a week she took an "interest course" at one of the city colleges. One day a week she did volunteer work for a hospital. In all these worthwhile activities she had tried at various times — without success — to enlist me. Something about that word "worthwhile" put me off. But "You mustn't *stagnate*, Anne," she kept saying earnestly. To which the subversive in me longed to say, "Why not?" However, by this time, because she was basically kind, she had pretty well accepted the fact that I was beyond salvation, and as a consequence was kinder to me than ever.

Certainly I'd never done anything to deserve such a perfect neighbour. From the day I first ran to her for help, eighteen-month-old Martha having locked herself into the bathroom, Margaret had been the ideal friend, calm, cheerful, and efficient. And yet it was Margaret, ironically enough, who was responsible — indirectly of course — for the worst row Ross and I ever had. Like most marital battles it was about nothing, and yet about everything, and it left trivial wounds that would perhaps never heal.

"I suppose you wouldn't by any chance like a Siamese kitten?" she asked me over coffee one morning soon after Hugh was born. "A friend of mine out in Mississauga breeds them. She's keen to get rid of this last litter before they go away on sabbatical, and apparently this one's the last. He's going cheap, in other words. Ten weeks old, seal point, male. And he's got a pedigree that makes me feel like a peasant."

"Oh, I don't really think . . ." I said cautiously. It had gradually been borne in on me that prudence wasn't my strong point, and this created a vague sense of guilt. But, even as I spoke, I remembered that Ross had a birthday coming up in a few days and I hadn't been able to find any present nice enough to buy for him. Just the same, I strongly suspected he would not approve of a kitten, so I added, "No, I don't think we really need a cat, with all we've got to cope with around here. We didn't really need a basset hound either, of course; but when you find a stray actually starving in the streets . . . anyhow, Ross was all set to turn her over to the city pound, but when we found out how they finish them off, he took her to the vet instead. A hundred dollars later she was spayed, vaccinated, tagged, and all ours. And I sometimes think he likes her more than he does the children. She doesn't make half the noise or mess, that's sure."

"Well, a kitten's no problem, as far as that goes," said Margaret briskly. "This one's house-trained, of course. You could let it out for exercise in your little garden here. They're terrific company, you know — bright and very affectionate. I'd take it myself, but cats make Harvey sneeze. Tell you what, why don't we drive out there this afternoon, just for fun, and have a look at it?"

"Sure, if you like. But I'm not going to buy any cats."

Four hours later I was back home with a wicker basket containing a kitten with sapphire eyes and a loud, dictatorial voice. For an hour or more he sniffed over every inch of the premises, critically inspected the furniture, tasted one or two of the house plants, and terrorized Violet, who fled upstairs and hid under a bed. To offers of food or other blandishments he was totally deaf; he was clearly too busy. Finally he went to the litter-box I'd put down and used it with dignity, his blue eyes austerely fixed on the middle distance. After long and fastidious scrapings, he suddenly shot out of the box and climbed me like a tree. A couple of whisks round after his tail; then he settled on my shoulder and began to purr.

Ross was very late getting home that evening, and we both fell asleep in the armchair waiting for him. The scrape of his key in the lock roused us, and the kitten sat upright on my knee, his dark ears pricked.

The stooped figure with the briefcase paused in the doorway. "Where the hell did that come from?" it inquired crossly.

"He's from me to you. Happy birthday, love."

Ross disappeared to drop his case and hang up his coat. He then went out to the kitchen and ran a glass of water. While out there, he evidently gave himself stern orders about self-control, because when he got back to us he had that disagreeable, swollen look that goes with keeping one's temper.

"Now, I know you'll probably raise objections," I began with a disarming smile, "but this creature is really too special for that. So loving you wouldn't believe. And he can retrieve a paper ball. I didn't teach him — he just does it. And see how beautiful."

But Ross, mouth set in a tight line, had settled in the armchair opposite and opened the *Star* with a crackle.

I began to feel affronted in a personal kind of way. The kitten jumped off my knee and went over to sniff at Ross's shoes. He paid no attention to it, and my blood began to simmer. Nothing could be more insulting than the dignified coldness Ross had inherited from all those successful ancestors of his. "Well, is that all you have to say?" I demanded.

His glasses came around the edge of the newspaper. "Anne, there is nothing to say. Wherever that cat came from, it's going back. I've got enough on my plate as it is. One more thing to be responsible for I do *not* need."

"Are you implying I'm a dead weight? You know damn well Professor Stein's promised to take me back at the lab as soon as Hugh's weaned. I think you're being unnecessarily bloody, anyhow, about a birthday present — when it was the nicest thing I could find to give you."

"I am not going to fight with you, Anne. Only that cat goes back."

"What you mean is, you don't give a shit what I think or how I feel, right?"

The hand gripping the paper shook; then he threw it to the carpet, startling the kitten into a sideways leap.

"What I mean is," he shouted, "I'm fed up with you tanking over me as if I didn't exist. When do I ever get to vote around here? About *anything*? The mood takes you to paint the kitchen purple or adopt a dog, and I'm supposed to tag along, Mr. Yes Dear. Well, I'm not going to do it any more. I warn you, I'm fed up. Dangerously fed up."

The violence of this attack shook me, and to my own disgust I heard a querulous little voice say, "I thought you liked cats."

"For Christ's sake, what's that got to do with it! You're a woman supposed to have brains, but you can be so *dumb* —"

"It's not dumb to wonder why anybody would get into such a fizz just because his wife gives him a birthday present."

He took a deep breath and tried to get hold of himself. "This present of yours — if you insist on bringing it down to cases — it's going to do nothing for me but run up vet's bills, eat the plants, and wreck the furniture your father's probably still paying for. Now, I don't know about you, but if Max and Billie came here for dinner and found the chairs in rags, I would personally be embarrassed. It's bad enough to be under an obligation like that in the first place, or have you forgotten that another man's had to furnish my house?''

"So that's it. Why didn't you say all this in the first place, then? I'd have been glad to live with Goodwill cast-offs if I'd known you felt that way. But I thought you were big enough to be grateful to Max, not sour and jealous. After all, you accept those cheques your mother keeps on leaving around the house cheerfully enough, don't you?''

"Will you just leave my mother the hell out of this! Among the other things I'm fed up with is you making a face like sucking lemons every time she comes here, or is even mentioned. You seem to take it as a personal insult every time she does something nice for us.''

"Yes, because she does it for you, not me. She makes it so clear she's sorry for you, handcuffed to me, you poor victim!''

"Well, maybe that's not such a way-out view of it. For starters, it was *you* took *me* to bed, if you remember. I don't recall having a whole lot of choice there, either.''

"What a total, rotten lie! You know damn well *I* was the one that had no bloody choice!''

"Don't yell like that,'' he said, assembling the newspaper fussily.

"I'll yell all I like! You just don't want to admit you're married to your bloody mother, that's all!''

"You can sit here and scream at the walls if you like. I'm going up — I'll sleep in the study. And that animal goes back tomorrow, is that clear?''

"Tomorrow's Saturday, they'll be up at their ski place.''

"Monday, then."

And he continued mounting the stairs, back very stiff, the newspaper grasped like a sword in his dexter talon. The kitten watched him go, head on one side, and then began to sharpen its claws on the sofa. Upstairs Hugh woke and began to squall for his ten o'clock feed. Angrily rubbing tears off my face, I went up to him.

It was bad luck that the next day was Saturday, because that meant we had no chance to get away from each other and pretend nothing had happened. It was the first time we'd ever needed that kind of space. Until now, our fights had been short and sharp but, as it were, reversible. This time it was different. I woke up feeling sore all over, as if I'd been beaten. As for Ross, he spoke to me only when absolutely necessary, and with a cold politeness that was worse than abuse. He hung out the baby-wash, he amused Martha while I did another feed, all with a kind of glaze of reserve over him. He appeared not to notice the existence of the kitten, except once to pluck it off the kitchen counter where it was playing with an eggshell.

The day seemed to drag on forever. He went up to the study and worked for part of the morning, but lunchtime was another cold and silent encounter. In a tacit peace overture, I made creamed salmon on toast, a dish he liked, with chopped mushrooms, celery, and green onions in it, and cleared the kitchen table so we could sit down and eat, instead of leaning against the counter or wandering around the house with bowls. But Ross only threw a dismissive glance at the lunch and said briefly, "I'm not hungry."

Many vivid answers to that sprang to mind, but I swallowed them all, because it was clear too much had been said already, on both sides. Instead I scrubbed the kitchen floor with particular ferocity, wondering as I did so how much housewifely cleanliness came from the same bitter source.

When he said, early in the afternoon, "I'll take Martha over to the park with the dog," I thought, "Good. Don't hurry back." It was a relief to have him out of the house, even though the unnatural silence of the place lingered after him like a bad smell. Somehow I couldn't settle to anything. The book I was reading (it was *Pride and Prejudice*) seemed dull and silly; and I couldn't relax enough for a nap. I wandered around beginning one small tidying-up or cleaning job after another, only to leave it half done for some other chore like watering the plants, or sewing buttons on a little coat for Martha. And the superb weather only made everything worse. It was a flawless, early-winter day, still and mild, with a sky of that peculiarly radiant blue that suggests the world is a place infinitely too good for its masters.

At twilight, when Ross came back, he was still aloof and polite, and we ate dinner in total silence until I said, "Look, if you've got something more on your mind, for God's sake say it. Don't just sit there like a toad with the bellyache."

Without a word he pushed away his plate and left the table. I heard his footsteps climb the stairs and the study door close. I then threw down my knife and fork with such violence that my plate cracked into two pieces.

Sunday was a duplicate of Saturday, and I began to feel a muffled sort of panic beating under my skin. How long could this kind of thing go on? Surely it could only mean that there was nothing left between us, unless you counted this bitter mutual resentment. The hours crawled past. I caught myself sitting down in snatches or leaning against things for support like someone very old. The perpetual demands of the two babies struck me for the first time as monstrous. Outrageous. Colossal. I mouthed these and other words from time to time. By way of response, no doubt, to the atmosphere generally, Martha was impossibly cranky and demanding. She pattered from room to room whining or pulling at things, until in desperation I dressed her for a walk. While I was getting on my own coat, the phone rang.

"Hi, Anne. Is Ross there?"

"Hullo, Randy. Yes, just hold on. Ross — for you." My voice sounded as leaden as I felt, but when Ross lifted the upstairs extension and spoke, he sounded perfectly normal. As I shepherded Martha out, I heard him, chatty and cheerful, and I thought bitterly, "It's only me he hates."

Tediously the hours drained away. When I got back, Ross was downstairs reading, with a wailing, hungry Hugh in his arm. He handed the baby over silently and went on reading. I sat down and began to feed him. Martha stumped out to the kitchen and began to open cupboard doors, her favourite game. One after another she opened them and clapped them shut. The silence of the house was stretched so tight that little normal sounds like a dripping tap or a creaking floorboard cracked like pistol shots. Just as we neared the end of Hugh's feed, Martha trotted into the room carrying a saucepan and a wooden spoon.

"I make de din," she announced. Then added, "Pussy gone."

"What's that?" I asked.

"All gone."

"What do you mean? Martha, you haven't opened the back door, have you? Oh God." She had done exactly that; it stood wide, letting in a flood of late sunlight and cool air. There was no sign of the kitten. I searched the house, looking under beds and into cupboards, with no success. Martha trotted after me, beaming and busy, calling, "Puss, Puss." But the cat was gone. Ross, still assiduously reading, barely looked up when I said, "The kitten's got out. I'll have to go out and try to find it."

"All right."

"The thing is, it's so little — it will never find its way home if anything frightens it. I'll try the lane first."

But a survey of the lane and then our short cul-de-sac street produced nothing, though I poked under bushes and questioned random children and peered under front porches with rising anxiety. Finally I went back to the house.

"Any sign of it?" I asked Ross.

"No."

"Well, you'll have to help, I'm afraid. I'll leave the kids with June for an hour — we've got to find it. Soon it'll be dark; the poor little thing will get killed in the traffic."

He closed his book and got up with reluctance.

"If you head east and I take the other way, we can cover more ground," I told him. "Keep calling — it might hear you and come."

After depositing the kids at June's I set off, calling, "Puss, Puss," as seductively as I could; and after a while I heard the very cross, receding voice of Ross in the dusk saying, "Puss. Damn you. Puss."

An hour later we met at our own corner. "No luck?" I asked.

"No."

"Oh God. Nobody's seen it?"

"No."

"Oh, what are we going to do?"

"Keep looking, that's all. You check the kids. I'll go south this time."

The dusk thickened into dark. Behind a tangle of bare trees the evening star came out. The rush of post-weekend traffic on the downtown roads haunted me. But full dark came and the kitten was still nowhere to be found. Finally, cold and with a throbbing headache, I turned back to our street to retrieve the kids.

"I wouldn't worry if I was you," June said serenely. She was in the middle of giving herself a home permanent in front of the TV. "Cats always turn up."

"This one won't — it's only a baby. Well, thanks for coping. Come on home, Martha."

But I was just taking her coat off when Ross suddenly appeared. He had something inside his quilted jacket — something that could be heard loudly purring.

"Oh!" I said in a voice loud with relief.

"Found it crossing Bloor Street," he said. "Stopped the traffic cold and just strolled across like Boss Cat. When I called him, he came running up to me and started to climb my leg. I think maybe he could use some milk."

"Good idea. Could you do it while I put the kids to bed?"

I left him carefully heating up milk in a pan. And so ended the great battle of the cat. A day or two later he'd been christened Chairman Mao as a tribute to his masterful character, and nothing more was ever said about taking him back to Mississauga. But then nothing more was ever said about a number of major issues left on hold, but that didn't mean they'd ceased to exist. Far from it.

"Look, Anne," Margaret said, "if you're not doing anything special for lunch, why not come and have it with us? I'm unfreezing a quiche. Then I can show you that folder about the Science Club. You've simply got to join — it's all wrong for you to lose touch like this."

"I'd love to have lunch," I said. It occurred to me how odd it was, not to say discouraging, that women as unlike each other as June, Billie, and Margaret should so unite in their efforts to improve me. All of them unsuccessful. And yet in different ways I was dependent on all of them. Where would I be without Junie to despise, Billie to mother, and Margaret to admire? Specially since these equations were to some extent interchangeable, depending on my mood. But it was better not to pursue this line of thought too far. It would only end in self-analysis, tears, and heartburn, none of which I really wanted. So I packed the vegetable-bag into the pram and meekly fell into line behind Margaret.

"You sure this isn't too much trouble for you, Marg?"

"Not a bit. Give us a chance to hash over our arrangements for Baby Week. And you could use a little break, right? Come to that, so could I, after a weekend with my father's awful old aunt. Whenever I hear about sweet, frail little old ladies getting raped and killed, I wonder why it can't happen to Auntie Maud. I see you've been to the Liquor Board. Well, you can offer me a drink of whatever it is."

"I can?" I thought in some surprise. Discovering a tough and funny side to Margaret was a surprise, too, because if she'd always been like this, I was only now on the right wavelength to perceive it. In any case, I said, "If you mean I can do something for you for a change, great. Let's go."

As for the Science Club, or any other group she might try to rope me into, I told myself stoutly, "Who's afraid of Margaret Neilson?" and thought instead of the delicious hot meal that would come from her shining, immaculate kitchen, by comparison with which mine was a cave littered with bones.

After peeling the kids out of their snowsuits, I followed Margaret through to the kitchen, where I found her capably flicking switches and extracting containers from the frig. Her two polite girls took away my coat and laid the glass-topped breakfast table without being asked. Margaret wore a sweater and a pleated skirt that fitted her trim figure perfectly. The two silver wings of hair over her temples framed a face so serene and bland I thought I must have dreamed that remark about Auntie Maud.

When the older girl, Patricia, set out a plate of cupcakes iced in different colours, Martha's eyes brightened with greed and she reached out to take one. "No, honey," said Margaret firmly. "They are for after lunch." And such was that woman's calm strength of character that my daughter actually backed away from the table and came to lean against me, while I tried to look as if this was her normal behaviour.

"Gin and vermouth, eh?" said Margaret, inspecting the liquor bag. "Perfect. We'll have a nice dry martini."

"I shouldn't, of course. But I couldn't feel much worse than I do, so why not?"

"I always think the last week or so of it is the worst,"
she said tactfully. "Poor old Hughie's got another cold
hasn't he? Bad luck."

As if to oblige, Hugh produced the loose, rattling
cough I knew so well. Automatically I felt his forehead. No
temperature yet, but he'd probably have one before the day
was over.

Margaret set before us two pale, beaded glasses, each
with a tiny lemon twist, and we lifted them to each other. At
that instant, Martha seized two of the cupcakes and bolted,
stuffing them as totally as possible into her greedy, laughing
mouth. Hopelessly I lumbered after her, but she was already
halfway up the stairs. As she fled, her stumping little feet
trod icing energetically into the immaculate stair carpet. On
the landing Patricia caught her and tried to confiscate what
was left of the loot, but with a shriek of evil glee Martha bit
her and escaped. Through the bedroom door I glimpsed her
rolling in a cloud of cake crumbs across the Neilsons'
snow-white counterpane.

Pat looked with respect at the semicircle of tooth
marks in her arm and said, "Wow." I went back to the
kitchen. Some battles, it seemed to me, weren't really worth
winning. But of course it was too much to expect Margaret
to accept such anarchy.

"Sorry about that," I said apologetically.

"Of course, she's compensating for Ross," Margaret
remarked calmly. "Punishing you.".

"Well, maybe," I said unwillingly. Was it just dodg-
ing the truth to think that Martha would be exactly the same
kind of child if Ross had never taken off? She'd been raising
hell long before she could sit up alone, that was sure. And
all she'd ever said about it when I explained that Daddy

didn't sleep at home any more was, "Oh." It was Hugh, actually, who felt it more. I knew this because for the first five minutes of all Ross's visits, he kept his face turned away and wouldn't look at his father.

"On the other hand," Margaret said kindly, "it may be just a stage. Good martini, isn't it?"

"Perfect." And it was. Tensions, fears, frustrations, all seemed to drop off me like a set of chains. In seconds I became chatty and confidential, two things I've rarely been this winter, when depression has had to be hidden even from myself like some shameful secret.

"What's wrong with those last weeks of it is sheer, blind terror," I said. "You know. Spina bifida, cerebral palsy, Down's syndrome. Ugh, just saying the words could be bad magic." I dug out a Kleenex in haste from the jumble in my purse. "Don't let me be morbid. But the fact is, I can't remember feeling this guy move today. Maybe the poor thing's just stoned. Pay no attention, I'm getting tiddly. And it's heaven."

"Any chance of Ross coming to his senses, you think?" Margaret asked, topping up our drinks.

"None that I can see."

"Situation hasn't changed at all? I mean you'd think after five months — "

"No change. Or at least . . . well, all right, there is one. At the start, he was so open. You know, he'd talk about the whole thing. There was nothing he wouldn't discuss. We spent hours talking when he came to see the kids, or on the phone when he couldn't get over. But lately he doesn't come around so often. A lot less, in fact. And he has a lot less to say. I don't know, but I figure that may be a good sign, don't you? Maybe lovers can't be chums, or vice versa. Shouldn't even try. It was maybe better when we did more and talked less.''

Margaret got up to adjust the oven temperature. ''Well, let's face it, if he isn't communicating — '' There was a bright flush across her cheekbones and she blundered against her chair before sitting down on it again. Dear old Margaret, I thought with a surge of affection, was ever so slightly tiddly herself.

''I was married before Harvey, you know,'' she said suddenly.

''Were you really? I never knew that.''

Margaret's husband Harvey was a small man with a large pipe. He was so silent and so little given to action that I sometimes thought Margaret must dust him regularly like a piece of furniture. But the two of them had that rare thing, a perfect marriage. His antique shop on Avenue Road was as neat and clean as her kitchen. Like her, he dressed quietly, in perfect taste, and together they calmly, systematically attended the city's better cultural functions. They were like a pair of matched gloves, made of the same material and design, and I often thought of them with envy as I struggled to cope with the squabbling, complicated mess of my own married life. For Ross and me, marriage had been a crazy mistake from the start, while their partnership was wholly rational. Feelings — mine for Ross, his for me, no matter how violent — had nothing to do with it. I couldn't agree with Billie's definition of marriage as a deal; but I'd come to realize lately it was something that involved more tough concessions and trade-offs than I used to imagine. Unfortunately, this very practical angle of the thing was one I appreciated only when it was too late to be of any use.

". . . Yes, but it only lasted three years," Margaret was saying. "We had nothing at all in common."

"Right. That's what matters."

"Just the same, we — I mean, in spite of everything . . . but of course it's experience that teaches you, or ought to. The only answer was to break up. We were totally incompatible. I *know* that."

We lapsed into a thoughtful silence.

"But it's funny, isn't it, how knowing from experience doesn't help worth a damn when it comes to something like this," I said sadly. "I mean it's the wrong kind of knowledge to be any use."

She darted me a queer, almost furtive look.

"True. Because as a matter of fact I ran into Phil again just recently. At the Granite Club, of all places. Back in town after all this time. He's done very well . . . anyhow, we ended up having drinks and then lunch downtown, and . . ."

"And?" I said, deeply interested.

She drained the martini pitcher into her glass. After a quick glance around to make sure the kids were all out of earshot, she said calmly, "Yes, and."

"No kidding." Fascinated, I tried to imagine this kind of thing happening to Margaret in or even near the Granite Club. "And have you still got nothing in common?"

"Nothing, really. Except of course —"

"Ah yes. That."

"I've been going to his apartment twice a week. He's bought me a lot of clothes I keep there. We buy things for the place. Eat there sometimes. It's like having two lives, Anne. And you'd never believe how enjoyable . . . I mean it's awful — I'm horrified at myself — but I'm enjoying even the risk and the guilt. Of course, it's got to be some kind of crazy mid-life crisis. For one thing, how can I keep on doing this to Harvey?''

"Does he know about it?"

"Of course not. I'm not that crazy."

I looked at her with frank curiosity. There she sat, dignified, handsome, and guilty as hell. How it thrilled me to know that here was a liar, schemer, and pagan even more deplorable than myself.

"It's all my Aunt Maud's fault, really. She brought me up . . . my parents died when I was two. And she's the kind of woman who thinks everything to do with sex is dirty. And everything *is* to do with it, for people like that. Even *breathing*. That must be what's made me so greedy. Anyhow," (here she tilted the pitcher hopefully) "maybe it's not the worst thing that can happen to a marriage, after all." She tried to sound cool, but her voice trembled.

A wave of personal sorrow washed over me. "Oh Margaret, it's got to be pretty high on the list."

"Well, you could be right." We looked gloomily into our empty glasses and found no answers there. But then the timer pinged; the kids swooped in; Margaret got up to serve the lunch. We ate and I felt Hugh's forehead again. We talked about the girls' progress at Havergal. Traces of pink icing lingered around Martha's mouth as she grinned at me cheerfully.

"Now, before I forget, Anne," Margaret said briskly as she passed the salad bowl, "you've got to make an effort about this Science Club. They meet just once a month. You'd be in touch with all kinds of specialists, and hear interesting papers . . . just forget all that about not being a joiner. Somebody gave me a membership form the other day, and you're to take it away when you go. Got that?"

"Yes, Margaret." And the fetus under my ribs gave a hilarious kick. Maybe it already had a sense of humour.

Getting ready for Billie's visit was no problem. She never seemed to notice things like dust or clutter. So, while the kids napped, I sank into a deep chair, put up my swollen legs, and stole an hour's brief, ginny doze.

After that, all I had to do was set up the drinks tray and shut Violet into a bedroom. I wheeled the TV into the dining-room and, squatting breathlessly, managed to plug it in. There was even time before the kids woke to take a quick shower, have a rub with body lotion (glorious on the itchy, distended belly), and put on the least unattractive of my maternity smocks. By the time five o'clock rolled around, the kids were up and washed, and magnetized by the box, and I'd had a shot at improving my face with some green eyeshadow. Billie was always late, bless her. There was even time to get the mushroom canapés ready for the oven All this gave me the rare and welcome feeling of being serenely well-organized in the Margaret manner.

When Billie arrived, it was with her usual little shrieks of disgust at the weather. The wind had dropped and it was milder, but fat snowflakes had begun to coast down in a purposeful sort of way. She left on her handsome high leather boots, grumbling that one might as well wear them night and day in this awful climate. Then she touched a cool cheek to mine, saying, "Sweetie." To Mao, who sat on the hall table eyeing her with critical blue eyes, she cried, "Elegance!" and he closed them in gracious acknowledgement. After a quick visit to the downstairs loo, she peeped briefly at the children through the leaded-glass dining-room doors. Then, murmuring, "Don't disturb the dolls," she lowered herself into the most comfortable chair and hitched it closer to the fire. For just a second something about her caught at my attention — a darkish look under the eyes, was it? No, just a trick of the meagre winter light. She looked marvellous as ever in what she still called a "little black dress", her small feet crossed at the ankles and garnets twinkling in her ears.

"Well, this is nice," she said, after a quick, apprehensive glance into the hall. "That awful beast of yours isn't loose, is it?"

"No, shut up safely, licking her eczema. Will you mix your drink, or shall I?"

"Not to bother, sweetie — I very thoughtfully brought my own. Just a little ice, if you don't mind." On her last visit, there'd been nothing to drink in the house but some rather nasty sherry, and Billie did not lightly forget things like that. With a flash of her mischievous smile, she produced a large flask from her shoulder-bag.

"Oh, Billie, that's supposed to be a very bad sign."

Blandly not hearing, she poured herself a generous drink. "I know the beast has attractive Duncan Phyffe feet, but I can happily do without all the rest of it. Why has it got eczema — just to annoy?"

"She misses Ross."

"Which shows she is dim as well as dreadful. Why didn't he take the brute with him? Too smart, that's why. Well, anyhow, cheers, sweetie. You *and* your friend. God, it must be about ready to *walk* out, you're so enormous."

"Please don't ask me how I feel or when I'm due. I might scream."

"I'll change the subject, doll. But that's what *you*

should have done two years ago, if not before. Don't you want to hear my nice news?''

"Yes — yes — just let me stick the canapés on.''

But my chief purpose in hurrying to the kitchen was to hide an unpleasant flush of irritation. It was not kind of Billie to be so sharp at my expense. I had to stand at the window for quite a few minutes, staring at the snow clinging in white clots to the glass and biting my knuckles, before I could go back to her.

"Well, what's this great news, then?''

"Aren't you going to have a drink, sweetie?''

"Oh no; I had a martini with lunch, actually, and now both of us have hiccups. I'll have a glass of milk or something.''

"No, no, have another martini at once. Show it who's boss. Here, I'll fix it for you.''

Her little hands were incapable of sewing, changing gears, planting anything, or using any tool more complicated than a fork, but in two or three effortless, graceful gestures, they produced a perfect, silver-gilt cocktail. I took a resigned sip and with only partial success repressed a belch. "This is a mistake, I know,'' I muttered. But Billie was absorbed in a head-on-one-side contemplation of her own elegant legs. My own looked like cathedral pillars beside them, and I tucked them out of sight.

"Well, doll, you know how clever Max is with money,'' she began, spreading out her manicured fingers to the fire.

"Yes, I do.''

"Well, what Daddy left me was all invested in some rather dull stock, railways or something, and you know how the income from it has been quietly shrivelling away for a long time. But about three years ago, Max reinvested it all for me, and the stocks or margins went up or down, or whatever they do, and what do you think? It's coupon-cutting time, and I've made five thousand dollars' profit!"

"Heavens. How nice for you."

"Isn't it? And sweetie, I want it to be nice for you too. Have your drink." She refilled her own glass. "Now, I've got the most brilliant idea. Just picture this — you and me in Santa Lucia. Dwell on it, ducky. It's enough off the beaten track so the tourist man says there'll be no trouble getting reservations for the end of March. I intend to blow the whole lot, sweetie, and give you and me the holiday of our lives."

Roughly six different remarks occurred to me simultaneously. "You only got back from San Francisco a month ago" was one of the less agreeable ones. I put down my drink — it or something else was giving me severe indigestion — and said, "Yes, but Billie, it's a lovely idea, only you do realize I'll only just be out of hospital at the end of — "

"Exactly," she said with triumph.

"Then how in the world can you expect me to — "

"Now just listen carefully to me, doll. I have it all figured out, down to the smallest detail. You and Max never seem to realize how intensely practical I am. Now, I suppose you'll insist on breast-feeding this new one like the other two — though why anyone *would*, with bottles in this world, I'll never know — anyhow, much as I deplore this, Baby is invited too. At least it will be new, and sleep a lot. They have basket things for them on the plane, and stewardesses cope with diapers and all that. And once we get there, the island will be full of nice black girls to nanny it."

"And what about Martha and Hugh?"

"Well, I did wonder whether your nice neighbour might take them. It would only be for a few weeks, and you're always saying how good she is."

"Billie, nobody is that good. No, you cannot possibly do that to a neighbour. I'm sorry — it was a lovely idea, but — "

"Now just a minute, doll. Don't interrupt. That was just a passing thought. No, I've worked out all the angles. You know those people called Homemakers? — you just call up an agency and they send somebody around. Just like that; sleep in, full time, as long as you like; all bonded and guaranteed and everything. And it's all on me. Part of the deal. Now, aren't I marvellous?"

I stood up, feeling suddenly as if I might just crack into a whole lot of small, jagged pieces. Things were so hard and dangerous and sore with me at the moment that there was no time to wonder why Billie needed my company so much now when she had never seemed to need it before. My face felt hot and my tongue thick.

"Look, Billie — Homemakers — guaranteed for what? Who the hell are they? Do you think I'd leave my kids with a stranger, unless I had absolutely no choice? *I* am my children's home. You may think that's everybody's bad luck, and maybe it is; but there we are. Thanks anyway, but I can't go away. Not for a weekend, never mind weeks."

"I do wish you'd try not to be so Mother Rabbit about everything," she said crossly. "Ever since you got all these children you've gone primitive in the most boring way. I never thought you'd go to seed like this, a girl with your looks and intelligence. Good grief, Anne, you're not twenty-four yet, and you act like somebody's tedious old grandmother. What's worse, you *think* like one."

"I know you don't mean that for a compliment."

"Of course I don't."

Huffily she refilled her glass. Too late I caught a drift of smoke from the kitchen and hurried out to pull a pan of scorched canapés from the oven. Like the Happy Hour, they had not turned out well. I took them into the other room and, already ashamed of my bad temper, offered them with apologies.

"I'm sorry, Bill. You know I wish I could go, and it's a lovely, generous thought. Only it's just bloody well impossible, that's all." Even as I said this, some of the bad temper oozed back. Why, after all, should I feel guilty about refusing to leave my kids to the mercies of some Pamela from an agency in order to help Billie prop up a beachside bar?

"We'll say no more about it," she said with dignity, adjusting the garnet in her pierced ear. "I was simply trying to help. The very last thing on earth I'd ever do is interfere, you know that. You'll give me credit for that much, I hope. In your particular situation, I just thought it would be specially good for you to get away. After this ghastly winter and all the problems you've got, any intelligent person would agree that you need a holiday, if only for mental health. However, if you won't go, you won't, I wouldn't dream of pressing you. Let's change the subject. Max gave me this bracelet for my birthday — pretty, isn't it?"

I drew a mighty breath to reply, and then swallowed the words. There was absolutely no point in quarrelling with Billie. Better to try mustering a grin at her self-righteousness. She was Martha's grandmother, all right, whether she liked it or not.

"By the way," she added carelessly, "when I told

Max about the Santa Lucia idea, he said right away that it was just what you needed. I only mention it because I know you respect his opinion a lot more than mine."

"Please, Billie. Have another bloody mushroom thing and let mé see the bracelet properly. Did he get it at a dealer's?"

"Yes, of course. You know he's got friends under every rock."

I glanced at her, startled. It was not at all like Billie to be so acid, specially about Max.

". . . er . . . things not going well with you two?"

"Don't be silly. You know we've never had even a small tiff in all these years. We might just have one soon, though. He's been nagging me to have a check-up, and it gets on my nerves."

"A check-up? What for?"

"Nothing, absolutely nothing. I'm perfectly all right. Only Max is so neurotic about other people's organs. It's too boring." Crossly she brushed a crumb or two of canapé off her lap. I was keen to hear more about all this, but the thought of any more conflict was so daunting that I seized on what I thought would be a safer subject.

"Well, I just wondered . . . after all, a second marriage must be — tell me, what was my father like, Billie?"

"What, Daddy?"

"Yes, only why do you always call him that? It's such a kinky thing to call your husband."

"Well, he was ages older than me, you know."

"Yes, I know, but — "

"Well, it was one of those relationships, that's all. He liked me to be a little girl; and I needed a father. My own parents married horribly late, and they both popped off when I was fourteen. Most inconsiderate of them. So I grabbed at your father.''

"I see. Well, it should have worked out very well.''

"But it didn't, you know. Not at all.''

"Why was that, then?''

"Oh, mostly because he always had his head in a book. Then, of course, I immediately started you and was appalled. Nothing personal, sweetie — but you were never meant to happen. There's just nothing on this earth more totally boring than being pregnant and then looking after little kids. Fish have the right idea — just lay a few neat eggs and then take off. Fast.''

"I don't agree it's boring. But go on.''

"My own mother, poor creature, thought I was indigestion or the menopause for six whole months, you know. She actually fainted when the doctor told her.''

I tried not to, but Billie's flashing, crooked smile forced a laugh out of me.

"Well, I suppose scholars aren't easy people to be married to,'' I said, to bring her back to the real subject. "But you haven't told me yet what my father was *like*.''

She leaned forward and rubbed her fingers to warm them. A frown pinched her face and gave it a strained look. "Oh, Maurice was a creature of habit. Always in the library or somewhere like that. We had almost no social life except for ghastly dinners we had to go to, and then give back . . . oh, those colleagues of his, all of them arthritic or deaf, and their dreadful wives, only interested in the W.I., or breeding cockers . . . sometimes I thought I'd shriek out loud out of sheer, horrible boredom. So, what with one thing and another, we quarrelled all the time. No, it was a disaster, really. Miserable for both of us.''

"But you still haven't told me what he was really like."

She set down her glass with a sharp little clink.

"He was a cold man. Not just reserved or shy — I thought it was that at first. No, he was cold. Kept himself private. Even in bed."

"Oh. That must have been grim." It seemed to me that now at last I understood a little something about my parents, and consequently about myself. "So that's why after he died you travelled around so much. It must have been heaven to be free."

"It was nothing of the kind," she said.

Suddenly I felt uneasy, as if I were about to learn something not at all foreseen; something I might not be able to handle.

"No. When he died I was just about destroyed, if you want to know." She turned her head away. Her voice sounded thin and desolate, like the voice of a very old woman.

"Why do you think we kept on the move? — why was it always by the sea? Because I liked to look out and see no limits anywhere. That way I could think he was still *somewhere*, even if — Well, the only way I could keep going was to meet new people all the time in pubs and trains and places like that. Have a few laughs and keep sex casual. And in a way it's still like that. Although I'm very fond of Max, as you know."

I tipped down the last of my drink, though it had been clear for some time now that it was doing me no good whatever. My head felt unpleasantly disturbed, as if too many new ideas had crowded into it at once. I turned to Billie, but before I could speak, bedlam broke out in the next room. Of course, the only surprise about that was that it hadn't happened sooner. With a groan I got up and jerked open the dining-room door. Hugh had fallen (or more likely been pushed), and lay on his back howling and kicking in frustration, while Martha stamped around him chanting, "Crybaby cry! Crybaby cry!" At the sight of my expression she added in a small, pathetic voice, "He took my book."

When I hoisted Hugh up, I found he was indeed clinging to her book, a rather disgusting washable but unwashed affair depicting kittens. It was a book he liked, but this was rare self-assertion, and I muttered "Congratulations" as I plucked it away from him. I put it on the sideboard out of reach, feeling for a moment disoriented and a little dizzy. I didn't want to go back into the sitting-room. I didn't want to see Billie or remember what she'd told me.

Wiping off Hugh's face, I perched him on my arm and gave him a kiss. He was too warm. Temperature going up, without a doubt. Pull yourself together, I told myself, and said to the kids, "Come along and say hello to Billie."

"Has she got presents?" demanded Martha, cutting off a yell halfway.

"No, you horrible child, she has not. But you can have a nice mushroom thing. Let's go."

Billie, with a fresh drink in hand, had recovered enough equanimity to greet them with her usual rueful, ironic warmth.

"Don't touch my dress, sweeties," she warned them. "Sit down somewhere over there and I'll give you both something terribly nice." She then produced from her handbag two small boxes of maraschino chocolates, of all things. They tore off the ribbons and wrapping and at once began to stuff their mouths.

"I believe in giving people things that aren't good for them," she said with satisfaction. "What else are presents for?"

I looked at her and softened. With Billie, frivolity sometimes reached the point of wisdom.

"Thank you, Billie," I said loudly to the children.

"Sink you, Billie," murmured Martha behind a mask of chocolate. Hugh's smeared face beamed at us joyfully. Just in time, I prevented him from wiping his hand on the carpet.

"Disgusting little brutes," she said. "I'll just trot off to the little girls' room till they're finished."

The instant she was out of sight, I took the boxes away and tried to clean up their faces and hands. Martha immediately hurled herself prone and began to drum her head and heels on the floor. Billie, when she came back, looked so genuinely appalled at this performance that I dragged my child out of the room by one arm — rather more hoping to dislocate it than not — and in the kitchen doused her with a glassful of cold water. It didn't do much for the kitchen floor, but it cut off the tantrum like magic. Martha sat for a moment astonished in the puddle. Then she began to laugh in great, hoarse guffaws. Hugh tottered in, coughing, and his filthy face broke open in a wide grin that showed all his little chipmunk teeth.

"Well, sweetie, this seems like a good time to say goodbye to Sunnybrook Farm," said Billie, appearing in her smart little leather hat. "I'll catch a cab at the bottom of the street; there are always lots down there. So clever of you to live downtown. By the way, Max sent you his love, and he'll be in touch. Oh, is this for me? Thanks, doll. That reminds me, here's a little thing I picked up for you —

something nice and useless." She thrust into my hands a small box labelled Nina Ricci and, on a waft of her own spicy scent, made an exit uncomplicated by any embraces.

Miserably I wondered why our afternoon had been such a total and disturbing failure. Knowing I was in the right about Santa Lucia did nothing to comfort me. Just the same, as I lifted out the perfume bottle to sniff its faint, sweet fragrance, I too began to laugh weakly. Sunnybrook Farm. My dear Billie. Let's never really quarrel. Please, let's never.

The kids dawdled listlessly over their supper, and I felt too fagged myself to urge them to eat. I had no appetite either. The cheesy smell of the casserole vaguely depressed me, for no reason that made any sense except that I associated it with Karen, Bonnie's onetime roommate. Yes, that was it; the night I moved in to share their apartment, they were eating grilled-cheese sandwiches. There I stood at the door, loaded down with suitcases and typewriter, all wide-eyed and keen to begin my university education at last. I don't know what I expected, exactly — a cloistered hush of young intellectuals deep in great thoughts or what — but it was rather a surprise to find the place full of people eating, smoking, arguing, and laughing.

"Come on in," said Karen, with a wave of her cheese sandwich. "We're just getting the term off to a good start. Dump your stuff in your room and come meet people."

I did this very willingly, pausing only to smooth my hair briefly at the mirror. One swift glance around had already suggested to me that I should have spent more of Max's clothes allowance on clothes, instead of saving up for a microscope. Not that anyone there was dressed up; but

I'd been in Canada nearly a month by then — long enough to know the high price of those corduroy trousers, denim work-overalls, and casual blouses. It cost a lot of money to dress like the poor. Not to mention the fee for having one's hair cut into layers or permed into a frizzled blonde curtain like Karen's. When I edged shyly into the sitting-room, I was unhappily aware that my jeans were not the expensive pre-faded and tattered kind everybody else wore. Still, my new sneakers looked all right — or would when they got dirtier. At least I'd had the sense to get rid of my black lace-up oxfords. The standard school shoe all girls of my age wore in England were seen here only on old women with corns.

Bonnie thrust a can of beer into my hand and said buoyantly, "Happy days, Anne. Want something to eat? Hey, everybody, this is Anne Forrest, from London, England."

"Is there any other London?" I wondered in my innocence. But there was no time to ask; Bonnie was rapidly reeling off names; faces were turning to me and people were saying "Hi", to which I replied "Hi", having already learned that "How do you do" was considered stuck-up, like the English accent I was trying to lose for the same reason.

"Well, what d'you think of Canada, eh?" asked a tall girl in tight imitation-leather trousers.

"Oh, it's great. I mean literally. I can't get over the huge *size* of everything . . . cars and motorways and all that. And these enormous high-rise buildings. Doesn't it sometimes make you feel awfully dwarfed?"

"Not at all," said the leather girl coolly, and I remembered too late that when Canadians ask what you think of their country, they don't want an answer, they want a compliment.

"What courses you taking?" inquired a thin boy with a pipe that kept going out. He had dark hair and very blue eyes, but I hadn't caught his name. Ross something, was it? "I'm in General Science. Heading for Botany; I'd like to take the honours course."

"Ah. You'll get old Prof. MacAvey, then. He's really great, even if he does pinch girls' asses. Can't turn your back on him for a second, Karen says. Must liven up the lab a whole lot. We get no fun like that from the faculty at Osgoode Hall, believe me." He winked at me in a friendly way and moved off, knitting his fingers through Karen's.

Nobody else seemed to have any questions to ask me, and though I diffidently made a few approaches to various people, they always soon returned to their own group or their partner's in-chat, which was sometimes as baffling to me as a foreign language. Eventually I wandered along to the kitchen to look for a glass to drink my beer out of, but amid all the casual chaos of used crockery on the counters I could find nothing clean at all. The smell of grilled cheese made me vaguely hungry, and I opened the huge, humming frig which was crammed with food; but just then Bonnie danced in, hand-linked to a handsome West Indian.

"Don't bother with that leftover junk," she said. "We're sending out for Chinese. Here, dance with Charley; I'm going to the can."

I did dance with Charley, it being easy and fun to copy his loose, happy gyrations. Later I danced with one or two others, including the leather girl, who, it suddenly occurred to me, might actually be a boy. Eventually the Chinese food arrived in a number of warm cardboard containers, and everybody sat on the floor or on the arms of chairs to eat.

Conversations bubbled all around me, and I was happy to listen (in so far as I could follow it) to a long and vigorous argument about ESP and the occult generally.

"It may sound crazy to you," Karen said, "but I know this girl got involved with a bunch of guys in one of the fraternities running séances, and one night she just stood up in the middle of it and started to scream and scream. They caught her running down St. George Street like some kind of crazy, and it was days before she came out of it. I mean, it can be freaky, that kind of thing; it scares me."

"Aw, I know that kid; she was just having a bad trip."

"No, you're right, it can really blow your mind. One of the psych professors told a guy I know — you mess around with the subconscious and it can like trigger some kind of latent psychosis. No kidding, that chick spent a month after that locked up in Queen Street."

"And couldn't tell the difference from Vic College, I bet."

There was laughter and several people began to talk at once. Just then a bat fluttered in through the open window and began to blunder clumsily against the walls and the ceiling. There was a general outcry from the girls. Various people flapped things at it to drive it out again, but these attempts only terrified it into swooping wildly around the room.

"Let me out of here," shrieked Karen, clutching her perm.

"Don't be dumb, they don't get in your hair. That's an old wives' tale," someone told her, but she disappeared, saying, "I believe it, I *believe* it." Several other girls went out with her. A Japanese boy began to swat at the creature with a folded magazine.

"Oh, don't, you'll hurt it," I protested. "Hold on a

second — let it settle somewhere, and I'll catch it."

We waited a minute or two; then the bat lighted, clinging with its small claws to the top of the curtains. Having plucked off my shoes, I nipped up onto the sofa and with a vigorous swoop captured the beast. It struggled in my grasp, and its mouth stretched wide to let out a high, hissing little shriek of fear. Its agonized pulsing filled my hand. It tried to bite me with needle-sharp teeth.

"Look at that mean face, man," somebody said, stepping back.

"No, they're perfectly harmless. Better than that — they eat mosquitoes. Let me put it out quickly — I shouldn't hold it like this, the tribe might reject it or something, for smelling of people." One or two of them gave me an odd look at this, but nobody interfered when I leaned well out of the window and released the bat into the warm air that smelled of city dust and decaying leaves. It disappeared with a flick into the darkness. I wondered where it would go, and whether it would remember its invasion of another world; whether by some freak of taste it might have taken a fancy to living in the light, and might try to come in again, welcome or no.

By then it was well after one in the morning, and people began to drift toward the door for home. Absently I returned any goodnights that came my way. Thinking about tomorrow's nine-o'clock lecture in chemistry, and my pile of new textbooks, I hugged a delicious anticipation. Tomorrow the adventure would really start. The long, empty preamble of my childhood would be over at last.

When the three of us were left alone, I began to pick up some of the party débris, but they said, "Forget it, Anne;

not your first night. Tomorrow we'll work out a system, but tonight we'll clean up. You go get some sleep."

"Well, thanks . . . goodnight, then."

But I was too wound up to sleep, even after unpacking all my books and other belongings. In the kitchen just down the hall, Bonnie and Karen clattered dishes and laughed. Outside in the sultry September air a late tram ground along its track; cars squealed at intersections; a TV movie blattered. The apartment was full of unfamiliar smells — fried rice, beer, toasted cheese, and a sweetish kind of smoke. I lay on my back and tried to doze, but the room seemed terribly hot, even with the window wide open. No wonder; hopping up, I discovered that the radiator was sizzling. The place was even hotter than the Don Mills apartment Max and Billie had just moved into. But she adored central heating, while I found it oppressive.

Suddenly I felt a qualm that could only be an absurd kind of homesickness. I wondered, not for the first time, why Max had been the first to suggest I find a room or share digs downtown instead of staying with them. "You won't want to waste a couple of hours every day on buses," he said. "Besides, it will be a hundred times more fun for you, being on your own," added Billie. I agreed entirely with both of them, and yet . . . well, it was very late, and I was tired. Once more I tried to settle down, but the room was so unbearably stuffy that I finally got up and opened the door, hoping a little cooler air might find its way in. Back in bed, I turned on my side and curled up, only to find that the conversation of Karen and Bonnie in the kitchen was now too close for comfort. Especially since it was soon apparent they were talking about me.

". . . bit of an oddball, for sure, eh?"

"Yeah. These Brits. I wonder whether it was a good idea after all."

"I mean, that crazy *braid*. Somebody's got to tell her, poor kid."

"Charley told her he missed Trinidad, and she said, 'How frightful for you.' "

"No — you're kidding!" Under cover of their hilarious giggling, I closed the door quietly once more. Then, back in bed, I stared fiercely into the dark and made a number of resolutions. One was never to speak to either of them again. Another was to go at once to a hair-stylist and have my plait cut off, regardless of expense. Seconds later, of course, I reversed both decisions. This was much the nicest apartment I'd seen in the university area. Come to that, Karen and Bonnie were charmers, compared to some of the rock-jawed landladies I'd interviewed first. As for the hair, I would keep it just the way it was, and to hell with the whole lot of them.

But it was not so easy to accept the painful truth — that even in this country of aliens, I didn't belong, and perhaps never would. I'd been so sure the lonely past was over, but it was not, and might never be. Like that stupid bat, I'd been liberated, but I might never be truly free; never really at home anywhere now. Two small, hot tears ran down my cheeks, and then I fell asleep.

Minutes later, as I scrubbed at the crusty remains of cheese in the casserole dish, my wedding ring caught painfully under its rolled edge. I gave it some four-letter advice, but instead of bringing relief, this only released a sudden, violent rage. Roughly drying my hands on my smock (which did not improve its charm), I tried to twist the gold band off. That ring no longer had the slightest relevance — wearing it was both tasteless and stupid. How could I ever have allowed myself to be lassooed into the thing in the first place? Now, though I tugged and swore, I couldn't get it off. "I'll send it to you in the mail, Edwina Graham, finger and all," I thought vengefully. "Because if it hadn't been for you . . ."

The word "pregnant" caused her face to bleach and seconds later flush to a dusky red.

"Oh, Ross," she whimpered. Out came an initialled linen handkerchief with which she dabbed her eyes like someone cruelly and personally betrayed. "How . . . *could* you?"

"The usual way," I almost said angrily, but bit my tongue. It was now my turn to sit in silent dejection and look at the carpet.

"Oh dear, oh dear," she went on between dabs. "What a tragedy, Ross, just when you're starting out at Fraser and Dawson's . . . *what* a calamity. Your poor father, what ever would he have said?"

"Not much point wondering about that, is there, Mother? And please stop crying; that doesn't help either."

It seemed to buck her up to be bullied. She put the handkerchief away; but Ross began to pace up and down the room in a distraught sort of way, as if he might be the next to cry.

"Well, my boy," she said after a pause, drawing up her large bosom like a defensive shield. "I suppose there's only one . . . *decent* thing you can do, in the unfortunate circumstances. You'll have to marry her." The bland assumption that I was not there to be spoken to made me angrier than I'd ever been in my life before.

"Nobody has to do anything of the kind," I said loudly.

"But Anne, what else can be done?" And her question was so well aimed, right at the centre of my vulnerability, where Billie had struck more openly, that I felt slightly sick.

"Nobody has to marry me," I repeated fiercely, looking at Ross. But to my considerable surprise, a look of something like relief had come over his face.

"Anne, somebody might want to. Even insist." He came and sat on the arm of my chair. Edwina at once averted her eyes as if witnessing an indecency. He didn't touch me, but I could feel his legs trembling.

"It's money that's the chief problem," he said, trying to sound mature and judicious; but all of us knew he was only waiting for her to settle that question too. "I could try to get a job for a year or two and finish my articles later, but — "

His mother fumbled out the handkerchief again. Money, after all, was just as tender an issue as morality, if not more so. "No, no, Ross; that's *quite* out of the question. Your father — well, we did hope you'd wait till you were thirty to marry; that's why Herbert left your inheritance in trust. But when it's a question of your future like this, of course we'll have to talk to the executor. Dear old Mr. Campbell I'm sure won't raise any difficulties about making funds available now ... enough, say, for the down payment on a house, and some kind of monthly living allowance."

I could feel Ross trying to repress an attack of hiccups. He was subject to them when under stress. I sometimes wondered how he would manage in court. He still didn't look at me or take my hand. My jaws ached from holding in tears.

"Well, that's settled, then. I'll phone Ian Campbell tomorrow." Edwina put away the handkerchief once more.

"Yes; do that." He looked as pale as his own ghost, but his voice was firm.

"Look, Mrs. Graham, I don't want Ross to be pressured into —"

"Shut up, Anne."

Edwina smoothed her bosom. "Well, I can't say I'm delighted, with Ross just at the start of his career, but I suppose we must just make the best of it. After all, you're not the first couple to . . . hm. I'll get in touch with your . . . *parents* tomorrow, Anne, and we'll arrange a very . . . *quiet* wedding as soon as possible. Luckily," she added thoughtfully, "nearly everybody's away for the summer just now."

"Which will not prevent your friends from counting backwards the day I give birth," I thought. "Not if your friends are anything like you."

"I don't see any need at all for marriage to come into this," I remarked sulkily. Neither of them paid any attention to me. Edwina had now produced a number of sharp pencils and a block of paper. It seemed to cheer them both up greatly to have things to write down and figures to add up. Under her direction, Ross trotted to and fro fetching things they seemed to think mattered, like insurance policies and a calendar. Both of them grew more and more chatty. Ross even laughed once. They appeared to have forgotten my existence — which was actually rather a relief to me.

"Now I think some time around the fifth. That leaves three Sundays to call the banns. The licence you can get right away; I think it's fifty dollars. . . ."

I sat back in the armchair and drifted into a sort of half-doze. After all, it was a comfort to be in the hands of a woman as sure as Edwina that there was a Right Thing, and we were doing it. It was three years before I grew up enough to despise both of us for that.

After Cave Bears, we three dropped into sleep in our fireside nest of bedding. Hugh, full of baby aspirin, breathed loudly through his mouth. Mao curled himself up behind my knees, purring. The day's effort was over, and I gradually felt the approach of a slow, tidal peace. My fetus stretched drowsily in its water-bed. Together we listened sleepily to the muffled echoes of sound in an outer world — rumble of traffic, swish and gurgle of digestive tract, lub-dub rhythm of heart-beat, hiss of burning wood. Pictures formed and melted behind my closed eyes. Seagulls. Ten-month-old Martha, her fat face rosy with sun under a little white hat, smacking a tidal pool with her toy shovel, to scatter its tiny crab population. Our Gaspé holiday.

Ross squatted beside a driftwood fire he'd built on a flat rock. Yams wrapped in foil roasted in the embers, and he was now building the fire up to a blaze before grilling the steaks. The wind off the dark-blue water tousled his hair. His nose was peeling with sunburn.

"I love you a *hell* of a lot," I told him. His answering smile was shy. In his tattered denim shorts and checked shirt, he looked about six. I did wish beaches weren't such hopeless, gritty places for making love, because this one was beautifully deserted. As it was, I would have to wait till we got back to the motel.

"Get on with that steak, love. It's getting late."

He tossed a bit of seaweed at me. "I know what's on your mind, you sex maniac."

"Too right."

"Well, hold on. Let's eat first."

This was a perfectly acceptable arrangement. That cold, pure, salt-bright air stimulated all the appetites. We stayed on the beach eating till the sun was low and red. Martha fell asleep in her stroller as abruptly as a drunk passing out. The seagulls mewed and called with their greedy, yearning voices, their wings flashing over the green foam of an incoming tide. We finished a bottle of wine, hugging the thought that the motel was only ten minutes' walk away, and that the grim white nights of Martha's colic were far behind us. We walked back along the beach pushing the stroller, so close together we made one shadow.

"I am so damn happy with you it isn't decent," I told him minutes later while taking off his shirt. I began to tickle his neck and jaws with small, teasing kisses. He groaned with pleasure as I pushed him onto the bed and rolled over him.

"Mmm. Lovely. Oh God."

"Absolutely."

"Wait a sec, Anne —"

"What for?"

"You sure your whatsit is in?"

"Of course I'm sure."

"Okay, we just don't want any little accidents, right?"

"Oh, do stop. You're such a worrywart."

"I know. Sorry. Only since they took you off the pill, I can't help . . . I mean this diaphragm thing isn't all that foolproof, is it."

"Well, next to total abstinence, I'm told it is. Now will you stop it."

"Sorry."

"Mmm. Now where were we . . ."

A log in the fire broke, shooting up a bright lick of flame and wakening Mao, who uttered a querulous, sleepy yowl. I shifted Martha's weight off my arm and sat up, glad of the interruption. Remembering past and gone joy was about as rewarding as pulling out your own hair in handfuls. It would be much more helpful, I told myself grimly, to recall past miseries. Like, perhaps, the day we got home from that same Gaspé holiday.

I'd been having some discomfort and a little bleeding, so on our way through the city, Ross dropped me off at the doctor's. There, to my consternation, he found me pregnant.

"Oh Lord. So much for diaphragms."

"Well, you've got to put 'em in right side up, you know. Better talk this over with your husband, and if you decide . . ."

The instant Ross got home I told him the news, blurting it out in a desperate hurry while I still had the courage.

He pulled off his glasses and rubbed both eyes with the heels of his hands. "No — no — Anne, you said that next to total —"

"I know. Only it turns out I've been putting the damn thing in upside-down or something. Miller says he'll install an IUD next time. Please, please don't be sore about it. I'm awfully sorry about the timing; but after all, you wouldn't mind a son, would you? It just means we're having our family early, that's all. Lots of people say you might as well have another one right away when you're tied down anyhow with the first one. Please, you're not sore about it, are you?"

He tried with minimal success to smile, and he put his arm around me, but a worry-frown dragged at his forehead, and he gave a sigh like a sad and weary old man. His goodness made the tears roll richly down my cheeks. He patted my back.

"There now, honey, don't cry. It's all right. Come on, blow your nose. It's all right, I tell you. When does Miller say you're due?"

"Early December. Martha will be eighteen months. It won't be so bad. I can have her trained by then, and —"

"Well, you'd better get some rest now. Lie down, why don't you. I'll cope with Martha."

"Our bed's not made yet. Sheets and all that are down in the laundry room."

"I'll go get them. You take it easy."

Five minutes later he was back from the basement. His face was dead white with fury.

"Anne. Do you know where I found the laundry? In one great big wet lump. Covered with mould. In the drier. You forgot to switch it on. That whole horrible mess has been sitting there for two *weeks*!" His voice rose to a yell. "It's absolutely, bloody TYPICAL! I've told you again and again, but you never listen. This place is *chaos*! Your junk is all over the place — you're always making clothes in the kitchen or reading in the toilet, toys and pots and God knows what cluttering the stairs — it's disgusting! It makes me physically sick!"

"I'm sorry —"

But he flung out of the room, still furious, and I thought, if we were being typical, how like him it was to make such an uproar about a few sheets. Just the same, I began to suspect for the first time that the trivial conflicts between us might be the ones, in the end, to prove true destroyers.

The red eye of the fire winked at me cynically, as if to remind me of the value of hindsight. Wide awake now, as it always was in the small hours, the unborn one flexed its spider limbs. In stages, like an old buffalo, I heaved to my feet and, one after the other, lugged the children up to their beds. As I climbed the stairs with Martha slung over my shoulder, I heard the faint echo of those gulls wistfully calling on the Gaspé beach.

A little later, when all of us had for some time been in our beds, I woke sharply to a noise like the coughing of some large, hoarse goat. Shivering, I groped along the creaking hall floor to the children's room. A big white moon like a face with toothache looked in at the window, and by its light I found Hugh wheezing and choking with croup. I lifted him out of the cot, wrapped his sweat-damp body in a blanket, and carried him to the phone.

"Next time, don't take him to Emergency," our pediatrician had told me. "Traumatizes the poor kid too much. Call me and I'll bring over our cold steamer." Luckily Jeff Reilly lived only a few blocks away.

"Anne Graham here. Sorry to bother you so late, Lynne, but is Jeff there?"

"Yes, he is. Hold on a minute."

"Jeff, our boy's having another bad go of croup."

"Argh. Well, bundle him up and take him out on the porch or somewhere — the cold air will help. I'll be there in ten minutes."

I struggled into a coat and swaddled Hugh in everything I could lay hands on before propping him up in the stroller and shoving it out onto the gritty little ornamental balcony that led off our bedroom. After a few minutes,

Hugh's hoarse struggle for breath eased, and I then seized the opportunity to blunder downstairs, turn on a light, and open the front door. (Poor old Junie: if the late movie had ended, she would miss this little drama.) Then I hurried back to peer at Hugh in the moonlight. He was still labouring to breathe, but the panic had died out of his eyes. "That's right, old man," I said, patting him. "You're all right now."

He gave me a quick, sweet look, and for a second I saw Ross there — vulnerable, loving, strong, and weak. For a second, the illusion that he was literally there, and needing me, was so sharp that I turned around, as if he might be standing behind me. With it went an uncanny impression of being outside my own body and somehow in his, wherever it might chance at the moment to be. I could feel his confusion, a sort of clashing gloom and distress, as if they were lodgers in my own mind. This kind of transference was not uncommon between us, but only once before had it been as powerful as this — one evening soon after we moved into this house.

With my hair bound up in a scarf, and wearing one of Ross's torn old shirts, I was painting the kitchen walls, working hard to have it done to surprise him when he came home. It was deeply satisfying to be working in my own house; the colour was an attractive plum blue; I should have been happy, but for some reason I was not. Some kind of uneasiness dragged at me, nagging and persistent; a kind of spiritual indigestion. I switched on the radio and found some lively music, but it didn't help. Vigorously I wielded the roller, smoothing on the fresh colour and expertly catching the drips; but still the malaise persisted. It grew so keen I almost called Ross at the office; but then I remembered the senior partner, old Mr. Fraser, might still be there — a tall old man with bleak eyes cynically hooded like the eyes of an aged turtle. Ross, I knew, was afraid of him.

The bad feeling was so pervasive that I told myself with great firmness its origin was simply the smell of paint. After all, I was six months pregnant and entitled to occasional qualms. The fact was, though, that I'd never had a moment's nausea and glowed with rude health from the very start.

Finally, to comfort myself, I put down the roller and wandered through the hall and into the living-room. Here we'd opened a wide archway to provide space, and in the dining-room, builders had made French doors onto a pleasant little brick patio brightened with tubs of geranium, lobelia, and ivy. The whole house was almost comically narrow, and it had been a real test of ingenuity to find ways of giving it charm. Yet with one accord we'd chosen this downtown, terraced house with its skylight and steep stair in preference to a prim Leaside bungalow or a sterile suburban condominium like the one Max and Billie owned. They both seemed perfectly happy in a twentieth-floor flat furnished and decorated throughout by Interiors, Inc., who chose the very china for the table. But Ross built book shelves (though he nearly sawed off his own thumb in the process), and I made curtains on a second-hand sewing machine. Together we white-painted the downstairs room and pasted enormous brilliant flowers cut out of fabric on the walls — in short, we had the best fun of our lives. Ross worked late into every evening, attempting to ingratiate himself with Mr. Fraser; but the instant he got home, he changed into paint-speckled clothes and happily joined me in scraping floors or painting woodwork. He was due now, in fact, overdue, and uneasiness squirmed in me more insist ently than ever as I waited for him.

By the time he actually arrived, I was so relieved to see him, apparently perfectly all right, that I hurried to the kitchen to make coffee. He did look extra tired.

"Here, love, have some of this, it will pick you up. Want something to eat?"

"No, no."

There was a dragging note in his voice. I looked at him sharply. "What's the matter, love? I've had this bad feeling for hours. Something's wrong, isn't it."

"No, there isn't. I'm just pooped, that's all."

"It's more than that. Tell me."

"Leave it, Anne. Just leave it. You've got enough on your mind, with baby coming and all. . . . Good God, what have you done to the kitchen?"

"What, don't you like it?"

"Oh, sure — sure — only that purply blue is a bit overpowering, don't you think?"

"Well, we could change it if you like. Maybe wallpaper would be better — "

"No, honey, actually it looks quite nice. Different, anyway. I'll get used to it." He put his arm around me, but when I leaned back against him, he was so tense it was like touching a high-tension wire.

"Ross, what's wrong?"

He jerked away from me and clapped down the mug of coffee, which he'd barely tasted. Hunching his shoulders irritably, he headed for the sitting-room. I followed him there and, cornered, he threw himself into a chair, only to leap out of it again as if it were on fire. He stood at the window staring out at the autumn sky in which great clusters of stars swarmed.

"Tell me," I said gently.

"Oh, it's nothing — I just get uptight about things, as you know. Only it's perfectly obvious that old man Fraser hates my *guts*, that's all. He only took me in because he knew my father. He despises me. Every day he finds some way to put me down, every single day. It's got so I dread going in to the office. He's completely different with Randy, but nothing I do is ever right. And I'm ashamed of being so scared of the old bugger. So it's a vicious circle."

"Go on."

"Well, I made up my mind today that I'd step right up to him. You know, man not mouse." His voice wobbled briefly and I longed to touch him, but didn't.

"Anyhow, I asked if I could see him, and he waved me into that office of his with the glass bookcase and the picture of Wilfrid Laurier, and I screwed myself up to ask him why Randy gets to help him with the Bennington case, instead of me. It's true we came into the firm at the same time, but I graduated with a damn sight better degree than Randy, and I stay late every night working my ass off while he puts his feet up at home. The old bastard knows all this perfectly well. It's time I was given more responsibility; he knows that too. It's so bloody *unfair*."

"What did he say to all that?"

"Well, he said — he said — 'Graham, the fact is that young Randall has more flair than you. Certainly he has more aptitude for corporate law. Frankly, I have more confidence in him. Perhaps in time . . . ' and he waffled on a bit about giving me time to mature and all that crap. And I went back to my desk and just sat there. How about that, being told you're in the wrong profession, after all those years hitting the books. Well, it's not the first time I've thought of it. Law attracts the failures — the guys not much good for anything."

"Ross, you know better than that. You have more perception and a better brain than Randy will ever have, and you know it. Fraser knows it too. He's simply jealous of both of you because you're young and bright — he feels *inferior*, don't you see; that's why he's trying to set the two of you against each other."

He shook his head. "Even if there's some truth in that, how can I go back to that office after today? How can I possibly, after what he said to me? But of course there's no way I can quit, either, not with you like this and the house to pay for . . . of course I'll just have to hack it the best way I can."

I went over and laid my arms around him, resting my face against his back between the shoulder-blades.

"Ross, you're not going to stay there and take any more. Not for long, anyhow. What's the point of heading for a nervous breakdown, even if Randy's in line for one next? There's got to be some way — move to another firm or something."

"No . . . word gets around Bay Street you're difficult or whatever, and . . . no, I'm stuck there for the next year, at the very least."

"Well, but after that —"

"After that what. It isn't as if I could dream of setting up on my own, not for ten years or so yet. If then. Me having no flair, and all that."

I rubbed my cheek on his back. "Now then. You know that's a lot of balls. Why shouldn't you set up on your own, as soon as your time with Fraser is up? You said yourself the other day that Tim Brian's looking around for partners — he was in your class, wasn't he? He's got access to his dad's money, and pots of it — you might not have to put that much in. I'm sure your mother would help, specially when she knows the story. Anything's better than dragging on there a minute longer than you have to.''

"Easy for you to say," he muttered; but he turned around and we held each other, the bulge that would soon be Martha pressed between us so firmly we could both feel her stir.

"We haven't done this room yet," I murmured. The reference was not to decoration. We had promised each other to make love in every room in the house, as a way of making it really ours, and by some inexplicable oversight hadn't yet used the sitting-room.

"Oh honey, I'm too tired."

"No, you're not."

He turned out to be almost right, just the same, and he fell asleep the instant we were finished, sprawled awkwardly half over me. I lay there for a long time buzzing here and there with pins and needles under his weight, because I couldn't bear to wake him.

A bang of the downstairs door announced the arrival of Jeff Reilly, M.D., a duffle coat slung on over worn jeans, and a Leafs hockey tuque jammed over his curly hair. There was something ridiculously boyish about Jeff — until he switched professional concentration like a bright light on his patient. He touched Hugh's face, peered at him closely, and listened critically to his hoarse cough. The moon looked over his shoulder as he shone a tiny flashlight into each of Hugh's ears.

"Yes; well, he's not too bad," he said, packing away the stethoscope after giving Hugh's cheek a friendly pinch. "Why don't we just keep him out here for a little while? He's over the worst already. I'll go plug in the steamer so we can put him to bed in a few minutes."

He was back shortly with a couple of chairs for us, which he placed cosily close together. "Now then, Annie, put your boots up and prepare for a small snort of medication. I have here a little of this wonder drug called Scotch."

With a wink he produced a flask and tiny cups from his duffle pocket.

"God, Jeff, I'd better not — what with one thing and another, I've had three martinis today, and my heartburn —"

"Do it the world of good," he said firmly. And to my surprise, it did just that. The first sip went down like a mouthful of sweet fire, warming my cold hands and feet and heart. Hugh's breathing was almost easy now, as if he felt comforted too.

"Oh, bless you, Jeff; that's so good."

He looked at me quickly and put his arm around me by way of answer. I relaxed against him gratefully. It was such a luxury to feel cherished for a rare and welcome change. Jeff and I had been warm friends ever since the days when Martha's five-month colic had driven us nearly mad together. I'd never dared tell po-faced old Dr. Marshall how her hours of nightly screaming drove me so nearly berserk that I was afraid of what I might do to her; but I could and did tell Jeff.

"Two good ounces of rye in a hot toddy," he said.

"What?"

"For you, dummy, not the baby. She'll scream on, but you'll feel a lot better."

From that moment I trusted as well as liked our Dr. Reilly. Hugh's many maladies had kept us in close touch since then, though socially as couples after the first year we hadn't seen much of each other. His wife, Lynne, was an intense girl, deeply into ecology. Unfortunately, like most people deeply into anything, she had a tendency to bore the pants off me.

In fact, I hadn't yet forgiven her for what she did to our first real dinner-party. It was to be a sort of mini-housewarming, just for four couples, and I spent hours preparing cocktail dips, casserole dishes, and a great salad bowl. The table looked elegant, set with all our wedding-present silver and crystal. We had scented candles burning everywhere to combat the lingering smell of fresh paint and varnish. I'd gone to the hairdresser, who made a crown of my thick gold braid, and Billie had bought me a delicious dress of green chiffon with innumerable tiny pleats gathered at the neck and falling loose to cover the by-then-considerable bulk of Martha. "Later on, if you ever get your waist back, you can wear it with a belt," she said. "Meanwhile the colour is gorgeous with those eyes of yours."

Jeff and Lynne were the last to arrive; and we had all begun on the punch, so the atmosphere was already jolly. Bonnie had a naval-reserve officer in tow, an amusing fellow; and Randy was euphoric because he'd just had both a legacy and a row with Fraser at the office, and had decided to leave. "No kidding, it's like being born again," he told me. "Never mind if Ross is the white-haired boy in there now, he'll have to get out too."

"I know." But this was no night for talking shop. I took the bottle of wine Jeff was holding out and gave Ross Lynne's coat to hang up. "Sorry we're late," Jeff said, "but I got a call from the hospital just before we left — Chinese baby damn near moribund with diarrhea. They will let the grandmothers at them with roots and things. Hey, the house looks great."

Ross and I squeezed hands privately. He ladelled out more punch, not forgetting his own glass. Soon he was at the head of the table carving beef, looking flushed and happy. When everybody had a full plate, Jeff raised his glass and proposed a toast to the house. It was a nice, rich burgundy, and it flew straight to my head, making me feel pleasantly muddled, but at the same time witty, wise, and wonderful. It was at this point that Lynne Reilly began to take over the conversation.

". . . been to the meeting? Concerned Citizens? — oh, you must have heard of them. We're pressuring the city to set up new by-laws about waste disposal. Do you realize that the domestic garbage of this city contains one hundred and fifty-nine thousand tons of metal, glass, and paper, all of it simply wasted? And that's not to mention another twenty-nine thousand tons of bones and vegetable matter, all of it recyclable one way or another. Now, if the law forced every householder not only to keep a compost heap, but to wrap separately all fats and bones — "

"Oh, dem bones," somebody sang.

"I'll bet you're making those statistics up."

"Won't you have some more meat, Lynne?"

"No, thanks. When you realize the cost per annum of shipping out all those cubic feet of garbage —"

"We flatten all our tin cans and take them to the depot place," said Randy's wife, "but I must say it's a bit of a drag."

"Well, I haven't got time, myself, to rush around bundling up newspapers," said Bonnie. "As for fats and bones, what are doggies for? My poodle Chi-Chi recycles all that kind of thing."

"No responsible person can afford to ignore this problem," said Lynne severely. She was a very tiny girl, but there was a ferocious curl to her nostrils and a masterful ring to her voice that was beginning to make more frivolous conversations about things like inflation fade out. "There's nobody who can't find the six minutes twice a week it would take to sort and pack household refuse for recycling."

"Six minutes?" somebody asked sceptically.

"That's all. It's simply a matter of organization. Plus, of course, awareness of the fact that ecology is the biggest single issue around. Is there anybody who can't find six minutes a week to preserve the planet?"

"Yes. Me," muttered Bonnie rebelliously. But Lynne heard her, and to everybody's surprise stood up, tossing down her table-napkin. "You don't think it can be done in six minutes, do you?" she demanded of us all. "Well, it's time somebody raised your consciousness, then. I'm going to show you how quick and easy it is."

"Lynne —" murmured Jeff, trying to detain her. But her eyes were flashing a challenge all round the table. "Now you come on out here, all of you," she said, "and I'll show you how one concerned citizen can make a contribution. Where's your garbage, Anne?"

Helplessly, two or three of us followed her out to the kitchen, where she seized the pedal-can and dumped out onto a sheet of newspaper God only knew how many cubic feet of potato peelings, ratty lettuce leaves, bits of packaging and plastic, coffee grounds, eggshells, and orange peel. These relics appeared to give her the most profound satisfaction. She pounced on an empty spray-tin with particular relish. "Look at that!" she cried. "Every time you push that button, you deplete the ozone layer and increase the rate of skin cancer, don't you know that?"

She pulled on a pair of my rubber gloves and began to sort the mass of our household waste into various unsavoury piles.

"I'm timing you, Lynne," Bonnie said, grinning.

The men all stayed at the table sensibly having more beef and refilling their glasses; but we women watched with unwilling fascination while Lynne demonstrated concerned citizenship amid the garbage. Over her head I caught sight of Ross, his eyebrows raised to their fullest extent, and made a cheerful face at him. But the six minutes seemed to extend themselves endlessly. Bonnie drifted away, bored; but I somehow felt obliged to stay until Lynne had everything sorted and packed to her satisfaction. At last she peeled off the gloves, saying, "You see? Six minutes precisely. Nothing to it."

"Amazing," I said bleakly.

She went back to the table again, and there all cheerful chatter abruptly ceased and one of those disastrous social silences dropped like a pall. Lynne had two helpings of dessert, but the party never really recovered, and I've had a grudge against ecology ever since.

"How is Lynne?" I asked Jeff.

"Oh, she's fine. You sound down, dear. Had a rough day?"

"Jesus, don't ask."

He rubbed his nose thoughtfully. "You know, I honestly can't figure Ross in all this. What the hell's happened to the guy this last year? He's the very last one I'd ever imagine would cop out like this. I mean, he was really bonded to you. And for another thing, at Ridley he used to be religious. Not smarmy with it — not your altar-boy type — but actually for real. He tried to be a decent guy. He was *respected*."

"He's still trying to be decent, Jeff."

"That's a joke, maybe?"

"No, I mean it. He thinks he can't do anything for me any more, and he's found somebody that he thinks needs him."

"That white rat Larine? After you? Come on."

"No, you don't get the point. You don't really know him."

"Look, we went through four years of boarding-school — if you don't know a guy after that —"

"This is different. Marriage is a whole new ball game, as you must know damn well."

He drew a little away from me and clinked the flask against his cup again. "Right," he said in a suddenly cooler voice.

"No, don't blame Ross. It's more me that's wrong. This whole mess is my fault, basically. He never wanted all these pregnancies. I mean, three of them in three years. It's all been just too bloody much. He can't understand why I've been so totally incompetent, and then so stubborn. No wonder he felt overwhelmed. Threatened, even."

Jeff shifted forward to have a look at Hugh, now fast asleep with his face turned blindly up to the moon.

"When we went to the gynecologist this last time — you know, Miller — he said, 'Believe it or not, you're at it again, Mrs. G. But how you've managed it I'll never know.' And poor old Ross had to sit down with his head between his knees. Another accident. Or blunder. Did I know the IUD had slipped out? I mean, Hugh was only seven months. . . . Then Miller asked his usual question, did we want an abortion. Both of us answered together. Only I said no, and Ross said yes. Pretty basic difference of opinion, right?''

Jeff grunted helplessly.

"So he took off just a month or two later. What's more, I don't blame him, Jeff. I mean that. The whole scene has done bad things to him, and he's built up a big resentment. Even fear. He says I'm too powerful. I fill up the whole house, he says, with all my kids and plants and books and animals and junk, till there isn't enough air for him to breathe. I know just what he's trying to say. I understand how he feels. And if I can, surely you can.''

A thick pepper of small, bright stars looked down at us, though a drifting snow-cloud hid the moon.

"Actually, I sometimes think I'm a touch obsessed — with all this kid business, I mean. Don't you think? With all the fool-proof contraception around . . . well, look at you and Lynne. Three years, isn't it, since —'' Their first baby had been found dead in her crib one morning, and they had had no more.

He cleared his throat. After a minute he said, "We've maybe got too many choices now. Lynne . . . she's got a thing about zero population. Two years ago she insisted on a tubal ligation.''

"Well, Lynne is a very intelligent girl.''

"Sure. We're actually talking about a trial separation. And you can't get much more intelligent than that.''

"I'm sorry.'' So I was, though not altogether surprised. But in fact I'd hardly taken in what he said. My thoughts had jumped back to the last stage of my sixteen-hour labour with Martha, who had characteristically tried to arrive in the breech position. After an age with poor, pale

Ross rubbing my back pain, they had to put me out so she could be turned. At the end, it took a whole medical team to get her out of there — nurses yawning wearily, the obstetrician sweating, Ross trembling as he coached me with the breathing. I was exhausted, battered with pain and high on several different kinds of dope. But when Ross lifted my head for the first look at that small, purple creature, its head swollen and bruised, its mouth open and furiously yelling, my whole life focussed and became perfectly simple. I had one purpose: to keep that ugly, helpless human thing safe. Total commitment. Adulthood at last.

"Anybody chooses to skip kids —" said Jeff, as if I'd spoken out loud. "I saw mine born and — well — without them you just go round in circles, polluted by your own ego. I can't get this through to Lynne. But to hell with zero population, I say."

"Me too."

Suddenly he turned to me and lifted my face so we could look directly at each other.

"Anne?"

"What?"

"I'm feeling unprofessional."

"Eh?"

"Yes. You don't realize, I know, the way you make me feel. But it's been like this for a long time. And it's a powerful feeling. It really is."

And before I could say, alarmed, "Don't," he kissed my eyes and cheeks and then my mouth. My heavy body lay against him, too astonished to move. But within seconds the stars began to buzz and jump like fireworks, and I pushed him away.

"Well, at least you've never called me Mother, like

that old pill Dr. Marshall,'' I said, pulling the sides of my coat together in a way I hoped he'd recognize as completely final.

"This isn't funny, Anne. Not to me," he said humbly. We looked at each other, ridiculously bundled in our winter gear under the lopsided moon, and nobody smiled. In a burst of desperate honesty I said, "Jeff baby, go home. You don't know how basic I feel."

"My poor, sweet Anne. How've you been managing? Hasn't there been anybody since Ross left?"

"Well, hardly, with me like this. So I manage in the obvious way. Not that it's any real substitute."

"You are so beautiful," he said slowly. "I never thought I could tell you this, but — Know what I've often wanted to do? I want to undo that hair of yours and let it all fall down around me like some gorgeous, golden tent. For years I've wanted to."

Suddenly I thought, "Dear Jeff." If intercourse had not at this stage been out of the question, I would probably have taken him to bed then and there, out of simple gratitude and affection. As it was, I turned my head and kissed his hand where it still rested on my shoulder. "That's twice in twenty-four hours," I thought dimly, "that I've felt loving-kindness for somebody who probably doesn't deserve it. I must be mad."

"We're going to talk more about this, Anne. And do something about it, too. But right now, you're worn out. Also a tiny bit smashed. Wait here and finish the Scotch. I'll put Hugh to bed." And expertly scooping up the baby, he went into the house.

Thanks to the pre-dawn hour and the whiskey, none of this seemed at all real. The stars were drifting around in lazy circles. My head buzzed with sleep. Jeff came back, helped me climb onto the broad, empty bed, and covered me with a blanket. A profound and blissful sleep overtook me at once. I didn't hear him go.

Wednesday

*E*DWINA HELD UP a limp lace veil banded across the forehead with tarnished silver flowers. "My dear mother and I both wore it," she said. "I think it will look very nice on you. . . . Of course, you won't have your hair in that braid." "Cut it off, I tell you," said Junie. With a weak little bleat the phone rang and I snatched up the receiver. "Anne, I'm coming home," said Ross's voice.

I struggled upright in bed, my heart drumming. The phone was silent. The veil was in a drawer somewhere, waiting for Martha, unless she proved a lot more agile and cunning than *her* dear mother had been. My mouth tasted of rusty metal, and a headache thumped between my ears. With some surprise, I noticed that I was wearing a coat; and with that came the memory of last night's regrettable encounter with Jeff. I rolled over and groaned into the pillows. Even for me, this was an extra stupid and pointless situation to get into. There was absolutely nothing to be gained from it, and much to be lost — namely a first-rate pediatrician.

This line of thought was so acutely disagreeable that I pulled the blanket up around my head and fixed my mind instead on Edwina's veil. When I showed it to Billie she gave a little scream of dismay.

"Oh you poor duck, how ghastly. And I suppose you can't very well refuse. Not only is it hideous, but it means you have to wear a long white dress, the whole damn business, complete with tulle garter. They can be so vulgar, actually, these old Upper Canada families. Still, it could be worse — she might have forced you into some awful satin gown made in the thirties. As it is, Max wants to give you a great triple strand of pearls, so you might as well have the lot, I suppose."

"I know. And we were going to keep everything so simple. All private and quiet, you know, because of what Edwina calls 'my Condition'. But the other night she and Ross began to make a list of all the relatives that apparently have to be invited. . . . There are *hordes* of them. All her sisters and their families, and Ross's Uncle Hugh and *his* lot out west; and of course Granny, and dear old Gwen, who looked after Ross when he was a baby . . . it's shaping up into a real circus."

The truth was, though, that all the arrangements about rings, flowers, and rehearsals fascinated me as much as it did Ross, and we put up only token resistance to the whole business.

"Then there's the best man," Edwina said, rubbing her forehead with a pencil. "I suppose it had better be your cousin Edwin."

Ross gave a groan and closed his eyes. "For God's sake, Mother. Ed takes fits."

"Very mild seizures, dear; well controlled. He'd be perfectly all right."

"No," he said firmly. "I can't stand to think what he might do with the ring. I'll have Jeff, or Randy. That is, if I have to have anybody."

Edwina frowned at her list. "And Anne will need at least one attendant. A maid of honour —"

"Maid meaning maiden?" I asked, unable to control myself. "Well, I doubt very much if my friend Bonnie would pass any test, but — "

She drew up her bosom in a warning sort of way, but went on blandly, "Perhaps, then, you know some . . . *nice* little girl, just to hold your flowers while the rings are exchanged."

By processes like these our wedding rapidly shaped into a clan gathering, a ritual in which Ross and I would be at once the most prominent and the least active figures, like those saints in effigy carried in religious processions.

"It's ridiculous," fretted Billie. "I hate churches, they're as bad as hospitals. When you aren't bored to tears in them, you're scared to death or horribly depressed. I don't know why the two of you don't just elope." Quietly but firmly she left all the arrangements to Edwina, who adored her double role as martyr and impressario. When I repeated Billie's suggestion about elopement, she only said, "Quite a . . . *sense of humour* your mother has," and went on to debate whether champagne or a sparkling rosé would be better for the breakfast. "And we must call Hugh tonight and ask if he'll propose the toast. He's a busy man, but I'm sure he'll make the effort." After a pause she added, "I do hope, though, he'll . . . *control* . . . his sense of humour."

Ross's head snapped up. "Good old Uncle Hugh," he said. "Will you ever forget that joke he told at Barbara's — "

"Quite," his mother said crisply. "I'll just have a quiet word beforehand with your Aunt Jean. Then there's Catriona. I'm afraid she'll expect to be asked to sing."

"Look," said Ross earnestly. "In no circumstances

will I let that cow sing 'O Perfect Love' anywhere *near* me, do you understand?''

"Well," she conceded with an unwilling little smile, "I must say I've always wondered why they're so proud she never had a lesson in her life."

This kind of thing was highly diverting; but the time soon came when I couldn't avoid noticing that Ross was growing day by day more silent and withdrawn. He tried to conceal it from me, but his sleep was thin and restless, his food disagreed with him, and when he thought no one was looking, he would put his head in his hands and sigh.

One morning at first light I woke to hear him pacing to and fro in the next room, and at last I faced the truth. We'd been like a couple of kids dressed up in their parents' shoes, playing a silly game that would have to stop at once. Hastily I pulled on some clothes and opened the door. Ross stood at the window and did not turn when I spoke.

"Listen," I said desperately. "I know how you feel."

His back went very still. He was listening with acute attention for something he wanted badly to hear.

"Ross, it's insane for us to get married, isn't it."

There was a silence. Then he said almost inaudibly, "It's nothing to do with how I feel about you."

"No, I know that. But it's not just all this chat about ushers that's getting you down, either."

"No."

It had to be said, and because I knew myself to be the tougher of us two by far, I was the one who had to say it.

"Well, then, for God's sake don't let's *do* it. We've been crazy to let ourselves get pushed this far. But nobody can make us go through with it."

"Yes, but all these goddam *arrangements* —"

"We cancel them. That's all."

"Yes, but Anne, there's this — there's your —"

"All right. That's strictly my problem, not yours. It's maybe not too late for me to do some thinking again about that, too. It could just be that everybody's right and I'm wrong about . . . Anyhow, that's my responsibility. Nothing to do with you, basically."

Ross turned away again. His shoulder bones stood out in two sharp blades.

"The thing is," he said in a low voice, "you and I are too . . . I mean it just wouldn't work. We both know it wouldn't. I'm cross in the morning when you're bursting with energy. I'm neat and you're sloppy. I'm a worrier, always analysing and hair-splitting; you just live by some kind of primitive radar. And without being bossy, you're so . . . anyhow, you know we'd started to fight even before we knew about your . . ." Another miserable pause. Then he burst out, "No, I just can't go through with it, that's all. What's the point, when it will all just end in some lousy divorce?"

"Right. Then it's finally settled. No wedding." All of a sudden I felt a crazy sort of relief; my voice sounded almost gay. But his was soft, sad, and final.

"It's no good; you see, I'm just not ready for it. I'm sorry, but I just can't."

"Don't apologize. I know we're not compatible. It would be lunacy for us to go through with the whole thing just for a lot of relatives. You'd better tell your mother right away. I'll cope with my parents. The caterers and all that jazz — they'll be too busy cancelling everything to work up a big scene."

"My mother will be plenty upset. I'd better go home for the weekend."

"Yes, do that. But she'll soon get used to the idea. The thought of you married to me appalled her anyhow, deep down."

"That is not *fair*, Anne. She's behaved damn well, and you know it."

A light shock of delicious anger tingled through me. "Of course she has. That's her speciality. But let's not kid ourselves; your mother *loathes* me."

"Please Anne, don't let's — "

"Why not?" I shouted. "What's wrong with a good loud row? What's there to lose now? You're out of it, whack, and so am I. We can afford a good brawl — maybe we even owe it to each other."

But Ross had darted into the other room, where he snatched up a few clothes and stuffed them into his brief-case. He was white in the face with anger and other kinds of distress.

"I'm off," he said in a breathless voice. "I can't take any more. I'm sorry, if that's any use to you. Sorry, but this is it. I'll be in touch some time later." And he crowded himself through the door without dignity and fumbled it shut between us.

Once he was gone, a superb sort of calm spread through me. Everything now seemed perfectly clear and simple. Some kind of pressure or constriction — maybe it was the bonds of holy matrimony — had dropped away, leaving me light and free. Free to do anything. There was no possibility any more it was impossible to confront. Dr. Miller's offer to schedule me for a hospital abortion was no doubt still open. This procedure no longer seemed like an unthinkable atrocity, but simply a matter of common sense. The alternative was twenty-odd years of single-parent responsibility for a being still just a cluster of cells. Almost light-headed with relief, I dialled Miller's answering service and was promised a call from his secretary at noon.

In the interval, I set about a fanatic clean-up of the apartment's two and a quarter rooms. Ross's drawers in the bureau we shared were models of neatness; mine were a snake's nest of belts, bras, aspirin, deodorant spray, keys, cologne bottles, pantyhose, ballpoint pens, loose change; even, inexplicably, a tennis shoe. I reduced all this to impeccable order before going on to vacuum under the bed, excavating in the process an air-letter, an apple core, and two overdue library books . . . all on my side. He was right about my sloppiness. And about everything else, too. We were socially, psychologically, every way incompatible. What a pity that in spite of this we'd become so horribly intertwined that his toothache made my molar stab; my thoughts printed out in his mind; there were no definable boundaries anywhere between us.

Fiercely I scoured the tiny kitchen and bathroom, it being a matter of pride to leave the entire place in a state of inhuman neatness. Finally I packed a small case to take with me to Don Mills, and filled cartons with all the rest of my clothes and books. By the time Miller's nurse called, I was breathless with all this activity and glad to sit down.

"You called, Miss Forrest?"

"Yes. I need an appointment with Dr. Miller right away."

"Is it an emergency?" she wanted to know.

"Yes, you could call it that."

There must have been something convincing in my voice, because after a short pause she said, "Right. Why don't you come in a bit before two, and I'll sneak you in before he sees anyone else."

"Thanks very much."

That gave me time to make up the bed with clean linen, leaving that arena also perfectly, primly pure. After a last look around to make sure no litter remained, I locked the door behind me and set out.

On Yonge Street the tall city towers were paralysed in a thick heat-haze. Car exhaust, dust, and hot-tar fumes hung in the heavy air. The sun was like a brass gong overhead. On the subway platform it was a little cooler, but the invading gusts of hot, gritty air reeked of scorched metal. "A perfect day for this trip," I thought grimly. "Couldn't be better." On the bench waiting was an old woman with an orthopaedic collar and swollen legs. Looking at her kept my desperation in mint condition. Life wasn't such a glittering prize, after all. Who was I to force it on anybody else?

At last a train came rumbling out of the tiled tube, bringing its own gush of hot air to boil around the platform. I walked back to the last car, which was not crowded like the rest. Inside, though it was stiflingly hot, my hands felt cold.

I flopped down on the nearest empty seat. The two benches running lengthwise down the car close to me each contained the recumbent figure of a teen-aged girl. Their bare and filthy feet confronted me at disagreeably close range. The girl on my right might have been thirteen. Her greasy hair hung to the floor in long strands. She had something in her hands which she silently held up to show me. With an involuntary little start, I saw that it was a large black-and-white rat. Before I could check the gesture, one of my hands jerked open instinctively to cover my belly. The girl smiled at me.

"You like rats?" she asked.

"Not all that much."

"Well, but this one is special. He's specially trained. I

give him the signal and he goes straight for your throat. You don't believe it?''

"Frankly, no." The train at this point slowed to a crawl. It swayed and creaked by inches through an apparently endless tunnel. Finally it stopped altogether with a discouraged hiss, and all the lights blinked out. I stood up with sweat pouring down my back. In the dark the girls giggled.

"Okay," the one nearest me said. "Okay, George. *Get her*."

The lights flicked on again to reveal George crouched on her knee, his pink and indecisive nose quivering as if in apology. I smiled weakly and moved over to stand at the doors. A woman across the aisle abruptly changed her seat for one at the other end of the car.

"Chi — i — cken!" both girls chanted in delight.

"Perhaps you know some *nice* little girl," Edwina's voice repeated fatuously. Poor fool, she hadn't realized yet they were an extinct species. When would this infernal train get to a station — any station?

"Here," the girl nearest me said to her friend as the train began to sway forward at last. "Catch!"

She tossed her rat across the aisle and the friend caught it, not very neatly. They threw the creature to and fro several times, eyeing me to enjoy the effect. The other passengers resolutely ignored the whole performance. I stood at the doors with one hand pressed over my belly. My heart was banging with fear, anger, life. I'd forgotten why I was making this trip. All I could contain was a keen and sweating anxiety to get myself and my own personal passenger out of this underworld.

When at last the train doors slid open, I crossed to

the opposite platform and rode back to my starting-point, climbing the stairs minutes later with a euphoric sense of triumph. The blaze of heat rising from the sidewalk felt superb. My back hurt; my eyes dazzled — everything ached; thoughts, feelings, everything — the existence of evil was a real and frightening thing. But I was alive and so was my embryo; nothing else mattered. Later I would call and cancel my appointment with death. At the moment it seemed overwhelmingly important to get back to the apartment. I hurried toward it as if pursued by something dangerous.

As I groped for my keys in the dark lobby, I almost fell over something blocking the lowest step of our walk-up — a hunched-over man who was evidently half asleep — Ross.

"Forgot my key," he mumbled. "Been here for ages. Well, an hour. Where were you?"

"Oh," I said, "nowhere much." We climbed the stairs, each with his bit of hand luggage, and on the landing swayed clumsily together. Drunkenly our faces and bodies blundered into contact, and we clutched each other. The delicate knuckles of his spine felt sharp under my hand.

"I am going to cook you a truly enormous dinner," I said.

"Give me the key so I can open up. What's the suitcase for?"

"I forget."

As we struggled in together, he said, "I mean, what's wrong with City Hall? It's just as legal. To hell with the veil and the ushers."

"Yes, to hell with them."

"*And* the maid of honour."

"Right. Oh, Ross, look at how bloody neat everything is. Even the drawers. You won't believe the drawers."

"I'm a fussy old maid. You'll just have to forgive."

"Get your clothes off," I advised him.

I went into the bathroom briefly to wash my face, which was richly flushed and slobbered with tears. My eyes met the judge's eyes in the mirror without apology. I knew that if I really loved Ross, I would let him go, whatever the cost to myself. But I couldn't afford this kind of generosity. My need was too big. I could keep him safe — but who would protect him from me? That was a question too hard to answer then, or perhaps ever.

". . . on the other hand," he was saying from the bedroom, "my Uncle Hugh is a real gas. This wedding might even turn out to be fun. After all, you could call it an experience, I guess, to hear Catriona belt out 'O Perfect Love'."

This time the phone rang for real, but by the time I struggled out of bed and picked it up, there was nothing at the other end but an empty, electronic hum. While I still stood there stupidly listening to it, the sound of a key in the front door made me jump. Was that Ross at last? Occasionally he used to drop in on his way to the office, and certainly there were things we had to settle very soon about the week when I'd be in hospital. The arrangement was that he'd sleep here while Margaret coped in the daytime; but the details still had to be worked out. It wasn't like Ross to neglect details, I thought gratefully . . . but the head that emerged into the hall below was wearing a Leafs hockey tuque. At once I waddled swiftly back to bed and pulled the blankets high around my head.

Jeff's feet took the stairs two at a time. Hot face pushed deep into the pillow, I pretended to be asleep.

"Anne dear, I took the key off the bureau last night — didn't scare you, did I? Thought I'd come round and help get breakfast before I do rounds at Sick Kids. I want a look at Hugh, too. You don't mind, do you? I'll get the kids up and make coffee — you stay right there." He patted the large mound of my hip and went next door, calling "Wakey wakey" to the kids in a loud and cheerful voice. In a kind of dream I lay there listening to Mao yowling like ten cats to inform the world he expected to be fed before any insignificant brats of children. They, for their part, piercingly filled Jeff in, as he herded them downstairs, all about what they would and would not eat; and the poor devil actually seemed to be enjoying the whole experience.

With some urgency I tried to use this interlude to think of any way of escaping the consequences of my last-night's idiocy. But all I could think of was what would happen if Ross, by any unlikely chance, actually did drop in on us at this point. That confrontation would be so rich in various kinds of irony that picturing it made me shake with laughter under the bedclothes.

"All right now, that's enough," I had to say to myself at last with some severity. "Straighten up, you daft bitch, and make up your mind quickish how you're going to cope with this. Because it is a very ominous sign that Jeff is back here. As you well know." Hoping it might aid thought, I heaved into a sitting position and reached for a hairbrush. Getting the witch's tangles out of my long hair was a business as painful as penance. My arms and back ached cruelly as I tugged away, and by the time I got the whole mass braided again into its thick rope, I had to lie back against the pillows, feeling sick and exhausted. After a minute I put some perfume from Billie's bottle on my forehead, and the cool sting made me feel a bit better in body if not in mind. I still had not the remotest idea what I could say to Jeff to defuse the situation. The odd thing was that except for a sincere wish that he would just go away, I had no feelings about him now that I hadn't had for the last two years. But how to explain this to the poor sod?

When he came in with the coffee tray, I looked at him sombrely, and was touched to observe that he felt shy with me. If only there were some painless way to speed him off without damage. But none occurred to me. Meanwhile, he put his arms around me and nuzzled his face into my neck.

"Hugh's in good shape," he said. "Oh, you do smell so lovely."

"Don't be silly, I couldn't possibly." My voice sounded so ludicrously cross I nearly started to laugh again, and a big answering smile spread across his face.

"Anne, I haven't slept a wink, and I feel sort of unreal; but listen to me, love — I've never been so goddam happy in my life."

"Jeff, let me explain about last night —"

"Say you are too."

'No, I'm not. Far from it. I'm about to apologize to you in six different positions for the whole —"

He was kissing my neck and didn't appear to be listening.

"I couldn't wait to get back here and see you again. Crazy to feel like this, isn't it? But look, I want us to get things straight right away. After all, I've known Ross a long time. If he hadn't taken off, the whole thing would be impossible; but as it is — well, it simplifies everything. And, as you know, Lynne and I were calling it quits anyway; so that's all right too. It's just a question of —"

"Jeff, wait a minute."

"Now, I want you to relax, love. Your job right now is just to get a good baby here. Everything else you can leave to me. I'll try to get hold of Ross this morning and tell him how it is. Lynne's already in the picture. There's no reason why we can't start the legal side of it right away."

"Wait!" I said desperately.

"Eh?" He looked at me, startled.

"I mean, hold on. You mean divorces all round? No, no, Jeff. That would be . . . I mean, look — last night I was quite simply bombed out of my mind. I know I — but it was just one of those crazy impulses. I really am most humbly sorry."

His pleasant, snub-nosed face had gone very still. "What you mean is, you just want me to forget last night entirely?"

I put my hand on his back gently. "That's it."

"And what if I can't do that?"

"Of course you can. You will. I tell you it was just —"

"No, I won't, Anne. I never will."

"But I tried to explain to you how it is with Ross and me. I know how it looks, but we're not really apart. Not really."

"You're just not thinking straight, sweetheart, and no wonder, the way things have been with you. But you need me. And for the rest of it — you don't know how long I've wanted you. It's been years."

"Please. I'm getting along all right. Or was, until last night. That was my fault entirely, and I —"

"Anne, you don't understand." He took me by the shoulders just as Martha bustled into the room clasping a box of Cheerios half as big as herself. She had evidently conned Jeff into letting her wear her blue dress with its embroidered pinafore, but the skirt was kilted up at the back to reveal that he had not insisted on any underwear. "Here's some cereal for you, Mum," she announced. After an armpit-deep plunge into the box, she deposited a fistful of cereal on my tray.

"Lovely," said Jeff. "Now go down and help Hugh with his breakfast, okay?"

"No," said Martha.

"There's a good girl."

"Please?" I added.

"No."

"Take some Cheerios to Violet," he suggested craftily. Her face broke into a seraphic smile and she trotted off.

We talked a little faster now, in lower voices.

"Jeff, it was just one of those things that happen sometimes — you mustn't take it seriously. You wouldn't if we'd actually ... you'd never give it a second thought if you and Lynne were —"

"No, look; are you really trying to tell me it meant nothing when you —"

In trotted Martha again, the box still clutched to her belly. "Violet didn't want any. She ate the butter instead."

"Oh Christ."

"Then go and give the cat some," said Jeff.

"No."

"Please."

"No."

"Martha, *go downstairs*," said Jeff. A vein in his neck was swelling dangerously. "I want to talk to Mummy."

"Okay, talk." With a heave she lobbed the box of cereal onto the bed and clambered up after it, with a generous display of bare pink bum.

He shot me a look in which there was no remaining trace of tenderness, and I was once more seized by a wild urge to laugh. Silently blessing Martha, I pretended helplessness and sighed. At the same instant a powerful contraction made me wince for real.

"You all right?" he asked.

"Sure. Just a cramp. They come and go, these days. Anyhow, you'd better get going on your rounds. There's nothing more to say, except I'm sorry. Truly."

He began to speak, but Martha cut him off. "My mother's got a baby inside her. I'd rather have a hamster. We'd call it June or Albert, and it would eat up all the Cheerios."

"No kidding," Jeff said bleakly. "Well, it's after nine. I've got to go. But Anne, I'll call you tonight. We've got to talk."

"Talking won't make one bit of difference. Dr. Reilly dear, please know that."

He looked at me hungrily, but Martha's unblinking gaze was fastened on him. He drew back. Setting his lips in a tight line, he walked out of the room and went downstairs, one at a time. Violet greeted his departure as she had his arrival, with an outburst of witless barking, and we both distinctly heard him say "Fucking dog" before banging the front door behind him.

A piece of torn newspaper, several Cheerios, and a doll littered the stairs, and I paused on my way down to retrieve them all laboriously, though it was much too late for neatness to help me at all. En route to the kitchen I read the scrap of newsprint. "Martinique. A prisoner locked in his cell was the sole survivor of an earthquake in the village of — '' The rest was missing. But what a neat little paradox. It suggested something profoundly true about both liberty and bondage, and I greatly wished I had the wisdom to see what it was. Because for a long time now the concept of prison had come to seem central to my whole life. That was why, the day Ross left, I helped him pack.

"Why not? I'm not your jailer."

He looked at me with bitter annoyance. "You're supposed to be crying. As usual. Or yelling and cursing. Not folding my goddam shirts. Or is this just another way of cutting me up?"

"Don't. I'm trying to get it across that I know I have no right to try hanging onto you by force. Do you want this old brown sweater?"

"Well, I have no right to walk out on you, but I'm doing it."

"Will you get it through your head I'm not blaming you."

"I'll send you money at the end of the week. And regularly after that. Forward all the bills to me at the office. If Mother calls, tell her anything you like."

"That will be the day."

"Why not. Here's the chance you've been waiting for all these years."

Suddenly I yawned. This new pregnancy caused spells of acute sleepiness that overtook me at the most unlikely moments. He immediately yawned too. Then he said, "Sorry. I know damn well I'm the one that's failed here. You're no more to blame than the cat is for being a cat. Better say nothing yet to Mother. God, I'm so tired. I feel as if I hadn't slept for years."

"Well, you haven't, much."

"You despise me. That's why I have to get out."

"Don't forget your antacid pills."

"I won't."

"Where will you stay — with Randy and Jill?"

"No." He cleared his throat. "One of the girls in the office — she shares a house with some people on Prince John Street. It's right near work. I can have a room there for practically nothing."

"Which girl?"

"Larine."

"Oh. I see." What I saw, with painful clarity, was that our love might survive in some form for a long time yet, but our friendship had taken a damaging blow.

The kitchen window framed a frowning grey sky. I crumpled up the torn bit of newspaper and shot it into the garbage tin. Was that prisoner's survival a victory or a defeat? Was freedom actually a kind of prison, and vice versa? But questions like these could easily drive someone in my position completely around the twist, and what good would that do me or anyone else?

I began to stack the dishwasher, sternly forbidding myself to cry. Outside a pallid gleam of sun was now trying to melt honeycomb holes in yesterday's snow. The skinny black squirrel that lived in our back-yard maple left deep pits as he hopped across to June's patio for the crusts her kids threw out. He scampered up the tree, whisking his tail jauntily. I stared at him so intently I could almost count his fleas.

Ah, Christ, that my love were in my arms, I thought. If only there were some way back for Ross and me to those sunny, blissful afternoons in his narrow student bed. O western wind, when wilt thou blow? Never, kid. Never again.

The phone trilled and I snatched it up on the first ring. It had to be Ross.

"Hello?"

The words at the other end of the line were so coldly and deliberately obscene that at first I couldn't take in their meaning at all. Only after the caller hung up did I recognize the voice. It was Lynne Reilly, the conservationist. She mentioned her husband. She also advised me to get stuffed, among other fanciful variations. Suddenly I burst out laughing as if a joke of cosmic dimensions had been revealed, beautifully timed, and gloriously, tragically funny.

With the kids glued to *Sesame Street*, I went down to the basement for the daily diaper-folding and set about it, trying to ignore the pain like a stab wound in my lower back. It nagged until I dragged over a chair to finish the job sitting down. But nothing would help me much, I realized grimly, until I came to grips with June's question — "What are you going to do about that guy?" — instead of moaning over the snows of yesteryear, or shaking with insane laughter because life was a joke. After five months of passive waiting, it was high time I came up with some kind of action. Unfortunately, the things I wanted to do were all illegal, or immoral, or both. That left only the things I didn't want to do, like marrying Jeff. No need to waste time analysing that decision; it was final. But how could I *reach* Ross? Between us, like some bloody human traffic-jam, stood not only his mother and our kids, born and unborn, but Larine. It was hard to say which was the most threatening of them, except that her Monday visit had left me inclined to take away Edwina's prize for first place.

No, on points, of course, the real opponent had to be Larine, and not just because he was sleeping with her instead of with me. That pale face materialized in my mind's eye: receding chin, small, fishlike mouth, nose sharp as if whittled with a Scout knife. She was far from beautiful, but that was precisely the threat. She was pathetic with her thin little arms, her pale hair, and her tiny breasts. She made Ross feel strong. Ripe, rosy, big, masterful, I made him feel weak. That was a huge tactical disadvantage, and I knew it. But how could I overcome? Obscene phone calls? Blackmailing letters? A punch in the mouth? None of these had much real appeal, except maybe the last. Anyhow, I had little confidence in planned campaigns. The last time I tried to use strategy to lure Ross back home, the attempt could not be called a success.

Of course, seduction was perhaps a bit obvious as tactics go; but it seemed to me worth a try. At that point I wasn't breast-feeding anybody, and hadn't yet reached anything like my present massive size. Consequently I felt quite capable of seducing pretty well anyone, given a reasonable chance. So one evening when I knew he was coming over, I put the kids to bed early, bribed with bottles of sweetened juice, and took a long, leisurely bath before putting on the long blue gown he liked. My newly washed hair smelled of sandalwood. I put a bottle of his favourite hock in the frig, and a stack of Nana Mouskouri ballads on the stereo. He was late, so I had time for a refreshing little catnap before his key rattled in the door.

Two months and half a mile of space away from all

the rashes, teething, and diarrhoea of his married life had smoothed out Ross's face and removed some of its greyish look. He even smiled occasionally.

"Have a glass of wine, why don't you," I said, lifting the dewy bottle invitingly.

"Well, maybe just one. Kids asleep yet? They all right? I'll go on up and have a look at them."

"Don't wake them up."

I arranged myself as attractively as possible in a corner of the sofa, and when he came back downstairs, he sat down in the other corner after only a second's hesitation. We sipped our wine. Nana did her thing. The house was quiet and peaceful.

"Things going all right at the office? What happened about the Bailey case?"

"We won it."

"Oh, good."

"The guy was guilty as hell, too. So Tim was really pleased. So was I, actually. I like winning the Legal Aid ones."

"You hungry, by any chance? There's some of that moussaka you like left over."

"No . . . no thanks." But he made no protest when I refilled his glass. Nor did he withdraw when I slipped my hand into his.

"Been in touch with your mother lately?" I asked him.

"Yes, she's enjoying Florida."

"You haven't actually told her about us yet, have you. I wonder why."

"No, it's just . . . I thought I'd wait till she gets home. No point in spoiling her holiday."

With care I let that pass without comment. Then I put

down my glass, moved closer to him, and gave him a kiss intended to speak louder than words. He accepted it with mild surprise, but no unfriendliness. It was a minute before he drew away.

"Hold on, you are fogging my glasses. What is all this?"

"What does it feel like?"

"Well, but —"

"Why shouldn't we? After all, we're still married."

"Yes, but —"

"Then come on. What's wrong with here and now."

He was already in no condition to put up much resistance, as both of us were well aware; but he did mutter, "Okay, but no strings attached, right? No complications — no regrets after I've gone?"

"Of course not."

"Well, let's go up, then. This sofa's too small. And I'm too old to use the floor any more."

We stopped several times along the way, and by the time we reached the bed in our room, his resistance, such as it was, had completely vanished. Our familiar bed was warm, deliciously warm. The wine had turned my head into a helium balloon, floating somewhere above my drowsy, happy body, tickled by his lips and hands. Strange how very sleepy I felt, in spite of that catnap. Terribly sleepy . . .

My eyes blinked open to find him knotting his tie at the mirror. The face reflected there looked austere.

"There you are," I mumbled. "What are you doing?"

"Go back to sleep," he said.

"Oh. Was I asleep? You mean I —"

"Right in the very middle of it, to be exact."

"It's this crazy pregnancy. I do it all the time." Something warned me this was no time to laugh, but how I wished one or both of us could. Instead I said, "I *am* sorry. You wouldn't care to have another shot at it, I suppose?"

"No thanks," he said with dignity.

So that was that. The ploy that failed, I thought, lumbering up the basement steps with the laundry basket. Just as I reached the top, the phone shrilled. I lunged for the receiver before Martha could grab it. This time it had to be Ross.

"Anne? I saw the doctor at your place this morning. Everything all right?" It was Junie's flat voice. The jabbing pain in my back returned with vehemence.

"Yes, I . . . *had* the pediatrician, as my mother-in-law would put it."

"Oh, him." June's voice was already fading into boredom.

"Hugh had croup in the night. It's lucky for us that Reilly lives so near. He just dropped in to check on Hugh before going to work. He's terrific like that."

"Yeah. Gee, I don't know, such a lot seems to happen to you."

"None of it's good, though, kid."

"Yeah, but at least you're —" A note crept into her voice that I'd never heard there so clearly before — a sort of flat despair. "You know, sometimes I wake up mornings, here's another day, and I just think, *is this all?* You know?"

"Poor bitch," I thought. But all I could think of to say was "Cheer up. At least your mother didn't come to see you yesterday."

"Yeah. I saw your mum. Ever a lovely pair of boots she has."

"Aren't they."

Mail thumped through the letter-box and both children ran to get it. In the race, Hugh fell, or more likely was pushed, and lay in the hall howling, and in the fracas somebody must have stepped on Violet, who added to the din by a frenzied yelping. How glorious it would be to wake up one morning stone deaf, I thought, as I clamped the receiver in position with one shoulder and fanned through the mail. It was all bills.

"There's a sale of boots today at Simpson's," June was saying. "I sure wouldn't mind going down there for a look. Would you mind a whole lot taking my two just for an hour or so this aft.? I better not leave them alone. Last time Darryl built a fire on the kitchen floor. Nothing, really, but Clive got sore. At me, not Darryl. Typical."

"Sure, I don't mind. What's another couple of kids? Send 'em along. The more the merrier. Happy shopping."

"Gee, thanks," she said almost warmly. "Do the same for you next time, Anne. They'll be over right after lunch. See you."

"'Bye, Junie."

In the middle of making my bed, I had to sit down on it suddenly, hit by depression that reached right out of that brief conversation and caught me behind the knees. The kids played serenely around my legs with some Matchbox cars. Mao scrambled onto my shoulder, purring. A copy of Trollope's *Can You Forgive Her?* was pushed half under the pillow, and I pulled it out for comfort. His heroine was just as big a problem to everybody as I was; but any number of good people rallied round energetically to make her happy in the end, in spite of herself. The perfect plot. The book opened at my favourite sentence: "There are things which happen in a day which it would take a lifetime to explain."

"How true," I thought. Take my today, for instance. Every single nasty thing in it had its roots back there somewhere in that shifting childhood of mine. Explaining is easy. Understanding is something else again. Take Gary, the milkman, for instance, who let me ride with him on his rounds. . . .

Moving around as we constantly did often meant I had no friends, so I spent a lot of time on my own in public places, shops, hotel lounges, cinemas, rather like a stray dog. Sometimes casually encountered grown-ups were kind and spoiled my appetite with sweets; but some were threatening and mean as you might be to a stray, because it's already in trouble. I knew by the time I was eight which ones you could trust, and Gary was one of them. He had grey hair, but his face was pink and young, he could whistle with trills, and I loved him.

We had a lot of good conversations as the bottles jingled behind us. "There's an old lady in our hotel with whiskers, and she says God sees every single thing you do. Specially the bad things. I took an apple off the fruit dish before lunch yesterday, and she said God was watching. And he has a place full of fire that melts people's bones if they steal."

"Mean-minded old trout," said Gary. "If there is a place like that — *which* I doubt — she'll go there, not you."

It was a considerable relief to me to hear this. Gary knew pretty well everything, and he always told the truth, unlike a lot of old people who told lies. They said, for instance, that carrots would make your hair curl, and doctors brought babies in their black bags. I never touched carrots and my thick hair was wildly curly. As for babies, everybody knew that mothers vomited them up.

Gary was a great talker, always about interesting things, too, instead of the dull stuff schools were always on about. He liked to talk about pigeons, betting on the greyhound races, how to tell the weather from clouds, and why the price of milk kept going up. He told me a lot about his life: he'd been a Barnardo's orphan, put out to work at fourteen. He'd had lots of interesting jobs in ice-cream factories and stables and places like that; and he said it had been a great life, really — couldn't ask for a better. The one thing he regretted was that he'd married, he said, too young. It was a pity, really, he said, because him and the old woman didn't get on; not at all. What he often dreamed of was having some rich, beautiful woman fall in love with him, a real high-class woman, like Greer Garson used to be on the flicks.

Then one day an old woman suddenly appeared at the side of the float. She had a straw hat skewered to her grey hair, and a large, cracked handbag; and she seemed inexplicably furious with Gary.

"Wot's the matter, then, old lady?" he asked, setting down his basket of pints.

"You know wot's the matter, all right, you dirty animal! Get out, you dirty thing! I wonder you're not afraid of the police, I do. Think I don't know you. Picking up little kids. Always girls. Think I don't know you?" She hissed all this at him with such force that her spit made a little spray in the bright morning air.

"No, Rita," he said. "That's enough." But his face had gone red in strange patches. "Better hop off now," he said to me. "Run on home, then."

"That's right, get on out of it, you little bitch," she

180

said, turning viciously on me. I scrambled out of the float, scraping one knee painfully in my haste. She seized my arm and stooped to bring her face frighteningly close to mine. She smelled of pepper and onions and rage. "If ever I see you again, I'll 'ave your guts, understand? Dirty little beast, you're old enough to know better. Now get out of it, and remember what I tell yer."

I got out of it. I never saw Gary again. And I never knew which of them was the pervert. To the best of my recollection, he had never touched me, while she certainly had. But that was not really the point, then or now. The one thing clear was that somehow I was the guilty one. Exactly what I had done wrong was too hard to put into words. But to be alone like this was more than just my misfortune; it was my fault, for who else was there to blame for it? I scrubbed at my bleeding knee with a grubby handkerchief and went back to the hotel, where I was more careful than usual to avoid the old Christian with the whiskers. Billie was at the hairdresser's. I never told her or anyone else about Gary.

"We go to work on Monday and Tuesday," murmured Martha, running a small ambulance painfully over my foot; and with a start I put Trollope away. Today was surely Wednesday. And that reminded me there were at least twenty household jobs that urgently needed attention before I went into hospital. The thought of Margaret's clear eyes — not to mention Ross's expression — when they saw my linen-cupboard/pantry/clothes-closets/frig/kids' room was enough to fire me with a resolve at least to vacuum the entire downstairs before lunch. Unfortunately I hated our vacuum cleaner with the kind of personal and intense bitterness some people bring to politics or religion. It was a moral victory just to open the cupboard door under the stairs and drag the machine out, squealing, its long cord vindictively pulling forth all sorts of unrelated objects. When the phone rang during the process, I answered it in the brisk, resentful voice of one deeply engaged in important business.

"Yes?"

"Mrs. Graham?"

"Yes."

"It's Sharon in Dr. Mohammed's office calling. Just to remind you about your dental-hygiene appointment tomorrow at four."

What I would like to have said was it couldn't matter less if all my teeth fell out simultaneously like hailstones, as they might well do in the near future. Instead, I said meekly (Sharon being a very large girl, and mistress of many implements of torture), "Yes, thanks, Sharon; I'll be there."

I hung up brusquely. The vacuum cleaner grinned sardonically as I disentangled its cord from a collection of pull-toys and several pieces of material — unfinished night-gowns for the new baby, I discovered on inspection. Two months ago I'd run them up on the machine and begun to smock them around the neck and wrists; then I'd run out of embroidery cotton and somehow lost track of the whole project. But the fact was this baby needed clothes badly. Hugh's and Martha's outgrown things were too exhausted to be of any use a third time round. And though it was a bit odd to feel under an obligation to someone whose face you had yet to see, I did consider that this third error of mine deserved a wardrobe of its own, as a kind of compensation for being so randomly begun. It was this feeling that had made me buy four yards of blue flannelette printed with cheerful small birds in flight, and set to work.

There was not much left to do on the little gowns. I

could finish them off in an hour or so. And suddenly this seemed like a better investment of time than any amount of vacuuming. With my foot I pushed the machine back into the closet, threw the toys after it, and called, "Come on, kids. We're going to see the Loom Lady."

As we approached the Craft Shop, we fell in behind two women who had been hovering at the window looking in at Jennifer's patchwork cushions. They opened the door and were about to step in when Jen emerged from the back regions and they saw her colour. Instantly they stepped back and turned away, all but trampling my kids in their haste to escape.

"Cows," I said to Jen by way of greeting.

"Ah well," she said calmly. "They're entitled. It's a free country."

"But it must madden you, that people like that are still around."

"No point in getting mad. It's just one of those things. I reckon it will always be this way — human nature. The Bible's got it right: 'Can the Ethiopian change his skin, or the leopard his spots?' No, they damn well can't, either of them. So what can I do for you today? Come to buy a loom?"

"Funny lady."

The kids disappeared to inspect the baby, who could be heard making faint, chirping noises in the background.

"No, I just need some blue cotton for smocking."

"Right. Choose your blue." She plucked a handful of little skeins out of a drawer and held them out to me. With a sigh I tried to identify which one matched my sample thread.

"Feeling low?" she asked.

"Don't ask, Jen. Lower than a monkey's ass."

"Oh, come on. Life without men — think how simple. How serene. I mean, full of fringe benefits like that."

"Sure. So's a catatonic trance."

Jenny laughed, her whole face breaking open. "I saw your husband yesterday, actually. Went past the window here fast. He looked mad."

"Oh, really?" I could find no good news in this message, and Jenny didn't try to manufacture any. Instead she said, "How about a cup of tea?"

"Thanks, but I have to get back. My neighbour's kids are coming over for the afternoon. I wish they weren't and I could."

"Another time," she said calmly. And it hurt to think how little it meant to her whether I went or stayed; how self-sufficient she was; how insulated. She seemed to need nothing from me or anyone else, whereas I . . . Then I caught sight of her profile, turned to glance at the door where another customer was poised. Her lips were firmly closed, her eyes hooded, and I realized for the first time at how high a price she'd come to terms with her own solitude.

"Children! We're going. Wait, Jen; I've got the right change. Take you up on that tea offer soon. Come *on*, Hugh."

I herded them out onto the pavement, where a thin drift of last year's brown leaves scrabbled ahead of the wind. A woman hurried past us, head ducked low, adjusting a pair of dark glasses, and I said, surprised, "Hullo there, Marga —" but she went on without turning. Two things about this intrigued me greatly. One was that it was certainly Margaret behind those shades. The other was that before she slipped them on, I had distinctly seen that they covered a whopping black eye. My depression lifted dramatically as I tugged the kids homeward. How fascinating it was to speculate which one of her husbands had given it to her, and in the course of what kind of uncivilized debate. Did one of them want a divorce, and if so, which? Maddening to think that I might never know. On the other hand, maybe it was more fun to be kept guessing.

On our corner, someone had carelessly dropped a whole bag of baker's cookies, and a flotilla of pigeons busily bobbed and pivoted around the split brown paper and mess of crumbs. Martha at once ran toward them, doubtless with the idea of sharing the loot, but the birds flashed up into the cold air at her approach with such a clatter of stiff, dark-feathered wings that she paused, frightened.

And without warning there came into my memory, whole and vivid, my father's face, forgotten since my seventh year. There it was, long-boned, pale, a frown bitten between the grey-green, long-sighted eyes. Something about birds — what was it? — he was telling me about birds. The dry, academic timbre of his voice, a salt taste of tears . . . yes, I'd been sent to bed for some crime or other, perhaps for making a noise. Because surely he was ill then; he wore some kind of nightwear — a dressing-gown with rather grand velvet lapels. He drew open the curtains to let in a pinkish evening light.

"Anne? You're not still crying, are you?"

"No," I lied, trying not to sniffle.

He was a remote person, severe with himself and everyone else. His anger was rare, but freezing and devastating when it descended, as it had on me that afternoon. Dimly I could recall baby games and cuddling; but in the last year or two my dimples had disappeared; I grew leggy and lost all my top teeth. It was my private opinion that he was disappointed I'd grown so ugly. It was a surprise when, lowering himself stiffly, he sat down on the edge of my bed.

"Use your handkerchief," he said.

Damply I obeyed. There was a pause, as if he wasn't sure what to do or say next.

"Would you like me to read to you, or tell a story?"

"Tell, please."

Again there was a silence, teased only by the birds chirping sleepily to each other in the garden.

"When I was a very young man," he began slowly, "I had an illness, and the doctors thought it would do me good to go to a different climate — somewhere dry and warm. So I was sent across to Canada. In those days it took nearly two weeks to cross the Atlantic, even in a big ship, and when I landed in Halifax I got on a train and travelled days and days more across the country till I reached the west. It's a very huge country, and a good deal of it in those days was still wild, covered with virgin forest and completely empty. You could go for miles and miles without seeing a single house or a living person. If it hadn't been for the railway itself, you might think the human race hadn't been invented yet. That huge sky and the emptiness might have disturbed some people, but I found it healing, somehow. I started to get well." He paused here to cough.

My thumb stole furtively into my mouth. He was talking to himself rather than to me, as adults so rarely do to children, and this created a sort of person-to-person intimacy we'd never shared before.

"Then one evening," he went on "— it was somewhere in the prairie provinces — I went for a long walk alone and came to the edge of a small lake. It was perfectly still, an evening rather like this, but with a kind of brilliant air you get in Canada — new, as it were, not soft and blurred like the air here. All the colours and shapes look brighter and harder, even at a quiet time like twilight. Anyhow, all of a sudden, I heard a great sort of rustling noise, and I looked up to find the whole sky over me dark with an enormous flock of wild geese. Huge birds migrating south for the winter. They poured across the air on their big wings, calling to each other . . . I've never forgotten them. Ever since then Canada's meant something special to me . . . naturalness . . . a kind of wild innocence — It's a pity I was too hidebound to stay there. My life might have been entirely different. I might have been different." He coughed again, bending his long, thin back, and the door opened with a jerk.

"Maurice, what on *earth* are you doing out of bed!" cried Billie. Her voice and her face were sharp with anxiety. My father got rather laboriously to his feet, and I gave a frustrated kick under the bedclothes.

"You *heard* what the doctor said," she scolded. "Sitting here in this draughty room with your temperature high as it is — you bad girl, Anne, you know how ill he is — how could you let him do it?" Still scolding, she led him away, but he stopped at the door, gripping the handle of it for support.

"Good night, Anne."

"Good night, Daddy."

I never spoke to him again. He grew much worse that night, and a day or two later he was dead. The house filled up with undertakers, neighbours, and my red-eyed old aunts. Billie became invisible. For a little while I thought she'd died, too. Nobody had time to explain anything to me.

Otherwise I might not have formed the vague but oppressive suspicion that somehow I'd killed my father. Perhaps that was why for all these years I'd forgotten about those birds, and his voice and face when he talked about them, and about freedom.

At lunchtime we had a bowl of the soup I'd made from Sunday's chicken, and after it, for a treat, I played an old Burl Ives tape for the kids. This made Martha feel so benign that she put a kiss into the air near Hugh's head as he sat on the floor munching a graham cracker and rocking to the music.

Violet was scratching herself desperately, so I got out the ointment and began to spread it over her red patches, rubbing the tarry stuff well in to prevent her licking it off and then being sick. She lay belly up on the kitchen floor, groaning with satisfaction. As I worked on her, I began to feel a sort of groundless optimism steal over me; a folk belief, left over from my days of innocence, suggesting that because I was doing a good deed, somebody would in the near future surely do something nice for me. Recapping the ointment and levering myself by heavy stages back to my feet, I waited for these natural dynamics to work. The sun promptly went in and a flurry of sleet hissed against the window. The phone, though I looked at it hopefully, was mute. Outside the front door I heard a thump and scuffle announcing the arrival of June's kids. At the same minute a powerful contraction caught me with such force I gave a gasp. *Thank you, God.*

The instant the Williamson kids got into the house, one went to the frig and opened it, while the other turned on the

TV. They were chronically hungry, owing to Junie's ideas about slavery, though it probably wasn't only malnutrition that made Darryl so flabby, or Charleen so undersized and vacant-eyed. I firmly removed her hand from the freezer where it groped for ice cream, and spread bread for them with Health Shop peanut butter. "Where's the Coke?" demanded Darryl.

"Milk is all we've got," I returned briefly.

My two eyed our guests without enthusiasm. Hugh quietly hid his favourite fire-truck under his own bottom, while Mao gave a low and eerie yowl of depression, and disappeared under the sofa. I wished with all my heart I could join him.

But the phone rang like a reward, just as I finished cleaning up the lunch mess.

"Bonnie speaking, Anne. This a good time to call, or not?"

The children had drifted off toward the TV, and now an ad for kitten-soft toilet-paper blasted out, making the house tremble.

"As good a time as any, Bon. *Turn that set down, Darryl.* Nice to hear your voice — now that I can."

Bonnie's telephone manner these days tickled me, because it had become crisp, even a bit chilly, to match her executive horn-rims and the two phones on her huge new desk. Her office, on the thirtieth floor of a glass harbour-front tower, looked down on a city full of women like me, plodding to and fro and spreading peanut butter. It wasn't a distance easy to bridge, but we were still good enough friends to manage it. Bonnie would never, I thought, develop into the frigid career-girl stereotype; she still loved a giggle, and cried when her poodle got a cold. Many things had happened to both of us since she was the small-town undertaker's daughter sure that the streets of Toronto teemed with white-slavers armed with hypodermic needles, and I was the Botany Department's white hope who didn't know how to boil an egg. We both expected her to marry and me to become the Professional Woman; but when it happened the other way around, we became closer than we were before, and interested each other more.

It gave me pleasure untainted by the slightest envy that Bonnie was now editor of the house organ for a huge chemical company, and did her work with surpassing energy and skill. It even gave me a vicarious satisfaction that she kept her long, flat figure trim in a fitness class, and dressed elegantly in the latest boutique clothes. For her part, she liked to eat my meals and admire the early Canadian furniture we collected. Sometimes she took her god-daughter to a puppet show or the Santa Claus parade, and at every opportunity she showered the kids with presents. They amused and intrigued her, and she had a strong if unsentimental affection for both of them.

"Well, how are you, me old dear?" I asked, easing my backside onto a stool to take the weight off my aching legs.

"Getting ulcers. And you?"

"Bloody awful. Delivering next week."

Bonnie and I both had enough self-respect to allow open bitching and whining at frequent intervals. We could afford to complain to each other because our definitions of happiness were almost totally different.

"I've got the dumbest pair of assistants in the universe," she said. "And budget problems up to here. Anything new from Ross?"

"Nothing. But I have a feeling there will be soon.

Don't ask me why; I just do.''

"Well, things can't just drag on like this forever, he must damn well know that. And so must you.''

Darryl slouched back into the kitchen and hung about, picking his nose and hoping, I suppose, to hear something about sex. To indulge him and at the same time change the subject, I said, "Bonnie, let's talk about Margaret Trudeau instead.''

"No, actually, I can't chat, Anne; got a full afternoon. What I called to say is there's a job up for grabs with the Department of the Environment at Queen's Park. It's absolutely your thing. I just heard about it at lunchtime, and here I am — faithful dog with juicy bone.''

"A job?'' I said feebly, looking at the unfinished nightgowns, the diaper basket, etc. And I thought sadly, "You too, Bonnie, trying to do missionary work on Poor Anne? Ah, you disappoint me.''

"Yes. What it is, actually, they've got a grant for somebody to write a handbook about all the provincial conservation areas — you know, list facilities, describe flora and fauna, and all that. Exactly your thing. I mentioned your name to Chris Wagram, he's assistant to the big cheese down there. I mean they need somebody a bit special — not just for the natural-history part, but somebody that can write English. So why don't you grab a pencil and take down the details. They'll want a letter of application, references, and all that, but you're still in touch with Professor Stein, aren't you? The best thing is, you see, it would be sort of a part-time thing. You could go down there just two or three times a week, and the travel part would be possible, even if you had to take the kids, now that summer's coming. If it ever does.''

I listened patiently to all this, twisting the phone cord round and round my elbow.

"Sorry, Bonnie. But it just isn't possible, not while I'm single-parenting all this lot here. On top of all that, I'll be breast-feeding again . . . no, it just wouldn't work. Nice of you to think of me, though. One of these years . . . but in the meantime . . . it's not that I don't appreciate it."

"Okay, that's that," she said crisply. But I knew she wasn't offended. Unlike most favours, hers never had strings of obligation or ego-commitment tied to them. And she was one of the few people I knew who could change a subject with speed, grace, and finality.

"Got a great new guy I'll tell you about soon. Met him at the Squash Club. He's been married twice and doesn't want any more of *that*, thank you very much. Perfect. We're doing some discos tonight. He's fun."

"Great. Oh Bonnie, dancing sounds like heaven from here."

"It is, ducky. It is. But I've got to run. Shirley and Maura are due back from lunch." These were her much-harassed assistants, a pair of pale girls in black nail-polish who often had to adjourn to the washroom and cry into the roller-towel, so inadequate were their personalities to cope with hers. She was often very kind to them, which of course made their predicament harder, not easier. It was Bonnie's only real vice, as far as I knew. There was no Envy, Greed, or Covetousness in her; but she sharpened her claws on those girls, all right, in a form of Pride.

"So give your brats a hug from me, and I'll see you in Maternity one of these weeks, all right, kid? Ross will let me know when there's news."

"Yes, I suppose he will. Thanks for the call, Bonnie.

It will be great to see you."

"Right. Till then." And with admirable timing she rang off just as a rending crash from the sitting-room announced that Hugh had pulled the standard lamp over on himself again.

Well, I thought, waddling rapidly down the hall, this motherhood thing may be a career that lacks glamour, but at least it leaves no time for bad habits like Pride. Envy and Sloth, I also thought it fair to say, were more Junie's sins than mine. (With a few energetic swoops I righted the lamp and restored some vestiges of order to the sitting-room.) The older kids sprawled around the TV watching a woman cry with joy as she was given a hair-dryer, a food-blender, and a micro-wave oven for winning a three-legged race tied to someone else's husband. I switched off the set, ignoring the kids' protests, and unearthed some puzzles and games for them out of a drawer. Hugh I led away for safekeeping to the kitchen playpen, which I made more attractive by tossing raisins into the four corners for him to find.

With a sigh I settled in the big wicker chair near the window to finish the small nightgowns. As I threaded the needle I continued to think idly about the Seven Deadly Sins. Sloth and Gluttony — what quaint choices, with the whole canon of human evil to choose from. Of course, like most of the race, I was often guilty of those vices of torpor. As for Wrath, who could live without it? But what was the last of the seven, anyhow? I couldn't remember. Nor was there time for this or any other form of meditation: Charleen's voice was now uplifted in a loud wail.

Once more I lumbered down the hall. She was sitting, thumb in mouth, amid uncountable fragments of jigsaw puzzle. Darryl had evidently hit her over the head with a

1,000-piece view of Peggy's Cove. With one hand he was now unconcernedly rolling dice, and with the other, playing with himself. Martha was somewhat smugly giving a private doll's tea party behind the wing armchair.

"He hit me," snivelled Charleen.

"Why did you do that?" I asked him.

He simply shrugged, as if to say, "Because she was there." While I had no illusions about the goodness of little children in general, young Darryl seemed to have genuine promise as a criminal. On the other hand, Charleen was so much the wet, whining victim that it was hard to feel at all sorry for her. "Come on, cheer up," I said bracingly. "Play dolls with Martha."

"She won't let me."

"Well, then, do this rabbit puzzle, it's a nice, easy one. Darryl is going to pick up all these pieces, aren't you, Darryl?"

"Nah."

"*Or else*, buster."

"Yah. Okay. Later."

"Now." Under my basilisk eye he abandoned the dice and with his free hand began languidly to drop bits of the puzzle one by one into the box.

"I got nothing to do-oo-oo," moaned Charleen.

"Oh, watch bloody TV, then."

"I don' wanna."

"Christ. Come on out to the kitchen then, and help me make a shepherd's pie."

Her pudding face brightened faintly as she took charge of a vegetable peeler and some carrots. A lovely silence fell, broken only by her adenoidal breathing, while I got on with my smocking. Darryl and Martha stayed in the front room, mesmerised by a police show. The sun dropped out of a cloudbank into a lake of blue sky. Violet wagged her tail at the bowl of leftover potatoes on the counter. Hails of bullets and running feet echoed from the TV; then a wild scream rang out, making me start in alarm. Charleen's brow was furrowed as she mashed up the potatoes with milk; she appeared to hear nothing. Normally I would have turned off the program — not out of any impulse to censor violence, of which on the whole I approve, but for the practical reason that I'd noticed both my children got tense and irritable after watching that kind of show. Today, however, I smocked away resignedly and let them all get on with it.

In the distance a factory whistle announced five o'clock. Where on earth, I wondered, was June? She could hardly have been trying on boots all this time. No, she'd probably been home for the last couple of hours, watching her soaps with feet up and a beer in hand. But just then the doorbell rang.

"Go see who that is, Char — it's probably your mum."

Charleen thumped off. A minute later she came back with Clive. In a bulky-knit sweater, his hunched shoulders looked massive as a gorilla's, and the effect was heightened by a new haircut that made his head look abnormally small.

"Oh hi, Clive."

"Thanks for taking the kids."

"A pleasure," I lied.

She oughta be home looking after her own kids."

"No, it's all right, really. We help each other out."

"Where'd she go anyway?"

"Downtown to a sale. She ought to be back any minute."

"The bitch. Suit me okay if she never gets back." His voice was so casually vicious and at the same time so loud that I couldn't keep the surprise off my face. Involuntarily I glanced at Charleen, who was poking toys through the bars to Hugh. Her thumb was in her mouth, but I hoped maybe she hadn't been following the conversation — if you could call it that.

"You wouldn't happen to have a beer around, would you? We're all out." What for Clive was a winning smile bared a row of crowded, feral-looking teeth. Truly, Junie, I thought, you shouldn't want to get into something kinky — you're already there.

"Yes, I'm sure we've got a can somewhere . . . " I stooped to extricate a beer from the frig. When I straightened up, it was to find Clive in the leisurely act of looking up my legs. His bright rogue's eye caught mine in a wink. With one meaty hand he opened and tilted can to mouth, saying, "Cheers."

By way of a hint, I got busy browning hamburger for the shepherd's pie, but Clive appeared to be in no hurry to finish and go. With rising annoyance I became aware that his gaze was still on me. Specifically on my breasts this time, though God knows they were so conspicuous that perhaps he couldn't help it. I began to feel distinctly uncomfortable. It was impossible to ignore the fact that a noticeable and impressive bulge had appeared in Clive's faded jeans. As a replacement for small talk, I suppose this demonstration had its merits; but what on earth did he expect to happen next? And the shaming thing was that I had to make a heroic effort to tear my eyes away from the silent hulk of him and pretend to look in the oven to hide my flushed face.

"I'm afraid we're just about to have supper now," I said, trying to sound casual. "So if you don't mind — "

"Sure," he said. "Come on, Char. Get your stuff on and call Darryl."

"I'll help you," I said, hastily following her down the hall. But before finally padding off to his own house after the kids, he looked back at me once more with a sleepy lust in which there was a distinct gleam of ridicule. With a shock I realized that inside that hairy bulk lived a sharp intelligence — sharp enough to mock at mine. I wished I hadn't seen it.

Only when the Williamsons were all mercifully gone did I remember what was the Seventh Deadly Sin. Lechery, of course. Did it rank at the top or the bottom of the list? Well, perhaps that didn't matter. But it was a bit sad to realize that the Seven Deadlies were shared around more equally than I'd thought between me and my neighbours.

When the doorbell rang an hour later, I jumped as if bitten by a wasp. Who the devil could that be? A vision of Clive Williamson presented itself, complete with bulge and satiric wink, standing out there in the snow with subversive intentions. We were all half-undressed for bed, which didn't help tranquillize me. I decided the best thing to do was simply not answer. The bell rang again.

"I get it, Mummy," said Martha helpfully, and though I grabbed at her, she slipped through my hands and ran naked downstairs to open the door. I wallowed after her, muttering indecencies as I pulled on a dressing-gown.

There in the open doorway stood Max in a dark coat with a fur collar I hadn't seen before. His white hair was bright as the snow, and the smile in those dark eyes of his was like balm on a stinging wound.

"Oh Max!" I threw my arms around him in a great

hug. He smelled of the lavender water he used as shaving-lotion, and of the cigars he kept in his breast pocket.

"Easy there, kid, I'm a married man. Come on, let's get this crazy Miss Canada in out of the snow." Gently pushing us all back into the hall, he rubbed my back lovingly with one hand and put up the door chain with the other, clicking his tongue at it with disapproval. "Now, now, Annie, the very sight of me makes you bawl? Lucky thing I don't drop by too often." While I blew my nose, he swung Hugh up for a kiss. "After this, you lock up the door for your careless mum, and keep out the bad guys."

For some reason, this remark struck Hugh as brilliantly funny, and he lolled over Max's arm in a fit of ecstatic laughter.

"Oh Max, it's so great to see you. Billie mentioned that you might drop in, but I —"

"Well, I meant to call first, but there wasn't time. Here, let me get my coat off, you guys." He shrugged it off while Martha jealously tried to climb his leg.

"Lift me up!" she demanded. "I want to laugh too."

Hugh rolled on the floor, still weakly giggling. "I was just getting them ready for bed. I suppose — Max, could you stand it if we gave them a bath? They need a good soak, and I can't lift them out of the tub any more by myself."

"Sure, sweetie. Only tell me what to do. I'm no expert with babies." But Max was born knowing how to be a parent. He hoisted Martha up to ride his shoulders, and tucked the shrieking Hugh under one arm like a parcel. Somewhat laboriously he began to mount the stairs with them, Martha steering him by the hair and Hugh still drunkenly laughing. On the landing he paused, breathing hard.

"Ouf. Comes to me a bit late in life, this grandfather bit. Hang on there, honey — "

A few minutes later we had them one at each end of the long, old-fashioned tub, splashing luxuriously belly-deep in bubbles. They were perfectly silent now. This was too great a pleasure to be taken lightly. Hugh's face was grave as he steered a small plastic tugboat through the water. I had caught up Martha's hair off her nape with a bit of pink ribbon, and her profile was thoughtful as she bent over the ripples made by her own fat knees.

"What a pair of beauties, eh?" said Max, looking at the children proudly. He wiped his hands with an air of accomplishment on the big towel I'd pinned around his middle.

"Yes, they are." But another strong contraction just as I spoke steered me sharply away from sentiment. Surely there'd been more than usual of these damned spasms today? I frowned, trying to remember. Perhaps it might be a good idea to time them. Not that it could mean anything, really; not this soon. Both of my other deliveries had been late, not early.

"You okay, Anne?" Max asked in his slow, warm voice, and instantly I was, perfectly okay, even happy, though before his arrival, this awful day, so full of abrasive encounters, had left me feeling physically battered. This was Max's great personal gift. His combination of affection, horse sense, and ghetto humour made a safety zone where people as different as Billie and I could both rest and be eased.

We each dried a naked, fragrant child and put it into clean night things. Relaxed and warm, Hugh lay back on Max's lap, his soft mouth open, eyelids sinking shut as if pulled down by weights. Martha perched on my knee, chatting Max up in a grave, sweet voice she never used with me. Her fat hands moved in delicate gestures as she told him a number of shocking lies about tigers. From time to time she gave him a devastating, sidelong glance with glimmering blue eyes.

"At three already this one could give lessons to Bardot," he said, shaking his head. "Wonderful and scary how little girls are born with that old female magic."

"Don't I know it. And they never waste it on women. Ross, for instance, really believes she's as angelic as she looks — she can con him into anything. Right, shall we tuck them in now?"

"Yes, and then I am going to make my girl Anne a great big hot pot of tea, and we'll have it in the kitchen with our shoes off, and a good talk."

"Lovely. Oh Max, I'm so *bloody* glad to see you."

"No more with the tears now, doll, they make me nervous. I'm always afraid women want something from me when they cry."

"Well, this one doesn't." But of course I was lying. I wanted from Max now what I'd always wanted: nothing less than his total concern, his whole presence, the fatherly comfort and warmth of him. But at the moment I craved these things in a starved, almost dangerous way, and we both knew it. A sort of constraint suddenly made us shy with each other, and we went downstairs talking about the price of oil and gripping topics of that kind.

In the kitchen Max rolled up the sleeves of his white silk shirt and made tea in the brown kitchen pot. He established me in a rocker filched from the sitting-room, with a cushion deftly wedged against my backache. My feet he slipped gently out of their battered Roots shoes and lifted onto another chair.

"There," he said. "How's that now?"

"Marvellous."

"Good. Because the fact is, I got a bit of a confession to make."

"Oh?"

He poured the tea carefully into Coalport cups, having waved away kitchen mugs. ("Tastes better in good china.") His voice seemed to come from a long way away, or else it was thinned by a kind of diffidence rare in him. "This whole business with Ross. Now I've kept my nose strictly out of it, all this time. But it's been on my mind, believe me; it could make an ulcer there. Here you are about to go through labour again, struggling all by yourself, looking like hell — I mean it's too much. I've been your father too long. So for the first time I called him up today."

"And?" I said.

"Well, after winding up my nerves for a week to do it, the guy was out. I left a message to call me back. That was first thing this morning. And he hasn't called. Now Anne dear, that can only mean one thing. No need for me to say a word to him after all. I mean, no point in any of us hanging on hoping for the best any more. You're a young and beautiful woman. We get you a divorce and you'll marry again, this time a real man, with any kind of luck. Maybe I'm out of date, but I figure a woman needs a husband to look after her. Specially when she's got three kids. Tell me at least you'll think about it, honey."

"I'll think about it," I muttered.

"What you mean is, go to hell. Sorry. I know it's none of my — "

"Max, it isn't that. Only right now I honestly don't know what I'm going to do. I just have no idea. I feel as if there's only today. I mean, as if there might not be any tomorrow."

"Hey, that's no way to talk, at your age." His voice was sharp, and when I glanced at him I found his whole face dark with a frown that made him look frightened. He added crossly, "Women don't die in childbirth any more. I read an article."

"Of course not. Don't be silly."

But I said this without much real conviction. Giving birth, as I'd had two chances to discover, could bring you unpleasantly close to that hooded character with the scythe. My ward-mate after Martha was born lost her nine-pound boy on the second day — a plug of mucus in the airway — crazy bad luck, and fatal. They told her behind drawn curtains, and in nightmares I could still hear that terrible, animal howl of hers. As for me, I started to hemorrhage after Hugh . . . not, probably, very dangerously, but zip went those curtains, they cranked my bed up fast, they gave injections, and urgent hands massaged my abdomen. A little later I heard the gynecologist tell a young intern, "They can empty in half an hour; you have to watch 'em like a hawk." Out of kindness I spared Max these reminiscences, but there were times — and this was one of them — when I thought I'd been not brave but dotty to choose these risks instead of the nice clean curettage everybody so warmly recommended.

"After all," I said, trying to dismiss the subject lightly, "dying can't be worse than living, so why not be a good sport about it."

"No, it's not that I mind it, really, for myself," Max said slowly. And I remembered that he was sixty. It could be that in spite of my adventures in maternity, he'd given death more thought than I had. I tried to imagine the world without Max in it and gave a sudden shiver.

"What's the point in whining about it," he went on. "After all, we were given life for free in the first place; it's not decent to complain. But what I'd like is the chance to die for some good reason, you know? Not some stupid accident or a physical screw-up like cancer. Hardly anybody does die for a good reason, if you think of it. Maybe some in wars. In fact, that may be why wars keep on being popular. Seems to me you have to respect even those nuts killing each other in Belfast or Zimbabwe-Rhodesia, because they're dying for something, and that gives them some kind of dignity, even if the cause is stupid."

In spite of the rather morbid subject-matter, Max's slow, rich voice soothed me so profoundly I felt myself relaxing into an almost drowsy state of contentment.

"But enough of this philosophy. Time I got down to business. Because the fact is, dear, I'm the guy wants something here. I've come to ask a favour. Maybe you already figured that."

My eyes snapped open. "Eh? What favour?"

"Well," he said, stirring his tea carefully, "first thing I saw when I got home last night was that Billie had been crying."

I frowned uneasily. Billie, for all her helpless, little-girl ways, was not a weeper. Indeed, I literally couldn't remember ever seeing her cry. And after what she'd told me yesterday, that simple fact seemed the most revealing thing I might ever know about my mother.

"Are you sure?" I said foolishly. "I mean, did she tell you why?"

"No need for that. Only the day before, she was all excited about this holiday plan to take you to Santa Lucia. Told me all about it, thrilled as a kid. So I'm no great detective to guess you turned the offer down, right?"

"Yes, Max, because I simply can't leave —"

"I know, I know."

"But why does everybody think it's so *abnormal* for me to want to look after my own kids?"

"Nobody said that, doll."

Long ago he'd picked up Billie's absurd set of endearments in the silly way married people echo each other's speech habits. It was one of the few things I disapproved of in Max.

"She *did* say that," I muttered sulkily. "She talked about my mental health."

Max's lips twitched, but he looked at me squarely under the black bar of his heavy eyebrows. "Tell me, did it strike you that Billie isn't looking too good these days?"

"No, it didn't."

"No?"

"Well — nobody looks good this time of year."

"There's something wrong with her, sweetie. I don't know what, but she's running to the bathroom every couple of hours these days. Gets up two or three times in the night. Now it could be those stingers, or a chill, or a little touch cystitis; no need to get all that worried, maybe. Just the same, I made her tell me about it, and I got her a doctor's appointment for Monday. I'll take her there in handcuffs if I have to. She's scared, Anne. So that's the story."

"Well, she should have seen a doctor ages ago, if it's like that. But what can I do?"

"You can make her happy. Go with her to the Islands."

Something in the straight line of Max's lips reminded me that rich men get that way by having plenty of well-founded confidence in their own will-power.

"Max, I explained to her that I simply can't leave my kids with some hired goon that could be anything — how can you tell? — a glue-sniffer, a religious nut, somebody with nits or the clap —"

"Boy, what a pessimist. Look, what if I tell you I know somebody could do the job, the worst you could say about her is she wears arch-supports."

"I'd still say —"

"Let me finish. Our cleaning lady's been sick all winter and her daughter's been coming over instead. Might be forty, big laugh, keeps everything so clean it squeaks. Looks around for curtains to wash, slip-covers . . . has half an hour to spare, she doesn't just go home, she knocks you out a great lemon pie. You drop a dime, she follows you all over the house to give it back. Brought up three of her own; one's a student at York. I took the trouble and got to know Hilda, because I'm like you, I don't trust just anybody in my house where I have people and things that matter to me. Now this is my suggestion. Or if you like to put it another way, this is what I want from you. Let Hilda come here while you take a holiday with your mother."

He hesitated a moment and then went on more quickly, "And after that, Anne, if Hilda's willing and you trust her, why don't you keep her on and go back to college for your doctor's degree? If Ross can't afford it, I can. It's a crime, and you know it, with that head of yours, not to be using it. With a Ph.D. you could get some high-class academic job, or a post at the Museum maybe, and get the hell out of this kitchen."

I looked at him grimly. He gave me a broad, ingenuous smile intended to disarm.

"So you want to rescue me, too. Take me away from all this. Arrange my future for my own good. Improve my mental health."

Long before I ran out of breath, his smile had disappeared.

"Now, doll, don't be sarcastic. It's not nice."

But I was so angry now I felt slightly drunk. "Max, will you do me a favour and get this straight. I *like* being at home with my children. I'm not a victim or a martyr. I'm a natural, normal woman. There is nothing being *wasted* here. Do you really think what happens in kitchens and bedrooms isn't important? I tell you, half of what goes on in labs and offices and classrooms is trivial by comparison. *This* is where it's all at, not out there. Anyhow, that's how I see it. For the next five years at least, these kids are going to need me here, and here is where I'm going to be. Full time. After that, sure, I might get a part-time job, or go back to graduate school. For God's sake, I'm barely twenty-four. So will you get it through your head, I'm not some poor victim in chains. Even if I were, I'd stay in them. My kids are not going to wander the streets with a door-key round their necks. They are not going to be entertained by the neighbourhood flasher while I'm somewhere else being liberated."

I concluded this tirade with the greatest firmness and dignity, and then burst into loud, childish sobbing. Max got up from his chair and held me, rocking me to and fro in silence. "There now, my poor baby," he said.

"You don't know what it was like for me," I blubbered, incoherent with the self-pity that had been festering silently for too many years. "With Billie — that life — it took away my childhood. You just don't know."

He pushed a clean handkerchief into my hand and turned away to pour more steaming tea into our cups.

"No," he said. "You're wrong. I know a lot about what it must have been like for you. Not that I'm blaming Billie. She couldn't do any different, being what she is. But that's why — well, it was one of the big things in my life that I could send you to university, give you the chance you needed to be somebody really special. For me, right from the first, you were no kidding some kind of princess I found in the cinders. It meant a lot to me, with no kids of my own, to sort of rescue you."

"Did it, Max?"

The bitter edge to my voice startled him. He tried to smile, but didn't make a very good job of it. "Well, it takes a guy born over a tailor's shop in Cabbagetown to appreciate a chance like that. I mean, to be a sort of Jewish Pygmalion."

But the truth was sour in my mouth. It was an act of egoism, then, all his goodness to me; not really love? I pushed the rocker into motion. It creaked with my double weight. My burning eyes closed. At the sink Max rinsed the teacups very quietly, as if it were important not to disturb anyone or anything.

The fetus kicked and twisted so restlessly I had to sit up. Max was putting on his jacket, twitching down his shirt-cuffs.

"Well, dear, time I took off. You go on up to bed — you need rest, the shape you're in. Only be damn sure you put the chain up on that front door first." He tried to make these banalities sound normal, in his calm, practical, parent's voice, but it didn't quite work.

"Yes, Max."

"And tomorrow I'll give you a ring and we'll maybe talk about Hilda. I'm not pressing you, mind. Talk it over with Ross, why don't you. I suppose he's in touch. See what he thinks about it. Plus other things."

My mouth opened and I closed it again. No, it was not possible to risk any more discussion with Max. Already too many delicate checks and balances between us had been threatened. There were heavy pouches under his eyes; I could see that in his way, he too was adjusting his defences, recovering balance. But the role each of us had for so long played for the other was irrevocably changed, and we both knew it.

"Give my love to Billie," I said.

"Right."

"And take care."

"Sure."

At the door he turned. "And cheer up, doll," he added. "Things could always be worse. You heard the one about the optimist fell off the top of a skyscraper? Some horrified guy in an office saw him falling past the window and gave a yell, but the optimist only smiled and yelled back, 'Okay so far!'"

I forced a smile. He patted my cheek and we parted, pretending that nothing of any significance had changed. What else, after all, could we do?

The door of Max's Lincoln chunked shut. His snow tires crunched over ice and faded off down the street. I wandered into the dark sitting-room and lay down on the sofa instead of going up to bed. It was only nine-thirty, after all. I was tired, but all my systems were electrically super-charged. As I lay there restlessly scratching my belly, I wondered whether Max would ever write me another letter. Would we ever be able to play that game again? Probably not.

At this point it seemed appropriate to give myself a severe talking-to along the following lines. Anne Graham, you will now, I mean immediately, stop snivelling just because you've discovered your father is a human being. Face it, all these years you've tried to cast him as a sort of hybrid of God and lover, exactly as you saw him at fifteen. Jocasta came to a bad end, right? So grow up, will you? Even if it hurts.

This lecture had a somewhat calming effect, but my nerves were still inclined to twitch. Far too much tea and philosophy. There was something grim and final about turning the dry eye of experience on myself and all my illusions, past and present. When the phone shrilled, I heaved myself over to it with alacrity. Any change in the old stream of consciousness would be welcome.

"Anne baby? How are you doing? It's Tim here. Not too late to call, I hope."

"Hi, Tim," I said without enthusiasm. I'd never much liked Ross's other partner. He had a husky adolescent voice and a crass, ebullient manner to match; but he was the toughest, the most mature, and much the meanest of the three. I'd often thought that Ross and Randy would sooner or later regret sharing the practice with him.

"Well, what's new with you, kid?" he demanded heartily.

"Oh, nothing very much. And you?"

"Just groovin' along. You know how it is." There was

a slight, uncomfortable pause.

"Jean and the kids okay?" I ventured.

"Sure, great. Just fine. They're at a movie."

"That's nice." I took a deep breath to ride out another strong contraction. Then I thought, All right; let's have it. "Everything all right at the office?"

"Ah, well now." He cleared his throat and then made a subdued, gulping sound that meant he had a drink beside him. The trouble was that liquor didn't change Tim, it only made him more intensely himself.

"Ah well, what?"

"Now Anne baby, don't get hostile. You've got to admit this isn't exactly one of your easy situations we've got here. I'm just trying to do my best for all of us."

"Just tell me what it is, Tim." Mentally I doodled a sketch of his wide, fleshy face. He had little or no neck, and his eyes were a formidably pale blue — the eyes of a winner. Just the same, there was a look of acute anxiety in them sometimes, perhaps because his father was a millionaire.

"Well, of course you realize with Ross and Larine in the same office . . . I mean this kind of thing just doesn't work, right? For a while they were very discreet and under-cover about it — come to that, Ross still is — but the trouble is Larine's been wagging her ass around here lately, making waves, bitching at the other two girls — you know the kind of thing. It's raising hell, anyhow. So much so I actually had to say something about it to Ross the other day. If it goes on, she'll have to get out of the office, that's all. Of course, he hit the roof when I told him that, but Randy agrees, and now he hardly speaks to either of us. So things are now pretty tense, I don't mind telling you."

"I'll bet you don't," I thought nastily. A few years

ago at a New Year's party (at that point I was between pregnancies and looking all right) Tim had made a pass at me in
the hall of somebody's apartment just outside the bathroom.
Feeling generous on some rather ghastly mulled wine, I'd
given him a light kiss, and out of sheer friendliness let him
feel my buttocks. That few seconds would have been perfectly
innocent, even good for both of us, except that just then his
tall wife Jean came out of the bathroom.

She harpooned him on a look so punitive that I wouldn't
have been surprised to see his balls drop off right on the
spot. Tim was a heavyset man, slow on his feet, but he
instantly vanished into the crowd as if dematerialized. She
picked her way past me as if I were some unusually nasty
insect, and the party roared on. I remember enjoying it very
much until we were gathered at the door to say goodnight,
everybody kissing everybody. Then, under Jean's frigid
eye, Tim actually shook hands with me, and I had to turn
away to hide a hysterical grin. Never did any husband in the
history of marriage look so abysmally guilty. If we'd been
caught naked in some exotic variation of the act in the
middle of Yonge Street, he could not have looked more
sheepish. He was the kind of man who deep down thought
fornication was a worse crime than murder. At the same
time, he thought of adultery as "scoring". It was hard to
think kindly about Tim, even when he wasn't there.

Anyhow, ever since that party, Tim had disliked me in
a subverted sort of way that masked itself under jovial
friendliness, even a kind of sly, sexual invitation. Not a
pleasant combination at all.

"Well, Tim, I don't know what I can do about it.
Damn all, I'm afraid. As you know, he doesn't live here
any more. In fact, I haven't even heard from him lately."

"Yeah. Well, Randy and I are pretty worried."

"I appreciate that. But —"

"If the bitch would only get out."

What absurd combination of feelings made me jump to Larine's defence I don't know; but I found myself doing it.

"Look, Tim, is there any real need to get your knickers in a twist about it? This is the first straight job she's ever had. She just can't handle the other side of it, that's all. Can't you talk to her, I mean without getting nasty and scaring her? She's been scared and threatened all her life, after all."

"Come on, I'm not a social worker, you know, or a shrink either. But I *have* talked to her. Had her into my office, like a Dutch uncle. Result? Zilch. Her attitude's been worse than ever. In fact, I wouldn't put it past the bitch to tell Ross I made a play for her. Which would be a fucking lie, of course. But that's maybe why he's freezing me out."

A vivid mental picture of Tim talking to Larine like a Dutch uncle formed in my mind. His hand was no doubt metaphorically on her buttocks the whole time. I smothered the laugh that was tickling me.

"No, they're certainly not playing the game, either of them," I said mildly. The innuendo luckily escaped him. Tim was suspicious of intelligent women and afraid of them when they had a sense of humour. Antagonizing him now would be silly, even dangerous, and I knew it.

"In fact," Tim was saying heavily, "the whole situation's got to the point where we're all finding it hard to carry on. Randy's tried, and so have I, but we can't seem to get through to Ross at all. He's like a guy on some other planet. Christ, is it so great between him and Larine that he can't tune in on anything else? When we started out together, the three of us, he used to be the keenest of us all. I just don't get it.''

Reluctantly I had to concede that Tim had a point there. I shifted my weight wearily. ''Tim, I wish I knew what to say. Or do.''

''Because,'' he went on, ''— well, I hate to say this, but — it could come to this, that Larine will have to get out, or Ross will.''

''Ah,'' I thought. ''Here's your real message at last.'' Gentle Randy would of course stand pretty well wherever Tim pushed him, so I understood with perfect clarity this was not just a hint; it was a threat.

''Have you put this ultimatum to Ross?'' I asked.

''Well, no — not —''

''Why not, then? Are you asking me to do it?''

''No, no, of course not. I'm only suggesting that when you see him, you could . . .''

''Could what?''

''Well, like use your influence —''

''My what? Look, if I had any influence left with Ross, you wouldn't be making this call, right?'' (One of the worst things about talking to Tim was that you couldn't help picking up his style.)

''Anne baby, you have all my sympathy. You know that.'' An unctuous leer began to creep into his voice. ''This whole thing makes me feel rotten mostly because it's such a raw deal for you. And you're such a sweet kid.''

When I made no reply, being preoccupied with another and sharper contraction, he assumed I was too moved for words. ''Look, baby,'' he went on, ''what say we meet somewhere for a drink tomorrow and talk this over properly. The phone's no good. A drink or two, a bite to eat, what do you say? We really need to get together. I mean, apart from everything, I haven't seen you for ages."

"Sure we could get together. You mean with Randy? Or maybe Jean?" Bitchy of me, but a backache of this intensity was enough to rot any woman's better nature. There was a huffy silence at the other end. I added, by way of apology, "Because any conference like that will have to wait till I come out of hospital. My new baby's due the end of next week."

"Oh. Yeah, of course. I mean, I forgot about that. Well, Anne, great talking to you. Just, when you see Ross, you could like pass it along, eh, how things are . . . how Randy and I feel. He'll listen to you."

"I doubt that. However."

Unable to think of any answer to that, he gave his bray of a laugh. "Ah-ha-ha-ha. Anyhow, baby, be hearing from you. Take care, now. Ciao. And all the best."

"Sure. Whatever that is."

He hung up with almost audible relief. I made a couple of hideous faces at the phone before putting it down, but they didn't help much.

Hardly any conversation in my life had been as disagreeable as this one, or in so many ways undermining. The more I thought about it, the worse I felt — the sort of reaction you get after stepping in dog crap. Not only is there always more of it than you thought at first, but you can't get rid of the smell of it, or the suspicion that this kind of thing could never have happened if you were a better person.

I wandered aimlessly from kitchen to dining-room to hall, nibbling a soda cracker to quiet a queasy stomach, and occasionally giving the telephone a finger-up signal to relieve other feelings. When my legs got tired, as they soon did, I sank down again in the rocker. Thank God I was alone, at least, without other people to preserve a face for. Hugh, for instance, if he caught me wearing certain expressions, was apt to burst into tears, while Martha would snap with military brusqueness: "Smile!"

The to-and-fro creak of the rocker gradually tranquillized me a little. Chairman Mao appeared from one of his lairs and leaped onto my shoulder. After a loud conversational squawk or two, he curled up against my neck. He had recently been eating fish, and the rhythmic flexing of his claws dug uncomfortably into my shoulder, but his companionship was comforting. It was easy to understand why people in solitary confinement made friends with cockroaches and rats and fellow-prisoners like that. Communication without demands, so unlike the kind the bloody telephone brought every day. Or didn't bring. The silent phone on the counter smirked at me. Beside it, in a litter of Lego bits and crayons, were a pile of bills and the car keys.

Suddenly, without any conscious process at all, I knew what I had to do now. Like all important decisions, it was classically simple. I couldn't think why I hadn't done it weeks and weeks ago. Mao yowled in protest as I struggled out of the chair, displacing him. The Neilsons' phone number came obligingly to mind, and I dialled it.

"Pat, is your mother there?" My watch said ten o'clock. It wasn't too outrageously late to call, in the circumstances.

"Yes, she's home — didn't go to French Conversation tonight. Hold on, I'll get her."

"Wait — don't bother her, Pat — it's one of you girls, actually, that I need. Just for an hour, to sit. Would you see if your parents will let you come over?"

"Well, I'll see."

"I know it's lateish, but I have to go out — there's something urgent I have to do. I'll send a cab for you."

"Just let me check — hold on, please."

In a few seconds her voice came back. "Okay. Daddy will run me over. Be there in two minutes."

I used them to struggle into my duffle coat, boots, and head scarf, in which outfit I had exactly the shape of those portly wooden dolls from Russia that contain other dolls in diminishing sizes. The bills and the car keys I stuffed into my purse before opening the door to Pat.

"Nice of you to come. I won't be more than an hour. The kids are asleep — you shouldn't have any trouble. Emergency numbers by the phone. Watch TV if you like, and eat anything you fancy in the frig."

She gave me a quick glance but was too well brought up to ask any questions about where a grossly pregnant woman could be going alone and on impulse at this hour. I, on the other hand, noticed that she had a slight limp, and, in the unfair manner of adults, didn't bother to repress curiosity.

"Hurt yourself, Pat?"

She pulled up her denim trouser-leg to reveal a raw scrape that ran the length of her shinbone.

"I got it shagging? The roads are neat for it these days. Got nearly the whole way to yoga class on the bumper of a sports car today. Don't mention it to Mum."

I looked at her in some bafflement. The days when I too practised the cool anarchy of the teens were so far behind me as to seem prehistoric. It was sad, perhaps even tragic, to lose that instinctive resistance to authority, that urge to live recklessly, that fellowship with all rebels and crazies. But from the moment Martha was born, I'd become a true-blue conservative, a supporter of the law, regular bowel movements, safety belts, and correct grammar. It's not a conversion I was really prepared for, then or now, and at moments like these it still gave me a vaguely bewildered feeling of being alienated from my own tribe. Even Pat's habit of making most statements into questions, as if it were stupid to be sure of anything, however trivial, reminded me how dogmatic motherhood had made me, how prematurely middle-aged. "When I have more time," I thought, fumbling with the car keys, "I may just worry about this. It could be important."

"See you, Pat," I said before stepping out into the frosty air. With caution I negotiated the snow-clotted steps. The moon was large and bright, lolling to one side as if a trifle drunk. The city air smelled of cats, exhaust, woodsmoke, and the sugar snow that lay fresh everywhere an inch or so deep. It was wonderfully good to be out of the house — marvellous to be alone and moving somewhere with intention. I breathed up the cold air in deep drags and stamped my booted feet in brisk rhythm as I walked along.

Around the corner where we rented parking-space at a gas station, I found and opened our shabby Volks crouching patiently there in the snow. Ross rarely used it, and it was weeks since I'd driven anywhere. Some kind of lethargy — or perhaps it was self-punishment — had kept me tethered to the immediate neighbourhood, or clinging to the security of home. But when I tried to squeeze behind the wheel, I discovered I'd expanded so much since last time that I wouldn't fit. Muttering, I stooped double and levered the seat back. Once more I tried to cram myself in behind the wheel — the Incredible Hulk in action. But struggle as

I would, I simply couldn't get in. The giggling this predicament brought on was a serious threat to bladder control, because of course I'd forgotten to attend to that before setting out. Finally I slammed the door shut and locked the car up, defeated. Luckily there was nobody around to watch this undignified retreat.

It was clear I would just have to walk it. Prince John Street wasn't more than ten or fifteen minutes away. Off I went, my breath preceding me in generous puffs; but the pavements were so slippery with ice under the fresh snow that several times I slipped, lurching like some derelict tanker in a heavy sea. A fall would be highly inconvenient, since once down I would probably be incapable of getting up again, so I slowed my gait to a sort of stately waddle. At that pace the distance seemed endless, but I dared go no faster.

At last, however, I drew in sight of the house. Downstairs through the sheer curtains of the front window I could see three or four heads watching the blue flicker of TV. Ross and Larine were not there. Upstairs one bedroom window made a bright square in the dark.

As I stood out there in the street, I felt a sudden burst of such basic fury that my blood literally seemed to boil. I would not knock at that door and stand waiting for someone to answer. Without stopping to think about it, I stooped awkwardly down, grasped as much sticky snow as I could pack into a ball, and hurled it at the lighted upstairs window. Hot and breathless, I barely waited for it to land on the pane with a loud and satisfying whack before launching another. And another. Both bull's-eyes. Between grunts of satisfaction, I puffed obscenities into the night air. Pat's face formed in my imagination grinning congratulations. I was briskly packing a fresh missile when the window-sash lifted with a scrape and Ross's head poked out.

"What the *hell* are you doing, Anne!" Between the moon and a nearby street-light, he had no trouble identifying me. "For Christ's sake," he added indignantly, "cut that out and come into the house. You'll have the whole neighbourhood —"

"Fuck the whole neighbourhood," I returned, not at all quietly, and shot another hard-packed ball after its predecessors. His head jerked out of sight. There were faces clustered now at the downstairs window, all alight with spectator interest — two girls, one of them Chinese, and a tall lad with a bush of fair hair — Jamie. Larine was nowhere to be seen, which was all right with me. It was not Larine I had anything to say to.

The front door opened and Ross came out, slinging a denim jacket over his shirt and jeans, which also had the air of clothes pulled on at top speed. At the sight of him close up, all the fierce, energetic anger suddenly died out of me and my legs felt light and weak. I dropped the last snowball and brushed my wet gloves together clumsily.

"Now will you kindly tell me what the hell you think you're doing?" hissed Ross in a low and furious voice. He looked so self-righteous, so morally outraged, that I couldn't hold back a hilarious grin.

"The same to you, whack," I mumbled, and because laughing made it difficult to keep my balance, I caught at his arm to steady myself. He wasn't ready to support that mammoth weight, though, and I had no choice but to sit down rather abruptly on the curb.

"Jesus Christ, Anne, will you get up! Hang onto my hands — now pull. You can't sit there."

But in spite of our joint efforts, I couldn't manage to get up, and he wasn't strong enough to haul me to my feet alone. The heads at the window watched us, fascinated. Behind them the TV flickered in vain competition with this more interesting show.

"I'll get Jamie to help," he said.

"No, don't. Sit down here with me for a second. I have one or two things to say to you, and it might as well be here, where we have a bit of privacy. Come on, sit down."

Reluctantly he did so, after first throwing the watchers a dignified glare intended to send them away. They didn't move. It gave me a grim satisfaction to know that his bottom on the icy pavement must be even colder and damper than mine.

"Well?" he said stiffly.

"You haven't been by for over a week, so here I am. There are some bloody bills to pay. And a couple of things to tell you."

"Yes; go on, then." He sat well apart from me, dignified even with his feet in the gutter. His face was aloof, the guarded eyes looking into the perspective of the dark street.

"The chief thing, Ross, is that Tim Brian called me up tonight. We had a long, horrible talk. What a shit he is. Anyhow, you may not know it, but he's getting ready to push you out of the office. Larine is only the excuse, of course. He's always wanted to be top banana down there, and now he sees a chance to force you out."

"Yes, I know."

"All right, then. I just thought if you didn't, I'd better warn you. Up to you, of course. Maybe she's worth it."

He said nothing. His head was lowered now and his hands were knotted together like a pair of wrestlers in deadlock. A woman with a Siamese cat on a leash strolled past us with an easy stride. She had a good-humoured, freckled face that opened in a wide grin at the sight of two adults sitting on their butts in the snow. I liked the look of her and grinned back. Somewhere a clock chimed the half-hour. The moon was high now and dropped a thin white light over the city's rooftops and bare trees.

"Actually," he said with some reluctance, "Larine's getting into Hare Krishna these days. Her friend Cheryl is one of them. Really into meditation and fasting and all that. She's thinking of quitting at the office anyway. There's nothing very transcendental about typing."

"Well, that makes it simpler, then. A bit."

"Not much, really. The thing is, these groups are bad news for people like Larine. All that fasting . . . I mean, the little fool could kill herself."

"She will, of course. In the end. You know that, don't you? One way or another. Sooner or later. Nobody can prevent it."

"You could be right. But I still feel — responsible."

"Sure, because you're like that. But you feel a lot more about her than that, right?"

"No, not really. Not any more. For quite a while now I've just felt sorry for her."

"I suppose that's what you were doing up there just now. Feeling sorry for her."

"Don't be coarse," he said primly.

"Well, as far as Hare Krishna goes, you know that poor old aunt of mine, the one that was always having nervous breakdowns and things. When she got to be sixty, she joined the Scientologists. Everybody was appalled. But it was quite marvellous, really. She got so happy and quite fat."

221

But Ross only shook his head gloomily. He was so Anglican that all other forms of belief embarrassed him. I wondered whether Larine realized what a serious mistake she was making.

"Well, is that all you want? We can't sit here —"

"Wait a minute. There's something else. Um — has Jeff Reilly by any chance been in touch with you today?"

"No, why? The kids all right?"

"They're fine. But you see . . . well, you may find this hard to believe — I do myself — but last night Jeff came to the house for Hugh's croup, and we . . . I mean he . . . well, the upshot is he's now talking about divorces all round." My face felt hot and I itched all over with embarrassment and shame. For one thing, I'd made up my mind very firmly never, in any circumstances whatever, to tell Ross about that regrettable little episode. For another, the whole thing sounded so ridiculous — perhaps even untrue. For still another, I knew perfectly well that in future Lynne Reilly was not going to allow her husband to walk to the corner alone, much less divorce her. Why on earth, then, had I ever mentioned it? Did I want to feel guilty — as guilty as Ross was? To make it easier for him? Was I prepared to stop at nothing to get him back? The answer to that was yes. The immorality of it was total. From somewhere there jigged into my head the phrase "In a vain head and double heart".

Ross had shot me one brief look of surprise and distaste. "Well, in my shoes I can hardly come all over the outraged husband, can I." After a pause he added in a louder voice, "Just the same, I *am* outraged."

"Love, so am I. If you only knew. But the thing is that poor old Jeff has been sort of emotionally involved for quite a while, only I didn't realize it till last night. Of course it's crazy. He'll recover. But at the moment he's going around in circles, rather."

"Well, he can go round and round till he disappears up his own backside. And much good may it do him."

"You wouldn't like to be free? I mean legally?"

"Of course not. Would you?"

"No. Certainly not."

"Well, at least we agree about something. Makes a change."

"Oh, Ross, I think you're almost as crazy as I am. It's a real bond. Blessed be the tie that binds."

When he smiled he looked as young as Hugh. I leaned on his shoulder and he braced himself to support my weight.

"What a pity we've made such a mess of it," I went on. "Because it's just been bad management, not — well, it's like that time you dislocated my jaw on our honeymoon. The one before we were married, I mean."

Unwilling to laugh, he pushed up his glasses and rubbed the bridge of his nose, frowning. On the night in question we'd been so keen and as yet so unskilled that in the throes Ross hit me hard on the jaw with his elbow or knee or something. "You remember that?" I asked, knowing that he did. "I actually saw a huge white star. It didn't interfere for a second, though, did it, with the business in hand. I mean that was one time when feeling sorry was more than enough."

In the milky light of the moon, I saw Ross's shoulders twitch. Suddenly he gave a great snort of laughter, hunching low over his own bony knees. "We were pretty gauche, all right. Remember those hiccups I had at the wedding? That old bishop with the sniff, I'll never forget how he glared at me."

"Ross, I want you the hell home," I said abruptly.

At once he stopped laughing. A cold little wind pushed at my back. He said nothing. But this was what I'd come here to tell him, and I was glad to have had the guts to say it at last.

"I need you. I can't cope alone. You think I'm powerful and tough, but I'm not. The way I feel about it, I'm ready to make any kind of deal, anything. I'll keep the house neater. This can be our last baby. Do you get the message?"

"Oh, Anne. You know it wouldn't — you couldn't — Look. Yesterday I went over to Jenny's place. I was going to ask about buying that loom you wanted. All set to make the big peace-offering. But on the way there, I got to thinking how goddam silly it was to put a loom in that dining-room where there isn't room to eat now, and I got so mad all over again about the whole scene that I got acid indigestion and walked right past the place. See what I mean? It's never going to be any different for us."

"I suppose you're right. Only maybe that doesn't matter. The thing is, even when we're at each other's throats, something's *there*, kicking like a wild horse. . . . Which is worse, to live with ulcers or boredom?" I shifted position. "You see, I think you —" But something was hurting me a lot, though I wasn't sure whether the pain was physical or metaphysical. Then, abruptly, I felt a warm gush and between my feet appeared a considerable puddle.

"Oh, will you look at this, I've disgraced meself —"

Before we could do more than look stupidly down at the pool in the gutter, a sharp blade of pain penetrated me. Its quality and meaning were things I well remembered. Ross looked quickly into my face, then gripped my shoulders to brace me. Turning his head to the window where one of the spectators still lingered, he called in a loud voice, "Jamie! Get out here quick!"

On the ebb of the pain I said, "All right. No panic. Just help me up and call Miller. I'll go home in a cab for my things and meet him at the hospital. There's plenty of time."

The tall boy with the hair had now come out of the house and somewhat cautiously approached us.

"There damn well *isn't* plenty of time," Ross said. He seemed ridiculously agitated. "You can't possibly go home. Jamie, I need a hand here. We've got to get her up and into the house. The waters just broke; she's in labour."

I started to say, "No, I'm not, it's too soon," but the fierce gripe of another contraction cut me off. My panting sounded hoarse in the sudden quiet of the night city. The two men hovered over me helplessly. Ross's knee bracing my back gave support as the spasm eased.

"All right now? Jamie, we'll have to hoist her up in a kind of fireman's seat —"

But at that point I had to wave them aside and lean forward to sick up a lot of tea and crackers into the gutter.

"Sorry," I muttered. "Couldn't help it. Or any of my sins. Just forgive."

"Shut up," said Ross. "Now grab my wrist like this, Jamie. Can you get one arm round my neck, Anne? Now the other one — that's it. Easy, now. Okay, Jamie? *Heave*."

"Sorry," I repeated, as they staggered under my weight.

"Hell, what for?" asked Jamie in a cracked, cheerful voice. "Okay now?"

Swaying and breathing hard they managed to totter with me up the icy path, and by slow degrees we all panted up the steps of the house, my disgraceful wet coat flapping in the wind. As we reached the front door, another spasm forced an animal moan out of me that made young Jamie's face under my arm turn paste-white. Nothing even in his experimental life had quite prepared him for this.

Interlocked like some triple-headed monster, we lurched at last into the living-room, where the TV still blinked. On the screen was a singer mouthing "More than a woman to me-ee-ee".

"On the sofa?" Jamie asked, his voice high. The two girls, one of them eating yogurt out of a plastic cup, stared astounded at the Laocoon group of us swaying there. The Chinese one said, "What's the matter with her?" but nobody answered her.

"No, no. On the floor," I insisted. I wanted to be on my hands and knees in a position to obey the primitive urge to push when it came, as it evidently very soon would. Once on all fours, I was seized by another strong contraction. When it eased off, I found the enormous house dog crouched in a mirror image of my own posture. It put its nose to mine and gazed into my eyes with concern.

"What's Miller's number?" Ross asked, squatting beside me. "He'll have to come here — I don't think there's going to be time to get you to the hospital, even. Looks like you're into one every minute already. For God's sake, somebody get this *dog* out of here."

"And call Margaret Neilson to stay with the kids." When I could focus again on anything external, I gave him both phone numbers and he disappeared. A furious sound of dialling followed. I rested briefly, forehead on the carpet, bottom in the air. A noisy struggle went on in the background while the two girls tried to drag the monster dog away. It growled. Somebody yelled at it. The girls broke into hysterical giggles. At last, with Jamie's help, the creature was dragged away, its claws scraping the floor, and shut up somewhere; but from time to time it let out a distant, lugubrious howl as if to encourage me.

"Can I do anything for you?" I opened my eyes to find Larine's wide-set hare's eyes and sharp nose in my line of vision. Her pale face was set in an aggressive frown, as if she had made up her mind to let no one but herself control this situation.

"Yes. Get some newspapers. For the rug."

Her pale eyes contracted in some shock as she took in the implications of this. "Oh," she said in the prim voice of a hostess whose guest has committed some unmentionable social error.

"Where's Ross?" I asked her.

"I think he's gone upstairs to be sick."

"Tell him there's no time for that."

Her long, lank fall of hair twitched out of sight, and without troubling to deliver any more bulletins, she began to spread sheets of the *Globe and Mail* around and under me. After grappling with another spasm, I found myself in a sea of newsprint adequate for the parturition of a whale. With reluctance I felt a sort of respect for Larine. She had made a gesture worthy of Edwina herself.

"Help me off with these boots and pants," I told her, adding, when I could, "Please," to show she wasn't the only lady around. "And could you boil a pair of sharp scissors." These instructions made Larine's lips thicken and pale, and she disappeared rather suddenly. One of the girls shyly knelt beside me to offer a pillow, and I wished there'd been time to smile at her, but there wasn't. The room was shifting and drifting in a surreal sort of way. The muscles in my thighs cramped miserably, and this trivial pain was harder to take than the long, rhythmic spasms of the expanding cervix.

Faces came and went. An elderly man in thick spectacles stared down at me in consternation, and disappeared. It bothered me a lot that I couldn't imagine who on earth he could be. Then with triumph I remembered the truss-maker who lived in the basement.

I asked for a glass of water, because panting dried my mouth. Young Jamie held it to my lips in a pair of deathly cold but steady hands. In a lucid interval I saw that Ross had returned.

"Be sure to call the Neilsons," I said.

"You told me that before. I've just done it. Margaret's with the kids now."

I looked at him.

"Were you sick?"

"No, of course not."

"Good."

Abruptly he squatted beside me and wiped my forehead. "Miller is sending an ambulance for you. It should be here any minute. Can you hang on? Everything's going to be all right."

Other voices faded, eddied, loomed close. "Cheryl, get a blanket, her legs are cold." . . . "Where's Larine?" . . . "Here. I'm right here. Oh God, why does she make that awful noise?" . . . "It's nothing; it's just automatic." (Ross, the veteran father) "Can't somebody kill that dog or something?" . . . "Why isn't that ambulance here?"

"I'll make some tea," said the little Chinese girl.

"Sorry — can't wait —" I gasped.

A hot smell of blood. Ross's voice sharp with fear and excitement. "We're crowning. By God, we're nearly there, love. Easy, now. Wait for it."

"Christ, is that the baby's head?" croaked Jamie.

"Larine, I want a big, clean towel, quick. Lar — what the hell's the matter?"

A glimpse of Larine's greenish face. A loud flop, like something wet falling. Their voices fading in and out.

"She's passed out. Jesus, just what we need." ... "Mei, get a wet cloth and bring her round." ... "I'll take her out to the kitchen." ... "Come on, Anne love, we're nearly there. One more, now. Somebody run get me that towel. Make sure it's clean. And I'll need those scissors, and a piece of string."

Running feet. Tingling warmth, a distended bursting and tearing; my hoarse panting. Then Ross supported the just-born head as one shoulder, then the whole body, slid out into his hands. His face was lit with a wordless joy as he lifted up to show me the red, wet child, still tethered to me by the navel cord. Jamie bent nearer to look at the squirming, snuffling creature, its wrinkled body sheathed in yellowish vernix, its eyes screwed shut against the light. His face, too, was lit up with delight. "Wonderful," he breathed. "Man, it's wonderful."

"Where's that towel? Look everybody! We've got a girl. A beautiful girl." She wasn't crying, but the snuffling breath was loud and strong. After the cord stopped pulsing, Ross cut and tied it with trembling hands. Then he laid the towel-wrapped bundle by my head. I was too tired to hold her, but she looked at me quietly and steadily, her large, calm eyes now wide open, and I looked at her. She had made an incalculably long and lonely journey in the last hour, and she lay there as if pondering this, one small fist clenched under her chin.

"Poor little girl," I thought. "And this is just the beginning for you. But maybe it's just as well not to have a poetic Lamaze introduction to this tough and dotty world. Face up to it right from the start. Things are not easy for the sisterhood."

As Ross and I looked at her, my sore body rested and my sore heart floated free in a brief half-sleep. Some time later Ross lifted my head and I drank hot, sweet tea that tasted like nectar. There was a muffled chatter of voices in the room.

"Ever a cute baby, eh?"

"Somebody's got the hiccups."

"Did you see those little, tiny *feet*, man?"

"I never knew it could be like this — so quick —"

"Where's Larine? She all right now?"

There was a brief gap nobody seemed to know how to fill. Then a voice said in a whisper, "She's split. Just took off out the back door."

"Yeah, well . . ."

"Wait till I tell my boyfriend about this. He's never even seen a kitten born."

"But God, did you see her face when he held the kid up to show her?"

"I mean imagine being so new you have no name yet."

"I think they ought to call her Bella. Or maybe Anna-belle."

"No," I thought drowsily, "not Annabelle. Of course, nobody could possibly call a helpless child Edwina; but doesn't she have a middle name? — yes, something quite possible, like Jane. Give the old girl a bit of a thrill, that would. I reckon she deserves it.''

The doorbell chimed. Two ambulance attendants, an interne, and a stretcher edged into the room. The baby was whisked away. The interne knelt down and checked me over swiftly. Cheryl and Mei hovered, fascinated, as he inspected the cord-tying job. The small red face in the towel opened in a great yawn, and everyone laughed. The attendants expertly trussed me in blankets and bound me on the stretcher. ''Righto,'' one of them said briskly. ''Off we go, then.'' Strapped down and helpless, I rose into the air like a bird. What was wrong with being in chains? I was dizzy with happiness.

''I'll take the baby,'' said the interne. ''Everything seems to be okay here. You can see your wife tomorrow.''

''No, I'm coming now,'' said Ross. ''And I'll carry my own baby. Some damn man will take her away from me soon enough.'' He walked beside the stretcher so I could see both of them.

Slowly the ragged little procession of us trailed out into the bright moonlight — the little Chinese girl carrying my boots, Jamie shambling with his long legs, the truss man, as if irresistibly compelled to join in, bringing up the rear. The huge dog, released from bondage, capered in uncouth gyrations from head to tail and back again of the parade. I kept my head turned not to lose sight of Ross, as I momentarily did while the ambulance doors were fastened back. The procession briefly halted. The moonlight formalized all its absurdities into something timeless, like the epilogue — or prologue — of something universally meaningful.

Headed by the newly born, the procession seemed to stretch back indefinitely far, and to possess a mute, mysterious dignity. For a second I had the illusion that my father's tall figure lingered on the fringes of the group, aloof yet involved, as if he had a share in something happening here that was both more and less than simply happy, and certainly not an ending. To the incidental music of Ross's hiccups as he climbed in to sit beside me, the huge dog, all paws and broad grin, barked hoarsely as it capered in the snow, and we moved away.